GHOST LIGHT

"You have to die," the little girl in a ghostly white dress said, in a voice audible only to Barbara.

Suddenly, she lunged forward, pushing the woman with all her might. All those who were watching thought Barbara had somehow lost her balance. Her thoughts filled with visions of fire and crashing timber. She tried desperately to grab for something. But there was nothing within her reach. Barbara Warner hit the floor so hard on impact that she never felt a thing.

ABOUT THE AUTHOR

CLARE McNALLY attended the Fashion Institute of Technology in New York City where she studied advertising and communications. She has worked on a children's wear magazine, freelanced as an advertising copy-writer and edited a technical magazine. She lives on Long Island.

Also by Clare McNally

GHOST HOUSE
GHOST HOUSE REVENGE
WHAT ABOUT THE BABY?
COME DOWN INTO DARKNESS
SOMEBODY COME AND PLAY

and published by Corgi Books

Ghost Light

Clare McNally

CORGI BOOKS

GHOST LIGHT

A CORGI BOOK   0 552 12400 1

First publication in Great Britain

PRINTING HISTORY

Corgi edition published 1984
Corgi edition reprinted 1986
Corgi edition reprinted 1987
Corgi edition reprinted 1989
Corgi edition reprinted 1990

Corgi Books are published by Transworld Publishers Ltd.,
61–63 Uxbridge Road, Ealing, London W5 5SA,
in Australia by Transworld Publishers (Australia) Pty. Ltd.,
15–23 Helles Avenue, Moorebank, NSW 2170, and in New
Zealand by Transworld Publishers (N.Z.) Ltd., Cnr. Moselle
and Waipareira Avenues, Henderson, Auckland.

Printed and bound in Great Britain by
BPCC Hazell Books
Aylesbury, Bucks, England
Member of BPCC Ltd.

For my mother and father,
Dorothy and William McNally,
with love

Special thanks for their expert advice and support to Denise Marcil, Marc Tantillo, Linda Price, and Michael Pastore.

GHOST LIGHT

PROLOGUE
December 12, 1921

She was such a darling child. Bonnie Jackson was the little girl everyone wanted—bright, pretty, talented. At the tender age of five she'd already made a name for herself on Broadway, charming both audiences and critics with her incredible voice range and talent for acting. Even other actors, who saw kids and animals as proverbial menaces, enjoyed working with this cheerful, appealing child.

Sometimes, though, Bonnie wasn't very cheerful. On a particularly gloomy day in late autumn she sat in her dressing room and stared solemnly at the reflection in her vanity as her mother tied a frothy white bow in the child's shoulder-length black hair.

Bonnie was sad because her parents had just had an argument, one that left Mommy's mouth set hard and Daddy searching the room for a flask of bootleg whiskey. Bonnie's pink lips turned down in a pout, and her round cheeks flushed as she fought her tears. She hated it when her parents fought.

"Why the hell does that guy have to follow us every theater?" Philip Jackson wanted to know.

"He's a friend, Phil," his wife answered. "Just a friend."

"I'm not an idiot, Margaret," Phil said. "I know what Aaron Milland means to you."

Bonnie looked up at her mother and in her desire to understand this argument dared to interrupt with a question.

"Do you like Aaron Milland, Mommy?"

Margaret glared at the reflection of her daughter's eyes, growing wider by the moment as Bonnie waited to be reprimanded. Sometimes Mommy became very angry with her. Sometimes, she even hurt her.

This time, however, she didn't say a word. Instead, she turned back to Phil.

"What does it matter, how Aaron and I feel about each other?" she demanded.

1

"Look," Phil said, "Bonnie shouldn't be hearing this. We can talk later in private."

Margaret sighed.

"All right, we'll talk later," she said. "Let's just concentrate on getting Bonnie ready for her debut."

As if by magic the stern look on her face fell away, replaced by a smile. Bonnie wished her mother would smile more often.

"Imagine," Margaret said, "our baby in the Winston Theater!"

"Only The Palace is bigger, Bonnie," Phil told his daughter.

Bonnie grinned at her father, her perfect white teeth glistening. He grinned back, caught a strand of his hair, and pushed it over his ear. It was plastered down with spice-smelling hair cream, parted in the middle and shining like the fender of a new Hudson Phaeton. Bonnie thought her daddy was very handsome. She loved him more than anyone, maybe even more than Mommy. Daddy never hit her, or yelled at her, or put her in dark places.

But she wouldn't think about the dark places. She'd think only of the songs she'd be singing tonight on the bright stage of the Winston Theater.

"Stand up now, darling," Margaret ordered.

Bonnie did as she was told, and modeled the new dress her father had ordered from Paris. Its hem was just fingertip length, and when she twirled around, rows and rows of lace ruffles fluttered like wispy clouds. Her parents admired her from head to toe, taking in her white bow, dress, stockings, and finally a pair of white Mary Janes with pearl buttons. It was when Margaret's eyes reached the shoes that her smile disappeared again.

Bonnie stopped dancing and stared at her mother with eyes that silently asked what she had done now. She was glad Daddy was here. Daddy wouldn't let her be hurt. He never did.

"My God, Phil!" Margaret cried. "Her shoes are scuffed, and she's on in five minutes!"

Bonnie looked down at the offending shoes and noticed that a few black streaks ran over the very tips of her toes.

"For crying out loud, Margaret," Phil said. "They're coming to hear her sing, not look at her shoes!"

"She has to be perfect," Margaret said. "I have to make her perfect."

She lifted Bonnie up and sat her on top of a black costume-trunk, quickly unbuckling the Mary Janes.

"Do you have any lighter fluid?"

Phil took out his silver flask of whiskey and joked, "This stuff'll set 'em on fire."

Bonnie giggled, and Margaret snapped, "I'm not amused!" And the little girl frowned again.

"Damn it," Phil said, reaching into the pocket of his pants. "Here, here's some lighter fluid. Jeez!"

Margaret went to work on the scuff marks. By the time she was done, Bonnie was being called on stage. Phil and Margaret took seats in the second row to watch her perform. The audience loved her here at the Winston Theater as had audiences everywhere else—they applauded and smiled and cheered the tiny performer. Some of the women and men even felt tears in their eyes.

But they didn't know the melancholy sweetness in her voice was not part of an act. All the while she was singing, Bonnie couldn't help thinking of the fight her parents had had. When she was finished, she met them in the wings, and holding Margaret's hand, she hurried back to her dressing room.

"You were terrific," Phil said. "Which you would have been with or without the scuff marks."

Margaret shot a look at him and pushed open the door to Bonnie's dressing room.

"As a matter of fact," Phil said, "a performance like that deserves a reward."

"I don't think that's necessary," Margaret said.

"Sure it is," Phil answered. "I'm going to head over to F.A.O. Schwartz and buy a new doll for you, Bonnie."

"Oh, Daddy!" the child squealed with delight. She ran to him and hugged him around the knees.

"I love you so much, Daddy," she said.

"And Daddy sure loves you," Phil replied.

Margaret stared icily at them, but said nothing. Phil took his trenchcoat down from its brass hook.

"I shouldn't be too long," he said. He reconsidered that

and glanced at his pocket watch. "Well, I guess the Christmas rush might delay me. Give me an hour."

"Phil, I think you're being foolish," Margaret commented.

But Phil only winked at Bonnie and left the room. Margaret began to see red, hating the fact that Bonnie was being rewarded simply for doing her job. What about Margaret? Why didn't Phil reward *her* for all the years she slaved to get the kid where she was? My God, she hadn't even wanted a baby! And look what sacrifices she'd made!

Her thoughts were cut off by a knock at the door. Bonnie watched her mother's face change once again from angry to cheerful as Aaron Milland walked into the room. The little girl shrank away from him, hating his gaunt cheeks and dark eyes. He reminded her of a skull. Ignoring Bonnie, Aaron pulled Margaret to him and kissed her neck.

"Mmm," she said. "Not here. Not here!"

She giggled and pushed him away.

Finally, Aaron noticed Bonnie. Bonnie didn't like Aaron Milland. He'd met her mommy last year during a preview run in Philadelphia, where he'd been stage manager. Now he followed them to every theater, always coming to see her mommy when her daddy wasn't around. Bonnie could sense there was something wrong with that.

"You kissed my mommy like my daddy used to," she said. "Why?"

Margaret gasped and put a hand to the low V-neck of her silky dress.

"How dare you ask such a question!" she cried. "Oh, Aaron, I'm so sorry. Sometimes she gets too big for her britches. It's 'his business, you know."

"That's okay," Aaron said. "No harm done. She's just a kid, Margaret."

"Nevertheless, I'd like you to excuse us," Margaret said.

Bonnie, though she didn't like Aaron, wished he wouldn't leave the room. What would her mother do to her? But he did, and now Margaret grabbed her by the arms, crushing the delicate organza of her puffed sleeves. Her long string of beads swayed forward, tapping the child's face lightly.

"You are rude, mean, and nasty," she hissed. "Aaron is my friend, and will be your daddy someday!"

"No!" Bonnie cried. "I only want my *real* daddy!"

Margaret slapped her little round cheek. Bonnie burst into tears and tried to pull away.

"You are a bad, bad girl," Margaret went on. "For being rude to Aaron, you'll stay in the closet until I come get you out!"

Bonnie kicked and protested with all her might as her mother pulled her toward the dark little closet. Why didn't anyone hear her? she wondered frantically. Why didn't one of the other performers come in and help, or even that Aaron? Bonnie decided then that she hated everyone in this theater. They didn't care what happened to her. They only cared if she made money for them.

Her mother shoved her into the closet. Bonnie's head struck the back wall, and she sat momentarily stunned as the door slammed shut and the lock clicked.

"Mommy, no!" Bonnie screamed. "No, please! I hate the dark! Please take the dark away!"

But the only reply was the sound of retreating footsteps and another door closing. Then laughter. Her mother was laughing, and so was Aaron! Bonnie recognized the deep voice of her mother's "friend."

"I hate you," she whispered, sniffling. "I hate you!"

She sat back and pulled her knees up to her chin, crying softly, rocking herself back and forth. Her daddy said he'd be right back. Maybe if she made herself small, if she closed her eyes, the monsters who hid in the closet wouldn't get her. Daddy would rescue her. Daddy always rescued her.

Cold and sick with fright, she collapsed into a deep sleep.

When her eyes opened again, it was darker in the closet than it had been earlier. Bonnie realized there was no light coming in from the room outside anymore. Had someone come and turned it off, not realizing she was in here? She crawled over to the door and tried to open it. Still locked.

"MOMMY!" she cried, pounding on the door. "MOMMY? PLEASE LET ME OUT!"

She would be good. She'd be a good girl if Mommy let her out. It was cold in here! And dark, so dark . . .

"I DON'T LIKE THE DARK, MOMMY!"

A door opened, there were footsteps, and suddenly Bonnie heard a key jangling in the closet lock. The door opened, but it was just as dark outside. She couldn't see who was there.

Strong arms lifted her, and Bonnie started to struggle. Who was it? Who was going to hurt her now?

"Hey, it's me!" a man's voice cried. "It's your daddy!"

Bonnie relaxed, as her small hands found the familiar comedy/tragedy pin he always wore on his coat.

"Oh, Daddy!" She buried her face in his shoulder and sobbed.

"Did your mother do this?"

Bonnie nodded. "She said I was rude to Aaron," Bonnie answered.

"Aaron?" Phil echoed. "Aaron was here?"

Again, the child nodded. "Daddy, why is it so dark?"

"We've lost all the lights. Must be a fuse, honey," Phil said. "Here, I'll light a candle."

Bonnie felt herself being placed on a velveteen loveseat. Her father kissed the top of her head, then went groping across the room to a chest of drawers. After a lot of rummaging noise, he found a candle and lit it. A soft glow illuminated the room, and Bonnie immediately felt better. Her daddy had brought the light.

"You wait here," he said. "Daddy's got a few words to say to Mommy."

"Daddy, where is everyone?" Bonnie asked. "Why didn't anyone hear me?"

"Everyone's gone home, darling," Phil said. He stopped and thought. "Didn't you know?"

"No, Daddy," Bonnie said. "I fell asleep."

Phil rubbed his eyes.

"You've been in that closet for three hours," he growled. "God, I'm sorry about that! I called your mother—she said everything was okay."

And all that time she was screwing Aaron . . .

"You just wait here," Phil said. "I'll be right back."

He opened a drawer in a tall cabinet, reached way into the back and pulled out a gun, grasping it firmly in a white-knuckled fist.

And then he left. Bonnie sat staring at the candle flame, waiting for him. But soon the candle burned out, and still her daddy hadn't returned. Terrified to be alone in the dark, Bonnie slid off the loveseat and decided she'd try to find him. She shuffled her way toward the door and opened it, entering the long hallway outside her dressing room. She could see nothing in either direction, but she could hear voices. Yelling voices—two men and a woman.

"If I follow them," she said out loud to reassure herself, "I'll find Daddy."

But it was so hard to tell where they were coming from in the theater's maze of pitch black hallways. Bonnie walked slowly, listening, turning when the sounds seemed to grow louder. But none of the doors she opened led to Daddy.

All of a sudden she heard the sound of running footsteps. And then her mother's voice crying, "That child is more trouble than she's worth! You keep her! I hate her!"

Bonnie's eyes filled with tears. Her mother really did hate her, didn't she?

And her mother was going to hurt her now. That's why she was running. To catch Bonnie. To hurt her.

Terrified, the child pulled open the nearest door. At first, when she felt some hanging sandbags and lengths of coiled rope, she thought it might be the stage. But no, this couldn't be the stage. There was no light here. Daddy told her that all stages had a "ghost light," a single bulb that always burned at the apron so that no one would walk off it in the dark. This had to be a storage room.

"BONNIE JACKSON, HOW DARE YOU RAT ON ME?"

Margaret's shriek resounded throughout the building. And then Phil's angry voice boomed out of the darkness.

"DON'T YOU HURT HER! I'll kill you if you touch my baby."

Bonnie prayed her daddy would come get her. She poked a thumb in her mouth (Mommy would smack her if she saw her) and started backing away from the door, afraid her mother would enter.

Suddenly, from some faraway part of the theater, came a loud, cracking noise. The sound of a gunshot startled Bonnie so that she lost her footing and tumbled backwards into a dark void. She screamed, realizing too late that the blackout had also claimed the ghost light. She crashed to the floor of the orchestra pit, her head striking a metal chair. Blackness came, and all the life and sweetness of the little girl who had charmed Broadway drained away—as easily as blood flows.

ONE

Music was playing, tinny as an old gramophone recording. And on a vast stage stood a beautiful, dark-haired child, singing sweetly to an invisible audience. To either side of her, gold and white curtains reached up toward colored lights. A man stood in the wings, feeling happy inside to hear her sweet voice. It was good, so very good.

And then the music stopped, abruptly, and darkness enshrouded the stage. The air grew hot and thick. The man felt his lungs tighten as he desperately sought to breathe. It was growing hotter by the moment, painfully hot. The little girl turned to him now with eyes that were huge with fear.

"Take the dark away! Please!" she screamed.

The man reached out, but he could not move. Flames illuminated the stage, racing around the man and teasing his pant legs. There was no escape. The child screamed and backed away from the fire. Suddenly he saw her small body disappear into the blackness of the orchestra pit.

"NNNNOOOO!!!"

The man broke free of the invisible force that held him and raced toward the apron of the stage, his arms outstretched. And then he, too, tripped down into the blackness, down and down, staring in horror as the fire claimed the gold and white curtains. He thrashed, feeling cloth entangle him. The curtains had torn from their rod, and he was entangled in them...

...in the comforter of a huge brass bed.

Nate Dysart sat up abruptly, a questioning noise escaping from between his chattering teeth. Confused, he looked around, trying to remember where he was. This wasn't his California apartment! This bed wasn't his! His room was never this dark before...

Trembling, he twisted the satin sheets and fought to calm himself. The room slowly began to look familiar. There was a tall armoire; there between two French windows stood a bookshelf. As his eyes adjusted to the light he saw a gold-framed painting on one wall. It was just a bedroom. The stage and the fire had been a dream.

But in his thirty-one years Nate had never been so unnerved by a nightmare. On the rare occasions he had them he was usually able to forget them and fall right back asleep again. But not tonight. He breathed heavily. He could hear his heart pound. He was soaked with sweat. Suddenly he realized where he was—in a bedroom of the Connecticut estate where he'd grown up. He'd arrived two days ago to attend his father's funeral.

But why would that make him dream about a little girl in a burning theater?

Groggily, needing to clear his head, Nate got out of bed and groped through the darkness to his bathroom. When the light went on, a pale and unshaven face stared at him from the mirror over the black marble sink. Nate groaned at his reflection and turned on the cold water faucet.

Like a slap driven to the face of an hysterical man, the icy liquid shocked him into complete wakefulness. Again and again he brought up his cupped palms, soaking himself until he had finally driven away much of the anxiety. With his eyes squeezed shut, he reached out to find a towel.

It seemed to come to him from midair, and as he took it Nate's hand brushed cool flesh.

"What the hell?!

He stumbled against the shower, grabbing for the curtains to steady himself as a familiar voice said, "I'm terribly sorry, sir. I didn't mean to startle you."

He rubbed his eyes and looked up at his father's butler, an old man named Carl. Sitting down on the edge of the tub, Nate said, "I must look like an idiot."

"Certainly not, sir," Carl said. He took the towel, folded it, and returned it to its brass rod. "I shouldn't have entered unannounced. But your father always insisted we servants remain silent unless spoken to."

"You know I'm not like my father, Carl," Nate said, standing up again. He was dressed only in his briefs, and the full-length bathroom mirror reflected a well-tanned, if slightly underweight, physique. Nate rejected the satin robe Carl was holding open for him. "I'm going right back to bed. What are you doing up, anyway?"

"I heard you cry out, sir," Carl said. "Did you have a nightmare?"

Nate's head nodded, a strand of hair falling over his forehead. Pushing it back, he said, "One of the worst in my life. It was so real. But I'll be okay."

Carl followed him into the bedroom, switching off the bathroom light.

"Under the circumstances," he said, turning on a lamp and readjusting the twisted covers of Nate's bed, "I'm not surprised. You must be terribly exhausted after traveling all the way from California, and then attending your father's wake."

"I'd rather not think about it," Nate said, sitting on the edge of the bed. "I'm here because my father's financial adviser talked me into it, not because I want to be. You know how I felt about my father, Carl."

"Yes, sir," Carl said softly, reading bitter hatred in the younger man's eyes. "Sir, the funeral is in just a few hours. I suggest you try to sleep again."

Nodding, Nate lay back and closed his eyes. He wished he would not have to attend the funeral, but knew he had no choice. Not when a sizable inheritance was at stake.

Nathaniel Dysart Jr. had spent the first twenty-six years of his life living under the same roof as his multimillionaire father, and yet in all that time he had never grown close to the man. How could he, when Nathaniel Sr. had nothing but contempt for him? The beautiful Sandra Dysart had died giving birth to Nate, and his father held the innocent child responsible. But he had promised Sandra, the only woman he'd ever loved, that he'd always see to the boy's welfare. And so Nate was kept in the big, opulent mansion—a poor little rich boy, as the cliché goes. He often wondered, as he looked back on a lonely childhood filled with days of ridicule and abuse, if he might have been better off with strangers. His father was no more to him. A stranger who refused him love.

Yet here he was, dressed in a dark suit, standing in a cemetery as the local minister read a eulogy to the old man. He stared, expressionless, at an ivory-inlaid coffin. My father is in there, he thought. Dead at age sixty-seven of a stroke, and soon to be buried. Nate wished they would hurry. He wanted to get back to California, to forget all this.

". . . a pillar of our community . . ."

The minister's nasal twang cut through the chilly November air. Of the three dozen people who had gathered for the funeral, not a single one had really cared for the old man. The senior Mr. Dysart had long ago alienated anyone he might have called "friend," with his miserly, temperamental ways.

No, they were all here to make an impression on Nate. And as far as the young man was concerned, they could all drop dead with his father. Including the pompous minister, who insisted upon telling them all how wonderful the old man had been. Maybe he hoped his church had been mentioned in the old man's will.

Lies, all lies, Nate thought.

He felt a hand on his shoulder and turned his head slightly to Jim Orland, his best friend. Without speaking, the stocky, curly-haired man was able to tell Nate he knew how hard it was to be here. He and Nate had been friends since early childhood, and Jim had often witnessed the cruel way Nate had been treated by his father. But he knew Nate was only here because his father's financial adviser had suggested it. As one of the few members left in the Dysart clan, he stood to inherit a great deal.

"That's a laugh," Nate had said to Jim at the wake. "If he left me anything, it'll be a few sticks of broken furniture or worthless stock."

"Then why'd you bother coming?"

Nate had shrugged. "I don't know. Maybe, after all that's happened, I'm still a hopeful kid. I'd still like to think my father had some affection for me, and any inheritance will make me believe that."

Here at the funeral there were others who had more than just a passing interest in Nathaniel Dysart Sr.'s will. The head of a major shipping company thought of the promise Dysart had made him for a considerable amount of money to bail him out of financial difficulties, and wondered if provisions had been made. Several people who had made large investments in Dysart Enterprises were so busy praying the old man's death wouldn't cause a dip in stock values that they didn't take time to pray for the deceased himself. And Nathaniel Sr.'s secretary, Lisa Bateson, was certain she would be fondly

remembered after thirty years of loyal service to the old
bastard.

Besides Nate, the only other relatives left behind were
Pearl and Vance Dysart. Because he was Nathaniel's only
nephew, forty-five-year-old Vance expected to take in a good
cut of the Dysart fortune. As far as he was concerned, he
deserved it more than Nate—who had been nothing but
trouble for his father from day one of his life. Now Vance
tilted his head back a little and stared across the coffin at his
cousin.

Look at him, he thought. Not a tear in his eye. He's glad
the old man is dead!

Nate caught him staring and held his eyes for a few
moments. Then he blinked and watched as the minister
splashed holy water on the ivory coffin. A faint aroma of
incense filled the air, followed by the jangling of bells.
Mesmerized by the minister's droning, Nate began to sway a
little. Suddenly, he was no longer looking at a white coffin.

In its place sat a simple pine casket, its only decoration a
gold cross. It was the coffin that had held his wife Meg five
years ago. He'd left for California right after that funeral.
Nate blinked, and the ivory casket was there again.

His mind wandered, carrying him back to the time when
Meg was alive. She had been so beautiful then, so happy.
Nate, Meg, and Jim had owned a tiny theater company
off-off-Broadway. But one day, there had been a terrible
accident, one that made Meg an invalid until her tragic death
several months later. He had wanted his own life to end, too.

Nate shook memories of that time from his head, letting a
cool gust of November air bring his senses back to him. He
watched grimly as four husky men, cemetery employees, took
the ends of the ropes that ran under the coffin. Carefully,
they lifted it up. The minister took Nate's hand and led him
to the grave's edge. Suddenly, Nate was reminded of the
orchestra pit in his dream, but the thought was lost when he
felt something cold in his hand. A shovel. He was expected to
throw in the first mound of dirt.

All of a sudden, a startled cry broke the solemnity of the
service, as one of the four men slipped on a slick patch of wet
grass. The rope flew from his hand, and the minister grabbed
desperately for it. But it was too late. The coffin fell off

balance and smashed to the ground below. It hit so hard on impact that the top half fell open, and the old man's head and arm flopped out.

Nate felt anger tighten his muscles as he looked into the pit at the thin old face. He hadn't wanted to see his father again, ever! In a moment of fury, he turned the shovel over and let dirt drop on the cadaver. For a second, he thought he saw the old man's lips curl into a sneer.

He's going to start yelling at me ...

It was an unbidden thought, one that Nate had had many times during his childhood. Hearing it, he felt a chill rush through him as he realized he was still fearful of the old man—even in death. As the cemetery workers tried to organize themselves again Nate squinted and backed away from the site.

Please, God, make this day end quickly!

He wrapped his arms around himself as if to control his fears and stared at his shoes for the rest of the ceremony.

Despite the fears he'd experienced at the funeral, Nate was going to be all right. About thirty-million-dollars' worth of all-right, according to the family lawyer, and that was after taxes. To his shock, he learned that he hadn't inherited only those broken pieces of furniture and worthless stocks. Every piece of furniture, every stock and bond, every inch of property was his—as soon as the will was out of probate.

Strangely, no one else had been included in the will—not Lisa Bates, not his cousins, or anyone else. Nate decided he'd give Lisa something in gratitude for her years of service. And he'd make certain all his father's debts were paid off. But, as far as his cousins Vance and Pearl were concerned, Nate didn't care what happened to them. He and his only cousin had never been close.

Nate spent hours each day going over his father's papers, trying to understand the wealth and responsibility that was now his, and making plans for the future. A few weeks after the funeral, he met Jim for lunch. Nate had a letter his father had written to him just before his death and felt Jim was the only one he could trust to read it.

"He's going to get a dig at me any way he can," Nate said.

"Don't worry about him anymore," Jim said. "He's dead.
Dead and gone."

"Just listen to this, anyway," Nate said. He held the letter
toward the window for better light. A bus, advertising a new
brand of liquor along its side, moved past his line of vision.
"'Though I detest you, and though I never called you "son,"
I am leaving my fortune to you. Long ago, your mother made
me promise all this would be yours. Because of my intense
love for her, I will respect her wishes.'"

"You can almost read 'choke on it,' in that," Jim commented.

Nate refolded the letter and shoved it into the pocket of his
western-style shirt.

"I can't imagine my father feeling intense love for anyone,"
he said.

Jim reached across the table and punched him lightly on
the chin.

"Hey, forget it," he said. "You shouldn't let the old man
bother you so much anymore. What do you care about him,
anyway? You've made a name for yourself as a director in
California, and all without a cent of his money."

"Yeah," Nate sighed. "Five years in California, directing
theater productions, living in two-room apartments. And now
I've got a mansion with more rooms than I can count."

"Do you intend to stay here in the East?"

Nate shook his head. "I don't know. There's no reason for
me to leave, now that my father's gone and everything is
taken care of back in California. I resigned from my job and
managed to get out of the lease for my apartment."

He lifted his coffee cup and drained it, then rubbed his
eyes.

Jim watched him, seeing weariness in his friend's expression, and he said, "There's been a lot on your mind, hasn't
there? You look like you haven't slept since you came here."

"I've slept," Nate said as a waitress came to refill his cup.
"But not too well. I keep having this weird nightmare."

"What about?"

"I'm standing in the wings of a theater," he said, "watching
this little girl sing."

"Who is she?"

Nate shrugged. "Beats me. In the dream, I know her. But I
don't recall her face when I wake up. Anyway, the theater

suddenly goes black, and catches fire. She falls into the orchestra pit, and I fall in after her."

"I think you're just overexerted these days. Once your father's will is out of probate, you'll be living so easy that you won't worry about a thing anymore."

Nate still looked worried.

"Hey, eat already," Jim said. "Forget about the dreams. You're old enough to know there ain't no boogey man. Now what are you going to do with all that money?"

Nate laughed and started eating again. With his free hand, he opened a copy of *Variety* that sat on the table.

"I've got an ad running in here today," he said. He found the page and turned it toward Jim. "See what you think."

Jim read the quarter-page ad, calling for people to back an original production to be presented by Nathaniel Dysart Jr. He nodded, approving.

"With all your money," he said, "you could almost back the thing yourself. But that would be financially disastrous, of course. Even if you are the best director-producer I know."

"Flattery won't get you any further than you are," Nate said. "You're already my best friend. And, I hope, you'll be my assistant when I open the theater."

"You can bet on it," Jim said. "Got any ideas where you'll rent?"

Nate shook his head. "I looked around a bit this morning, but nothing impressed me. Anyway, there's time."

"This is gonna be like old times," Jim said. "The way it was before you took off to California."

"You know why I left, Jim," Nate said. "I couldn't stand being in New York. Everything I looked at reminded me of Meg."

Jim could see Nate falling into a depression and quickly changed the subject. Nate was too melancholy these days, Jim thought. He would have to see to it that his friend cheered up a bit.

"Remember the first company we tried to start?" he asked. "I think we were about eighteen."

"It was in the basement of our church," Nate said, "and the Seriant twins were our stars."

"So tell me," Jim said, laughing. "Did we spend more hours working, or making out with those two?"

"I couldn't guess," Nate said. "We must have done some
work, because we managed to put on a play. God, we've
come a long way since then."

Jim nodded in agreement.

"It's hard to believe you're going to open your own Broadway
company," he said. "Even if you did make a name for yourself
in California theater. By the way, have you thought about the
play itself?"

"I want to do an original production of a comedy called
Making Good. I read the script before I left California. It's
great," Nate said. "And I'm going to get Sander Bernaux as
the lead."

Jim laughed and cuffed his chin again. "Are you kidding?"
he said. "Sander Bernaux is the biggest star on Broadway!"

"And you know how I've dreamed of working with him,"
Nate said. "My father used to say I'd never get to work with
him, that I was too untalented."

"Your father said a lot of things, Nate," Jim said.

"Yeah, well, I'm going to prove my talent," Nate replied.
"I'm going to get Sander Bernaux, no matter what. The part
is perfect for him."

In truth, Jim wondered if Nate could handle a man like
Bernaux. Sure, Nate was talented, dedicated, and hard-working.
When they'd had the off-off-Broadway production company a
few years ago, the critics were already noticing him. But
Sander Bernaux was mean-tempered and pathologically sus-
picious of everyone. Jim hoped Nate could cope with him.
But why not? He had coped with his father's temperament for
most of his life. Bernaux couldn't be much worse.

"Hey," he said finally, "I'll bet he begs to work with you."
He looked at his watch. "Speaking of work, I should remember I still belong to another production company. I've got to
get back to the theater, Nate."

"Need a ride?" Nate asked, standing. "I came to New York
in style today, you'll notice."

As he moved away from the table Jim looked out the
window to see an antique Rolls-Royce waiting at the curb.
Others had noticed it, too, for almost every passer-by on the
crowded street stopped to gape at it.

"Really getting into this money thing, aren't you?" he
teased as they walked towards the cashier.

"Oh, hell," Nate said. "You know I still prefer my jeans."

Jim laughed, knowing this was true. He couldn't really picture Nate as a member of the elite upper class, though his friend had been brought up surrounded by luxury. That luxury had never been shared between father and son.

They said good-bye outside the restaurant and walked in opposite directions. Nate climbed into the back of the Rolls and ordered George, his chauffeur, to head directly home. There was to be a meeting with his father's lawyers that afternoon, and Nate wanted to be ready for it. George nodded and turned on the ignition, easing the car into the street. Nate ignored the traffic, more interested in reading his copy of *Variety*. Suddenly, he felt a cold rush of wind and heard a voice say:

"I'm waiting for you!"

He looked up.

"What was that, George?"

"I didn't say anything, sir," George replied.

Nate let the matter drop, thinking it must have been one of the pedestrians crossing the street who had spoken. He turned a page of his trade paper and found the next one virtually blank, except for a small, two-line ad in its center. It gave an address, claiming this property was for sale.

"What a waste of space," Nate said. "They must be desperate to sell the place to take out an ad like this."

Still, the location was nearby, and he was intrigued. He ordered George to turn around and find it. The street was home for several theaters, office buildings, and restaurants. But there was no such number as the one given in the ad.

"Perhaps it's that empty lot we passed," George suggested.

"Let's take a look," Nate said.

After George had managed to find a parking space around the corner, Nate left the car and made his way back to the site. It was located between a restaurant and hotel, a dead spot on an otherwise lively street. Cinder blocks were scattered over its unkempt grass, a resting place for cigarette butts, tattered newspapers, and rusted cans. But there were no signs indicating the property was for sale.

Nate's eyes were drawn to a cloud of white smoke that hovered over the grass, then disappeared. He heard a small voice.

"We'll be together, soon."

It was a childish voice with a faint southwestern accent.

But when Nate looked around, he saw he was alone. None of the people walking by even looked at him.

"Funny," he said out loud, his words making clouds in the chilly air, "that's the second time I thought I heard voices."

But he wasn't going to worry about it. Like the dreams, it was probably caused by having so much on his mind. He knew what stress could do to you. Like after Meg died....

Suddenly, he felt someone touch his arm. He turned quickly to see a dirty, ragged old man gazing at him through filmy eyes that might once have been bright blue. But years of drinking had taken their toll, and Nate could smell the pungent aroma of stale wine when the man spoke.

"Bad t'ings happen at dis place," he said, his mouth toothless and slack.

He belched loudly, the sickening odor of his breath making Nate turn away with a grimace. The old man shook his head and shuffled off down the street, scratching the seat of his pants with fingers that poked through torn knit gloves.

"Crazy old man," Nate growled.

Well, he thought, weirdos like that came with the territory. They were all part of the ingredients that made New York interesting. If he built a theater right on this spot, it would just add to the fascination. And why shouldn't he do just that, he thought? He certainly had the money for it. He'd call the realtor this afternoon. Imagine, not only his own company, but his own theater, built to his own specifications, a building to last into the next century and to bear his name.

Nate climbed into the back of the Rolls and lifted his copy of *Variety* from the floor. He flipped through it, trying to find the ad. But it wasn't there anymore. Finally, after going over each page twice, he dropped it to the floor again. The page had probably fallen out when he'd opened the car door.

The address, though, had stuck in his mind. When he arrived home, he had his father's secretary call several dozen realtors until she finally located someone who claimed the property. It was for sale, they told Nate. But they were surprised to learn where he'd heard of it. No one at their office had put any ads in *Variety*.

TWO

The next weeks were the most hectic Nate had ever known. There were papers to be read and signed, contracts to be drawn up regarding purchase of the property, and contracting companies to be negotiated with to make the best deal possible for building his theater. But he didn't mind the fast pace. It left him so exhausted at night that only twice had he experienced that strange nightmare.

Finally, after the will came out of probate and he had signed the last paper necessary to make him owner of the vacant lot, Nate hired the best architect in New York to work with him on the theater's design. He sat with Fred Johnson now in his midtown Manhattan office, going over sketches laid out on a drafting table.

"I see you've incorporated the Art Nouveau theme I wanted," Nate said.

"What made you choose something so decorative?" Fred wanted to know. "These days, most of my clients want the Bauhaus style—steel and glass, that is."

"It's just something I've always liked," Nate said.

During a dark and ugly childhood he had developed a taste for beautiful things, but he did not discuss this with Fred.

The architect rummaged through the papers on his drafting table and pulled out a watercolor sketch.

"Look at this," he said, "it's my initial idea for the building's facade. I thought stone ivy would look good encircling the doors."

"Fine," Nate said. He clapped his hands together once, then slid off his three-legged stool. "Well! Since I want construction to begin as soon as possible, I'll leave you alone with your work. You're on the right track."

"I'll call you with a progress report in a few days," Fred said.

Nate left the office, feeling elated. Soon he would have his own theater. As he stood waiting for the elevator he hummed a tune. It almost masked the sound of a light voice calling out to him.

"I'm waiting for you!"

Nate looked behind and around himself, but the hallway was empty. Reasoning it must have come from one of the half-dozen offices along the hall, he was about to enter the elevator when he heard it again.

"Take the dark away, please! Please take the dark away!"

Nate shuddered and hurried onto the elevator. As the doors closed he tried to turn his thoughts elsewhere. But one fact kept haunting him. In the dream the little girl had said almost the same thing as that voice he'd just heard. It hadn't come from behind one of those office doors, but from his own mind. The dream was following him in daylight now.

"When the hell is this going to stop?" he asked the flashing elevator numerals.

In the lobby, he hurried out to the street and waited for George to arrive with the car. He would keep even busier than he'd been, he thought. That way, he would have no time for tricks of the mind.

Upstairs in the hallway outside Fred Johnson's office, a little girl walked, unseen by the two gossiping secretaries. She didn't like this big building, with its cold beige walls. But she had to be here. There were things to be done. She moved towards the door to Fred Johnson's office.

Fred put down his mechanical pencil and went to open the door. It was suddenly very stuffy in the room, and he thought he might get some cross-ventilation from the hallway. He should complain about the thermostat. They weren't supposed to let it get this hot in here anyway, were they? Energy conservation and all.

He rubbed his eyes and yawned.

"Don't know why I feel so tired," he said out loud, heading back to his drafting table.

For a moment he couldn't see the table or anything in front of him. It was as if a black curtain had been drawn down over his eyes. He swayed a little; his head felt very light. From somewhere deep in his mind he heard voices, voices that commanded him to return to work. In less than a minute Fred was sitting at the table again. He had no memory of his dizzy spell or even of getting up and opening his door. The temperature was normal again, and in Fred's mind it had never changed. He picked up his pencil and went to work again, so busy over the next hours that he did not stop to question why, when Nate had agreed the original designs were just fine, he was completely changing everything he'd drawn so far.

Nate could not stop thinking about the voice he'd heard. He was certain it had come from his mind, and yet it seemed external, as if someone unseen were following him around. He knew, though, that this was ridiculous. It was tension, just like everyone said it was. And now to ease some of it, he was lying in a room in his father's house (he wondered when he'd begin to think of all this as his) under the care of a masseuse.

Lulled by the kneading of his muscles, he soon fell into a deep sleep. But it was not a restful one. The dream came again. The little girl began to sing, surrounded by the gold and white curtains. And then the darkness came, and the heat and the fire and the falling...

"Wake up, Mr. Dysart!"

The masseuse was patting his cheek when Nate opened his eyes.

"You were dreaming again," she said. "You're really very tense, sir. Do you want me to set up the whirlpool?"

Nate rubbed his eyes and sat up, feeling weakened by the dream. When would they stop? He felt as if he were being maneuvered towards something, as if the dreams were trying to control him.

"No, I'll just take a shower," he mumbled as the masseuse helped him to his feet. Feeling like a helpless old man, he tried to put strength in his voice when he said, "Don't worry about me."

Everyone *was* worrying about him since his return East.

"Swimming in January," Jim said with wonder as he pulled himself up a steel ladder leading from Dysart Manor's enclosed pool. "This place never fails to amaze me."

Nate rubbed himself briskly with a towel.

"It's good for what ails you, anyway," he said. "I might consider keeping the housing up all year round."

"It's better to let the sun shine down unobstructed in the summer," Jim said.

The pool was just outside the mansion, and because of the cold weather, it had been covered by a movable glass and steel frame. There were dressing rooms at one end of it, and the two men headed to these. They spoke through a natural-wood divider as they dressed.

"Think you'll ever get used to calling this place your own?"

"I lived here for twenty-six years," Nate said. "I could live here another twenty-five, and still refer to everything as 'my father's.' I'm more at home in a theater, Jim."

He pulled a velour sweatshirt over his head and tucked it into his jeans, then walked barefoot from the cubicle, carrying his shoes. Jim was already sitting on a bench, tying his own.

"How's this theater of yours coming?" Jim asked.

"I've spoken to Fred Johnson a few times since our first meeting three weeks ago," Nate said. "He's really brilliant and dedicated to his work. He changed everything around from the originals because he thought he'd found a more effective design."

"Good for him," Jim said. He looked at his friend. "Did you like what he did?"

Nate shrugged. "Blueprints mean nothing to me. I'm waiting for him to do some drawings."

Jim stood up and started to roll his wet towel and bathing suit, but Nate stopped him.

"I've got maids to handle that sort of thing," he said. "Just leave it there."

"Big shot," Jim said, cuffing Nate's chin.

In the library Nate fixed drinks. Settling down in a huge leather rocking chair, Jim swiveled back and forth and looked around at the safari trophies on the walls.

"The idea of killing a wild animal disgusts me," he said. "When I was a kid, my favorite show was *Wild Kingdom*. It breaks my heart to see life destroyed just to decorate a wall."

Nate looked up at a bear's head.

"My father didn't sympathize with anything," he said, feeling the bitterness rise in him again. As if to wash it away, he took a long sip of his drink.

"Hey, easy with that stuff," Jim said. "That's good scotch you've got there."

"I just had a thought about my father," Nate said.

Jim lifted his glass.

"Then drink up," he said, "I thought I told you to forget about that old bastard. Exorcise his ghost. Why do you even think about him?"

"I don't know," Nate said. "It's hard to put it out of my mind. You know the funeral was barely two months ago and I've gotten a few nasty letters from people who thought they belonged in my father's will. They keep reminding me of him."

"They're crazy. Just think about your theater," Jim said. "That should be your only concern."

"Right," Nate said, finishing his drink.

The theater alone, he thought. No nightmares, no visions of his father. Just the theater.

Later that night, while going over papers in his father's study, Nate was interrupted by the jangling of the telephone. Still working as he said "hello," he did not hear the name mentioned at the other end.

"Pardon?" he asked, clicking his pen shut.

"Your cousin, Vance, Nate," a man's voice said. "Callin' to ask about your daddy's will."

"It's none of your business," Nate said.

"It sure as hell is!" Vance cried. "I figure it must be out of—of—what's that word? Predate?"

"Probate," Nate said.

"Well?" Vance drawled. Nate did not answer him directly, and so he went on. "Now, you listen. You know I was very close to dear Uncle Nathaniel. I've got to be one of his heirs!"

You hated his guts just like everyone else, Nate thought.

"I'm sorry," he said, "but you weren't included in the will."

Nate heard a sharp noise, like a fist striking a tabletop. He sighed and looked up at the elk's head over the door. Thank God he only had one relative!

"Some of that money is rightfully mine!" Vance yelled. "I was better to your father than you ever were! You couldn't have gotten all his money."

Impatiently, Nate slammed down the receiver. He was

too busy to bother with an idiot like Vance Dysart, a man who carried a perpetual chip on his shoulder.

Fred Johnson had been working on his sketches for Nate's theater for nearly three weeks when he finally decided he was satisfied with the finished product. He held a watercolor rendering at arm's distance and scrutinized it. It was perfect, right down to the gold filigree on the wainscotting, and about as opulent as Louis XIV's palace.

"I'm usually better at Bauhaus designs," he said. "God knows where I got the inspiration for this thing."

The room grew cold suddenly, as if an icy wind had found its way through the vents. Fred buttoned his sweater, unaware that he was being watched. When the cold snap passed, Fred went back to work, adding a few finishing touches here and there.

That afternoon, he met with Nate. The young producer rolled open the blueprints on the drafting table and held either end with his palms to keep them from snapping closed.

"That's an outer hallway," Fred said, pointing. "It should keep things flowing smoothly during performances."

"Good idea," Nate said.

The next blueprint was a cross-section.

"Why so much space between the first floor and basement?" he asked.

"Those are air passages," Fred explained, "for air conditioning and heating equipment."

Nate made a grunting comment and rerolled the papers. Fred Johnson was working for him because he was the best money could buy, and obviously he knew what he was talking about.

"Have you got any sketches of the finished theater?" he asked.

"There on my desk," Fred answered. "In the black portfolio."

Plastic pages slid to either side of metal rings as Nate opened the leather folder. He flipped back to the first page and studied the series of watercolor renderings Fred had done. The color that dominated all the pictures was gold. The seats were gold, the wainscotting, the trim along the balcony. A painting of the stage showed that its curtains were to be done in gold, too, with white designs woven through them.

"Very nice," Nate commented, turning the page.

But a second later, he turned back again. He studied the picture of the stage for a few moments. The dream. In the dream, the curtains were gold and white.

"Why did you choose this color scheme?" he asked, abruptly.

"You wanted it to be opulent," Fred answered. "What's more elegant than gold?"

"Crimson is regal-looking," Nate snapped.

"But I think gold works better," Fred pressed. He did not know why, but it seemed important not to change any details of his work.

"Forget it," Nate said. "Gold is fine."

He felt a little idiotic, having reacted so strongly to a simple color scheme. The fact that these curtains were gold and white was coincidental, of course!

"It's all very beautiful," he said, a little more calmly. "How soon will it be complete?"

"There are a few minor details left," Fred said. "But I should be through by the end of the week."

Nate pulled one of Jim Orland's business cards from his pocket and handed it to the architect.

"My stage manager will be handling this," he said. "You can have the finished drafts sent to his place."

With that, Nate left the studio and waited in the hallway for the elevator. To his relief, there were no voices to haunt him. When he left the building, he walked a few blocks to the nearest bus stop. It amused him that people would stand in the middle of the street watching for a bus, as if that would make it come faster. But after standing for five minutes, he understood their impatience. He wished he had brought the car today, but George had been sick and he had taken the train.

Finally, the bus arrived, very crowded. Though it was a cool March day, the bus was uncomfortably hot and Nate was glad when he reached his destination.

Whenever he came into New York, he liked to stop at the property he'd bought and imagine his theater there. He had been approached by quite a number of people willing to back his production. As Nate walked toward the lot he smiled to think some of those backers were acquaintances and contacts of his father's. The old man had had a great deal of disdain for the theater and would be turning over in his grave if he knew

how his business associates were fawning over the son he
hated.

It amused Nate to imagine how those stuffy old men would
cringe at the sight of the broken, gum-encrusted, littered
sidewalk that ran in front of the property their money had
helped buy. He stepped aside to let a bag lady get by, her
small brown eyes staring down at the toes of her pink
bedroom slippers. Suddenly, she looked up at the lot and
shook her head sadly, her thin lips forming a string of silent
words. Then she continued on her way, as if anxious to get
away, teetering back and forth between the loaded shopping
bags she held in either hand.

The chain-link fence was surrounded by tall planks of
wood, which were already covered with graffiti and posters.
Nate, who loved children, though it might be a nice gesture
to the city to allow some school kids to paint over it. Just as
this idea occurred to him he noticed a little girl watching
him, half-hidden in the doorway of the adjacent building.
Nate smiled at her.

"Hi," he said. "What're you doing there?"

The child whimpered and pulled herself further into the
doorway. Funny, one didn't usually see small children left
alone on the city streets. Sensing she might need help, Nate
approached her.

But the doorway was empty. Nate reached for the handle of
the door and tried to pull it open. It was locked.

"She must have gone inside," he rationalized. "I don't
know how kids move so fast."

But it wasn't his problem. He returned to the lot and
unlocked the gate, aware that curious passers-by were looking
at him, probably wondering what new building would be
erected there. Nate opened it and walked onto a stretch of
smooth dirt. At his orders, the place had been cleaned up
after its purchase. The dead grass had been plowed under,
the bottles and cinder blocks and litter had been hauled away.
Nate leaned back against the fence and shoved his hands into
his pockets, the words "Dysart Theater" coming to mind. He
smiled.

"Pretty soon," he said.

He left the site and locked the gate behind himself, then
headed over to Broadway to take a taxi to Grand Central

Station. A thousand people saw him, but no one would recall his face. No one but a little girl who stood on the sidewalk with her arms outstretched, watching him fade into the distance.

After Fred Johnson finished his work, Nate went over the plans with Jim and then sent them to the contracting company he'd hired. In the meantime, he began interviewing people to man his stage.

"I'm glad that's over with," Nate said after the final employee had been hired. "God, do you realize it's April already? I've never interviewed so many people in my life!"

"Hey, look," Jim said, "it keeps you off the streets. And you'd better get used to seeing people. You're a big producer now, Nate. We do things on a bigger scale here on Broadway than you did in California."

Nate squinted.

"Off-Broadway was never like this," he said.

There was a knock at the door, and Jim got up to answer it. Virginia Atwell, an older woman whom Nate had hired as casting director, entered the room.

"How's the deal with Sander Bernaux?" he asked.

"I've spoken to his agent half a dozen times," Virginia replied. "We're still negotiating his contract. He's tough."

"Give him whatever he wants," Nate said.

Jim folded his arms and said, "Nate, that kind of talk could get you into a lot of trouble."

"What do you mean?"

"I mean," Jim said, "if Bernaux sees you're desperate he'll milk you for everything he can get."

Virginia looked from Jim to Nate. "I agree," she said. "I've worked with him several times, and I know how ruthless he can be."

Nate turned to gaze out the window for a few moments before replying. Across the street, he could see a garment factory, where several dozen women were hunched over gray sewing machines.

"You also know how much it means to me to work with one of Broadway's greatest actors," he said, still watching the factory. "I've got to prove to my father that..."

"Nate, your father is dead," Jim interrupted. He waved a

hand at Virginia, dismissing her so that they could talk privately.

"Why do you have to prove something to a dead man?" he asked.

Nate finally met his eyes. "Maybe I'm trying to prove it to myself, then," he said.

"Prove what?" Jim demanded. "That you're good enough to work with a guy like Bernaux? You already know that's true."

"You know what my father used to say to me?" Nate said in reply. "Whenever he heard Meg and me talking about someday working with a star like Sander Bernaux, he'd start in with that crazy laugh of his and he'd say, 'Sander Bernaux wouldn't spit on you, let alone work with an untalented amateur!' And then he'd ask how I dared hope I'd ever be a success."

"Nate, your father was a jackass," Jim said, straightening. "Forget him, will you?"

"I can't," Nate insisted. "It's something embedded too deeply in me."

For a few moments, both men were silent. Jim watched Nate's expression, reading bitterness in his eyes. Nate would probably never get over the pain of his childhood, Jim thought. And those strange nightmares. What were they about? A little girl in a burning theater. Very symbolic. He was beginning to have an idea of what they meant.

"I've just figured something out," he said.

"What's that?"

"Maybe those dreams of yours have something to do with this obsession you have," he said. "Maybe that little girl isn't really a little girl at all, but represents something. The burning stage, too, and the orchestra pit."

Nate shook his head.

"I don't go for that supernatural stuff," he said.

"Listen to me," Jim pressed. He held up a hand and started pressing back his fingers with the other. "First, let's look at the kid. Could she be your career, begging to be started again? Second, the burning theater. Maybe that represents your fear that you might not be successful. It would make sense, considering how your father criticized you all the time."

"Sounds interesting," Nate said. He liked the idea that there might be a simple explanation to the nightmares and encouraged Jim to go on.

"Finally, there's the orchestra pit you fall into," Jim said. He cocked his hand back and forth, making a comparison. "Falling—plunging. You're plunging into a career no matter what the consequences. And I think that means, Nate, that you're going to do all right."

Nate grinned.

"You sound more like a psychiatrist than a stage manager," he said.

"But doesn't it make sense?" Jim asked.

"Yeah, I guess so," Nate shrugged.

But it made perfect sense. And Nate decided he would hold on to Jim's simple explanation. It was better than believing he was being tormented by some uncontrollable force.

THREE

Nate often visited the site where his new theater was being built, watching its progress with a feeling of excitement and pride. He ached for the day it would bear his name and decided to keep a record of the building stages so that he could look back on them one day and remember this happy time. He bought himself a camera and took pictures of the men digging the foundation, pouring the concrete, erecting the steel girders. The roll was completed about the same time as the building's frame, and Nate mailed it to a local developing studio. It was Jim who brought him the return package one morning, along with a pile of other mail.

"We've got an article in the *Times* today," he said, putting the pile on Nate's desk. "And another in *Architect's Digest*. That one has a four-color shot."

"Great," Nate said, removing the red-and-white photo envelope. "I'll take a look at it in a minute. First I want to see how my own pictures came out."

He slid them out, being careful not to drop the negatives, and started thumbing through them. The first few were good shots, taking in details such as a worker's hands on a drill or the date etched into the foundation's corner. Nate handed them up to Jim one at a time but stopped when he found a picture with a flaw, a white blur that hovered just above one of the girders. Further inspection showed that all of the other pictures were marked in the same way, though the blurs were in different places and varied in size.

"I'd better stick to directing," Nate joked. "I didn't do very well with my new camera."

"These pictures are fine," Jim said, holding up the first few. "What's wrong with those?"

He came around to Nate's side and looked at the remaining photos.

"Kind of looks like a person," he said. "See those two sticks coming out of the bottom? They could be legs."

"Hovering in midair?" Nate asked. "Hey, knock off the spooky stuff. You'll make me have those nightmares again."

Jim put the photos down on the desk.

"How long has it been since the last one?" he asked thoughtfully.

"A couple of months," Nate said, smiling. "Ever since you gave me that crazy explanation of yours."

"See what I told you?" Jim asked. "It was just your subconscious trying to relay a message to you. Now that the theater is going up, you don't need those dreams anymore."

"I *have* relaxed a great deal since the funeral," Nate agreed. "In spite of the annoying phone calls I keep getting from my cousin Vance. He doesn't really bother me, though. And I suppose the fact that Virginia's finally reached an agreement with Sander Bernaux's agent has something to do with it."

"When are you meeting with him?"

"After the preliminary auditions," Nate said. "I wish it could be sooner, but a man like Bernaux always has other commitments. But, since we have to wait for the theater to be completed anyway, it doesn't really matter."

Jim nodded. "So long as someone doesn't come along and steal him from us."

"Don't say that," Nate ordered. "I've got Sander Bernaux under contract, and that's that."

In the autumn of 1981 the finishing touches were put on the Dysart Theater, and at last Nate's lifelong dream became a reality. A small gathering of press people joined the employees of Nate's company, taking pictures and scribbling notes as they all watched the theater's name being chiseled into the stone above the doors.

"It's finally real," Nate whispered to Jim. "I can't believe it!"

"It's yours, all right," Jim said. "You've got your name up there to prove it."

"This theater is going to be the most famous on Broadway," Nate promised himself, out loud. "In a year's time, everyone will know its name."

"Good luck with it, Nate," Jim said.

Just then, as the last letter was carved, everyone burst into applause. Nate grinned, turning up his collar against the cold September air.

Nearby, an elderly wino took a swig from a bottle hidden in a paper bag. They'll be sorry, he thought. This was a bad place, an unlucky place. A lot had happened here.

But Nate and the others were too elated to think anything but good thoughts. The wino shook his head and staggered away, a piece of discarded newspaper rolling in the wind and catching his ankles. He bent down to pick it up and stuffed it into a torn pocket of his jacket. He felt a cold chill as he did so, but thought it was only another gust of wind.

"Dennis Richmond," a woman with a southern accent said loudly to the young boy seated beside her on the subway train, "why must you always carry that silly basketball?"

"It isn't silly," her eleven-year-old son replied. "Daddy sent it to me, and I like it."

"Don't sass me," Georgia Richmond scolded. "I'll tell you what's silly and what isn't. A boy your age couldn't possibly know."

Denny shifted on the hard plastic seat and looked up at his mother.

"I do so know," he said. "I know going to five auditions in two weeks is stupid. None of those TV guys wanted me—I'm sure. Same thing with that theater we went to.

"You just have to be patient, Denny," Georgia said, kissing the brown hair that hung loosely over his ears and forehead. "There hasn't been a chance for anyone to give us a call-back. Someone will hire you, of course. Remember how everyone praised your acting down home?"

"South Carolina isn't the same as New York City," Denny protested.

That was for certain, he thought, looking around at the unintelligible graffiti that completely covered the walls. Above a row of seats crammed with sour-faced passengers, someone had drawn private body parts on a woman clad in a bikini who was grinning out from a poster written in Spanish. If someone did that in his hometown, Denny thought, he'd spend a week in jail!

As the train came to a halt at the Forty-second Street station Georgia stood up and took Denny by the hand. People jostled them back and forth in a mad rush to the stairs. Georgia yelped as she felt someone pinch her backside. She pulled Denny close to her and quickened her pace. She held him tightly, afraid he'd come in contact with the walls, which were covered with filth sprayed from thousands of trains. As another train rumbled into the station, they reached a flight of stairs and hurried up them. Traffic was as insane as ever in busy Times Square, and Georgia was tempted to hang on to Denny to protect him from the taxi drivers who screeched around corners without looking.

"Button your jacket," Georgia ordered. "It's cold out here and I don't want you sniffling during your audition."

Denny shifted his basketball to his other arm, then buttoned his corduroy jacket, weaving in and out of the crowds as he did so. He thought it was funny that you could rarely walk a straight line in New York City.

"I sure hope we don't have to wait for two hours," he said, "like the last audition!"

"A good actor never gives up," Georgia said, taking his hand once more to cross the busy street.

At last they reached their destination. Georgia stopped momentarily to admire the facade of the theater, praying that her son might someday work inside it. Elaborate curvilinear motifs swirled around the glass doors which were trimmed in highly-polished wood. Georgia pushed through them and found a sign directing her to the auditions. Denny opened one of the vestibule's etched glass doors for her and together they entered a crowded lobby.

"My goodness," Georgia drawled. "I didn't expect it would be like this!"

The other auditions had been crowded, but the lobby of the Dysart Theater was so full of hopefuls that Georgia could hardly make her way to the line at the sign-in table. Determined, though, she pushed Denny ahead of her and took a place behind a red-haired woman. She tapped her on the shoulder and said, "Is this where we give our name?"

The young woman smiled.

"Yes, it is," she said. She looked at Denny. "Hi, I'm Adrian St. John. And I suppose you're trying out for the part of Jimmy Bertrand?"

"He sure is," Georgia said before Denny could speak. She kissed his freckled cheek, making him squirm a little. "My little Denny is going to make them forget every other kid here today."

Adrian laughed, seeing the way Denny rolled his eyes. She understood how embarrassed a kid his age could be by his mother, having several younger brothers of her own. Georgia, she thought, was like a character in her own comedy, with bleached-blonde hair and a bright multicolored dress. Adrian was glad to see Denny had worn a white shirt and dark slacks. Appearances meant a lot when you were competing with so many others.

"I'm trying out for the part of Jimmy's mother," she said, moving forward with the line. "Daisy Bertrand, that is."

"You're really calm," Denny said, in a southern accent not quite as thick as his mother's. "You must go to a lot of auditions."

Adrian held up a small hand to show him the trembling there.

"I could do this every day," she said, "and never get used to it."

"But you must have experience?" Georgia asked.

"A few heads off-Broadway," Adrian said. "And I had a minor role in Horace Rightwood's last production here on Broadway. But it was all comedy, so that gives me an edge here."

Adrian gave her name and address to the woman seated at the sign-in table and noticed there were quite a few other names listed under "Daisy". That meant she would have a little time to go out for some fresh air and calm down.

"Good luck," Georgia said as she moved off the line.

"You mean, 'break a leg,'" Adrian said with a smile. "Thanks. Maybe we'll work together, huh, Denny?"

The little boy nodded, then took his place in front of the table.

"Full name, please," the woman said, her pencil held over a yellow pad.

"Dennis Randall Richmond," Georgia said. "He's eleven years old, and..."

The woman looked up at her.

"I'd like the boy to speak for himself," she said. "Now, Dennis, where are you currently living?"

Denny told her, and the woman recorded the information. Then she pulled another pad in front of herself and wrote his name. Denny watched his name go under the subtitle "Jimmy" and saw the number fifty-eight go before it. The woman waved her pencil at him and said, "You can find a place to sit until we call you. And be sure to leave that basketball with your mother."

Before leaving, Georgia asked if there was a bathroom open.

"Upstairs," the woman said.

"I want you to try to go," Georgia said as she and Denny moved back into the clusters of waiting actors.

"Mom," Denny gasped. "Don't talk like that with so many people around!"

"I don't care," Georgia said, though she lowered her voice. "I want us to be right here when they start calling names. What will I say if you're off in the little boys' room then?"

"I'll be okay," Denny said. "For crying out loud, Mom. I'm not in diapers anymore!"

Georgia pointed toward the vast staircase and, with her expression, ordered obedience. Shaking his head, Denny handed her the basketball and headed toward the stairs, leaving her to talk to a young man. As soon as he started up the stairs, Denny forgot his embarrassment. He'd never seen stairs so huge in his entire life or a banister so polished.

"If I get hired, I'm going to slide down this thing," he promised himself.

He stopped at the top landing and folded his arms over the railing. From here, he could take in details of the crowded lobby. There was a huge concession stand at one end, trimmed with gold that swirled in a flowery pattern. Two bronze statues of Greek goddesses stood on either side of the etched glass doors leading into the auditorium. Denny's eyes moved to take in the bar, empty now, with three small chandeliers that hung from the ceiling, and a door at the far end marked No Admittance.

Then he saw his mother looking up at him and hurried away. But when he was certain she could no longer see him, he opened one of the doors leading into the mezzanine. It was chilly and dark inside, and Denny had to wait a moment for his eyes to adjust to the tiny lights that dotted the rows of seats. Holding out his arms to balance himself, he walked down toward the railing. What he saw there made him gasp with awe.

The stage was the biggest he'd ever seen in his life, draped with gold and white curtains that seemed to glitter like stars. A huge chandelier, which Denny was certain contained a few thousand pieces of crystal, swayed almost imperceptibly overhead. He raised his eyes further and saw a ceiling painted to resemble a sky. At each corner there was a painting that depicted one of the four seasons. Old man Winter blew clouds that whirled all around, Spring was wrapped in curling flowers, and Summer and Autumn carried on the same flowing theme.

"Gosh," Denny whispered.

Wondering what else there was to see, he turned toward the doors again. But as he did so, someone appeared in front of him in the dark. With a cry, Denny stumbled backward, landing hard on his rump.

From the stage down below, someone called, "Who's up there?"

Denny looked up to see a little girl. Realizing he was in no danger, except of getting in trouble for being there, he ignored the man on the stage and raced toward the door. When he got out in the hallway, he was surprised to see the little girl already there.

"Whatja go sneaking up on me like that for?" he demanded.

She did not reply. Denny sat on one of the velveteen chairs lining a wall and sighed. The child stood in front of him, staring at him with dark eyes. She was wearing a white dress layered with rows of frilly ruffles, and her dark hair was drawn to one side with a frothy white bow. Denny guessed she was in costume.

"What part are you trying out for?" he asked. "I don't remember seeing any other little girls in the lobby."

She shook her head.

"I'm all alone," she said. "This is my theater."

"Oh, I get it," Denny said. "Your Daddy owns the place."

His mother had told him that Nate Dysart was very rich. In his hometown in South Carolina the rich people always put their little girls in fussy dresses like the one this kid was wearing. He didn't like those rich, snobby kids. And he had already decided he didn't like this little girl. Why did she have to stare that way?

"Don't you have some place to go?" he asked.

"This is my place," she replied. "I'm always here."

Denny stood up and headed for the men's room, figuring she wouldn't follow him in there. But she did, and she leaned against a marble urinal as he unzipped his pants. He quickly closed them again and cried, "Will you get lost?"

"No," she said. "This is my theater, and you can't tell me what to do!"

"Boy, what a brat!" Denny said. "I'm going downstairs. Why don't you try to find your mother?"

His words upset the child so much that she started screaming, a high-pitched wail that made Denny cover his ears.

"Cut it out!" he ordered.

She glared at him.

"Don't want to see Mommy," she hissed. "Mommy made it dark and the dark hurt me!"

Denny watched her for a moment, then decided she was crazy and ran out of the bathroom. He did not look back as he bounded down the stairway, hoping he'd gotten rid of her. He decided then he was glad he didn't have any little sisters.

An hour and a half passed before Adrian's name was called. She said good-bye to Denny and entered the auditorium with several others, behind Virginia Atwell. Once on stage, she was handed a script and positioned up center. Adrian could see about a dozen people in the seats below, all holding black notebooks. They ranged in age from thirteen to eighty, representing a cross-section of people who might be found in any given audience. Adrian knew the "casting committee" had been selected so that the director could get an idea how an actor related to different audience types.

Now a handsome, blond-haired man in a plaid shirt spoke up, telling one of the other women to read the part of Daisy, and assigning the part of Jimmy to a young boy. The others, including Adrian, were given peripheral roles.

"You can start any time," Nate said, biting the end of his pencil.

Adrian was surprised to see he was such a young man, hardly older than her twenty-eight years. But he dismissed and replaced the people on stage with so little emotion that she knew he was completely professional. Still, it was his first Broadway production. When her turn came to read the part of Daisy, she put her all into it. She liked the idea of working with someone who was up-and-coming in the business.

"Why, if it hadn't been for this blessed crucifix," she said, picking up where the actress before her had left off," my little son Jimmy might well have died!"

She brought it to her lips and kissed it, a gesture not in the script but that came naturally to a woman who had attended twelve years of Catholic school. As she did this several of the people watching her took notes, and Nate said, "Nice touch, Miss, uh . . ." he looked at his list. "Miss St. John."

She paused, expecting to be dismissed.

"Go ahead, dear," Virginia said from the wings.

As Adrian continued her monologue Nate forgot the pad in

his hand and leaned forward to take in every moment of her
acting. She was the most talented woman he'd seen so far,
and she worked easily with everyone who came on stage. Not
only that, she was very attractive. Her wavy hair was a lovely
strawberry blonde, framing a fair, childish face that spoke of
Irish descent. Her green eyes sparkled under the stage
lights. She was small in stature, almost childlike, but her
voice was filled with flirtatious sensuality.

"I like the way she works," Virginia whispered. "She could
even con me into buying one of those phony crosses."

"Put her down for a call-back," Nate answered.

By the time Adrian was dismissed from the stage, everyone
in the casting committee agreed she should be considered for
the part. But Adrian didn't know what they were thinking,
and when she entered the lobby again her stomach knotted.
She thought of a dozen little things she should or shouldn't
have done and wished she could go back in and try again.

"Wow, they must have really liked you," Denny said. "You
were in there a long time!"

"I don't know," Adrian said. "I think I'm just going to go
home and wallow in self-pity."

"I'm sure you did just fine," Georgia insisted.

Outside it had started raining slightly, and of course she
did not have an umbrella. But maybe that was a good sign, a
portent that she'd done all right after all.

A smile spread over her face at the thought, and she stood
in front of the theater deciding which way to go. She noticed
a little girl huddled next to the row of doors, staring at her
with something like hatred in her eyes. But Adrian only
smiled at her, determined to think positively.

The wet, musty smell of fallen leaves rose thickly from the
ground as Jim Orland jogged through the park that sat just a
block away from his Connecticut home. He'd spent the
previous few weeks in Manhattan, renting a small apartment
so that he could easily get to the theater. After the hectic
pace of auditions, the tranquillity of this park seemed almost
surrealistic. Alone in this atmosphere, he was better able to
think about the way things were going for him. As far as Jim
was concerned, things couldn't have been more perfect. It
was great to work with Nate again after so many years. Funny

how sometimes the friendships that you formed as a kid were
the best ones of your life. During his other jobs in the
theater, Jim had been sort of an underdog, always careful not
to step on toes. But as Nate's right-hand-man, he held a
position of some authority—and if the play was a success, he
could make a name for himself. Jim looked forward to this
new production with the same delighted anticipation he felt
whenever he began a new job.

His mind elsewhere, Jim nearly tripped over the dog who
suddenly cut across his path. His sneakers made a sharp slap
on the pavement as he brought himself to a halt, stretching
his arms out from his sides to balance himself.

"Ho, Sport," he said.

The dog, a Heinz-57-Varieties type, picked up a stick with
its huge jaws and gazed at Jim imploringly. Jim hopped back
and forth, full of adrenaline from his run. He took the stick
and flung it, sending the mutt bounding into a clump of
bushes.

He began to run again. The dog kept pace with him,
cutting back and forth across the path, its curly tail wagging.
Jim, still running, took the stick and threw it again.

"Red!"

Suddenly, the dog stopped, perked up its ears. Hearing its
name again, it dropped the stick and gave one bark. In a
moment Jim saw a woman hurrying across the grass, her
canvas jacket flying open and the dog's leash dangling from
her hand.

"Red, what's the big idea?"

She crouched down and clicked the leash onto Red's collar.
Jim watched in wonder, unable to find even a single red hair
in the mongrel's coat. Finally, the woman looked up and
smiled at him.

"Red was making a pest of himself, I guess," she said,
apologizing.

"Not really," Jim replied. "It helps break the monotony of
jogging, anyway."

The woman, young and blonde and pretty, stood up. The
smile on her face widened.

"Wait a sec," she said. "I know who you are!"

"You do?" Jim asked, unable to recognize the woman.

"You work with the fellow who just inherited all that
money," she said. "Uh—sorry if I get your name wrong. Is it
Jim Orville?"

Jim laughed. "Orland. How'd you know?"

"Read it in the paper a few Sundays back," she said. "I'm
Debbi Natanson."

"Glad to meet you," Jim said. "And flattered too. This is
the first time I've ever been recognized."

For the next half hour Jim strolled through the park with
Debbi, happy to talk about his job and the new play. He
promised her a ticket for opening night, but he knew he
wouldn't want to wait that long to see her again. Reunited
with his best friend, working in a terrific job, and having a
beautiful woman in his future, Jim believed that things could
not have been more perfect.

FOUR

Both Denny and Adrian were called back to the final
auditions, but when two weeks went by without a word from
Virginia Atwell, Denny assumed he hadn't gotten the part.
His mother waited by the phone as much as possible, but
Denny had too much energy in him for that. So today, on a
cool September afternoon, he was outside playing with his
friends.

"Watch this," he said, aiming his basketball at the hoop
they'd set up on a telephone pole. The street was their court,
marked with yellow chalk to indicate boundaries. Denny let
the ball fly and executed a perfect shot.

"You gonna try out for the basketball team at school?"
Mikey Smith wanted to know.

"That's gonna be hard," Paul Kasson said. "He's got all this
actor stuff going on. How could he have time for sports?"

Denny bounced the basketball a few times and then threw
it to Mikey.

"I didn't get a part yet," he said. "I guess I might try out.
Might as well, since I don't seem to have much luck as an
actor."

"My mother says your mother is nuts for dragging you to Manhattan so much," Mikey said. "She says you'll probably miss too much school."

The little boy felt his collar tighten as Denny grabbed him and pulled him close.

"You tell your mom that she's got no right to talk like that," he said. "I'm gonna get a private tutor, and I bet I learn more than any of you."

He let go of Mikey and took his ball away. Paul knocked it away, laughed, and in a moment the three boys were playing happily again. A few minutes later the sound of a window scraping open alerted them to Denny's building. Normally, they wouldn't even pay attention, but it was too chilly a September day for anyone to open a window. Denny looked up to see his mother waving at him.

"Denny!" Georgia Richmond cried. "They called! You got the part! You're in Nate Dysart's play."

Denny's mouth dropped open in shock. He felt one of the other boys slap his back and barely heard Paul say, "Whoa, a big shot actor!"

Denny grinned and ran to the apartment building, where his mother greeted him with a big hug and kiss.

"Let's go out and celebrate," she said. "Here, put on your good shirt."

Denny changed into it, mumbling "I don't believe it" over and over. During the auditions, he hadn't dared hope he might be in the play. But it was true!

Across town Adrian St. John hung up her own telephone and went to the refrigerator to find a bottle of champagne. She'd been saving it for this moment, to celebrate her first leading role on Broadway. Pouring it into a crystal glass, she carried it over to a mirror and toasted her reflection.

"Way to go, lady," she said.

News like this was too good to keep to herself. Yet Adrian didn't have many friends here in New York. She spent so much time pursuing her career as an actress that her social life was rather quiet. Still, she was bursting with elation. She had to call her family in Ohio. They had been so worried when she came to New York, thinking she would only be disappointed. Yet she was about to play the female lead in a major Broadway production!

She was so jittery that she had to hang up and dial twice before getting the number right. She could hear faint sounds through the telephone wire, disembodied voices of thousands of people sharing the line. Then finally, there was a click, and then a series of faint-sounding rings. When her mother answered the phone, Adrian was surprised at how clear she sounded.

"Hi, it's your famous daughter!" she cried delightedly.

"Adrian!" Martha St. John replied. "It's so good to hear from you."

Adrian heard her telling someone who it was on the line.

"Your father wants to know when you're coming home," Martha said.

"Maybe never," Adrian said with a laugh. "Don't worry, Mom. I'm all right. In fact, I'm terrific. Guess what?"

Martha made some hesitant noises into the phone, and Adrian could imagine her waving a wooden spoon. More voices filled the background, youthful and excited.

"Is everyone there?" Adrian asked.

"Bill and Pat are in town," Martha said, referring to Adrian's oldest brothers. "But the other seven boys are right here sharing dinner with us. Sure wish you could be here, Adrian."

Adrian grinned. "Mom, wait till you hear what happened! I auditioned for a new play that's going to be right on Broadway. And I got the part!"

"Adrian!" Martha cried with delight.

Someone in the background asked what happened, and Martha told the family her daughter's news.

"Wait, there's more," Adrian said. "I'm the female lead—and I'm playing opposite Sander Bernaux!"

"Sander who?"

Martha's confusion made Adrian laugh again. "The most important actor on Broadway. Working with him is going to make me famous, and really help my career."

"Well, darling, that's wonderful," Martha said. "Wait, your father wants to talk to you."

Tom St. John sounded very serious over the phone, but Adrian knew that he was bursting with pride.

"How much are they paying you?" he asked.

"Lots," Adrian said. When she told her father the terms of contract, he whistled shrilly. "So you see, you don't have to worry about me."

There was a long pause, and then Tom said carefully, "You'll be real busy, huh?"

"Oh, yes," Adrian said. "Rehearsals start soon."

"Too busy to visit home?"

"Dad, why don't you and Mom come to New York?" Adrian suggested. "You could let Bill and Pat watch the little ones, and be here for my opening night in December."

"That sounds like a great idea," Tom said. "We'll talk about it, your mother and me."

Adrian finished the conversation off with a few trivial bits of news, then hung up the phone. She poured herself another little glass of champagne and laughed out loud.

"Small-town kid makes good," she said, grinning broadly.

In the Dysart Theater, Jim Orland was setting up for a little party to celebrate the fact that they were finally through with auditions.

Jim and Virginia were moving two metal tables onto the stage, working along with the others in the casting committee. Nate was busy in his office, doing a telephone interview for a national magazine.

"I always feel a great burden has been lifted when auditions are over," Virginia said, setting up a row of plastic utensils.

"Imagine how hard it is for the actors," Jim replied. He shrugged. "But it's the price you pay."

As they worked, the theater's mascot, a Siamese cat, who had rather mysteriously arrived, the day the theater opened, walked delicately around the orchestra pit railing. Suddenly, her ears lay back flat against her head, and her back hunched up. Jim and Virginia looked at each other, then turned to the cat. Cartier seemed to be staring at something in the orchestra pit.

"Don't tell me our brand-new theater has mice already," Virginia said.

Jim walked to the apron and looked down.

"There's nothing there," he said. He waved a hand at the cat. "Get lost, pest!"

Instead, Cartier turned and stared down the center aisle with saucer eyes that seemed to be watching something neither Virginia nor Jim could see. Just then, the door at the end of the middle aisle opened a little. Jim saw a small child's

silhouette and started to ask Virginia about her. But the
casting director had turned back to arranging the tables. At
first, Jim thought the little girl must belong to someone
working here. But she stood apart from the group for so long
that he wondered if she might need help. Finally, he left the
stage to ask her what was wrong.

A long hallway running alongside the auditorium led him
to the lobby, where he found the little girl. Approaching her
with a smile, he said, "Hi, honey. Where's your mom?"

She stepped back a little.

"Mommy's gone," she said.

"You don't have to be afraid of me," Jim told her. "I won't
hurt you. Want to wait for your mommy inside? We've got
some nice soda you can have."

The little girl shook her head and moved backward to the
winding staircase. Then, suddenly, she turned and raced up
them. Jim followed closely, trying to catch her. He didn't
want a small child alone upstairs. They didn't want any
unfortunate accidents when everything was going so well.

"Wait up!" he cried. "God, how can you move so fast?"

She ducked into a closet and slammed the door. Jim, losing
his patience, tugged it open and reached to pull her out.

The closet was empty.

"Wait a minute," he said, opening and closing his eyes.
"I'm sure I saw her go inside!"

He looked around and found the child standing clear across
the lobby, twisting the front of her ruffled white dress with
tiny fists.

"Hey, you can't be playing up here," Jim said. "Come on
and I'll take you downstairs."

"*No!*" the child cried.

Jim pointed a finger at her.

"Listen, I'm pretty patient with kids," he said. "But you're
cruising for a bruising. Either you come with me, or I'll tell
your mother you were up here."

He grabbed hold of her and lifted her into his arms. She
was very light, almost weightless, and he thought he would
have no more trouble from her.

"I'm sure your mommy is looking all over for you," he said.

Suddenly, she began to whimper.

"Don't want to see Mommy," she said.

"You have to, I'm afraid," Jim answered firmly.

"NNNNOOOO!!!!"

Her scream was so ear-piercing that Jim nearly dropped her. But she grabbed hold of his head and clung to him, her hands squeezing his temples. Now it was Jim's turn to scream, for a pain was seizing him, a burning pain more horrible than any he had ever known.

"I won't go to mommy!" the child cried. "I won't! I won't let the dark come again!"

Jim's mouth snapped open, and a gutteral choking sound came out as he collapsed to the floor. Hideous pain crept over his body, making his legs and arms quake involuntarily at his sides. The child straddled him, staring into his wide eyes with an eternity of hatred in her expression.

"You tried to hurt me," she hissed. "You want the dark to come again. Terrible man!"

Jim tried to speak, but a strange clicking noise was the only sound that escaped his throat. His body jerking, he watched the child rise above him like a demon, floating towards the carved ceiling. And then she was gone.

The pain stopped. Jim's eyes fluttered, and he lost consciousness.

Nate was smiling when he walked on stage. Someone insisted that he, as the head of the Dysart Theater, should do the honors of opening the champagne. Nate obliged, and in a moment the liquid was flowing into paper cups. Nate raised his own cup.

"To surviving three crazy weeks," he said. "And to a great group of people. Jim, want to come up here where I can see you?"

He scanned the group but did not see his friend.

"Where did he go?" he asked Virginia.

"I don't really know," she said. She had been so busy setting up for the party that she hadn't seen the stage manager leave.

Nate waved the back of his hand at the table.

"Go ahead everybody and drink," he said. "I'll try to find him."

As he was heading toward the down-right exit a strange

groaning noise filled the auditorium. Nate looked up and saw
Jim at the edge of the mezzanine, holding out his arms. Jim
seemed to be swaying unsteadily at the edge, but Nate
couldn't be sure because of the dim lights. He walked down
to the floor and called up to him.

"What's the matter?" he asked. "What are you doing up
there?"

But Jim did not reply. The pain that had made him pass out
a moment ago had returned, burning him, crawling over his
flesh. When he'd woken up, he had come in here to call for
help. But somehow, he had no voice. He reached out into the
air as if to grab his best friend, as if Nate could take the pain
away. Nate came closer and saw Jim more clearly. His face
was red, and sweat poured profusely over his skin, staining
the blue chambray shirt he wore and plastering his curly hair.
But his eyes were what made Nate break into a run to get
upstairs. They were wild eyes, filled with terror.

Nate took the steps two at a time and moved like lightning
into the mezzanine. Once inside, he caught hold of his
friend's arm, pulled him away from the edge, and tried to sit
him down. Instead, Jim backed further away and screamed.

"What the hell is wrong with you?" Nate demanded,
panicking. His friend had always been so easygoing, yet now
every muscle in his body was contracted in fear. "Jim, can't
you talk to me?"

Jim wanted to talk to his friend but couldn't. The pain
wouldn't let him. With a cry, he sank to the steps and closed
his eyes, tears spilling uncontrollably.

"Dear God," Nate whispered. He called to the people on
the stage below. "Virginia, get a doctor!"

He sat down next to Jim and carefully put an arm around
his shoulder. This time, Jim did not shrink away. He was
breathing heavily, and his sweat was pouring even more
profusely.

"God, I wish you could tell me what's wrong," Nate said.
"I'm your best friend, and I can't even help you!"

A few seconds later Virginia rushed through the mezzanine
door and down to them.

"I sent for an ambulance," she said. She looked into Jim's
dilated eyes. "Has he been able to say what's wrong?"

"He can't talk," Nate answered, frustrated at being unable to help.

They both looked at their friend again. Jim seemed to be staring at the stage below, his fixed pupils reflecting the light from the chandelier. But Jim didn't see the stagehands and assistants who stood near the tables that had been set up on stage. They were gone, the tables were gone, and in their place stood several groupings of actors in costume. The men wore loose-fitting suits, and the women wore flapper dresses, long fringe tickling their knees, and cloche hats encircled their heads. They moved about slowly, their lips parted as if in laughter, and yet no sound came out.

Jim moved his gaze down to the audience, so enthralled by the illusion that for the moment he did not feel his pain. It was as if his spirit had risen from his body, leaving pain in the empty shell. The audience was filled with people dressed in evening clothes. There were people in the mezzanine, too. Jim looked into the blue eyes of the girl next to him, seeing not Virginia, but a young woman dressed in a satin gown that showed off every curve of her figure. She smiled at him, then turned her eyes back to the stage below. She started to applaud, her small white hands coming together and yet making no sound. Jim, too, looked down at the stage. There was a child there, standing at its apron, dressed in white ruffles . . .

"Jim?"

Nate's voice traveled to him from far away, breaking the spell that had held Jim captive. The pain returned again, and with it a feeling of dread even greater than before. How could he have seen a theater filled with people dressed in 1920s styles?

"Jim, can't you tell us what happened to you?" Nate pleaded.

The little girl, Jim thought. *It was a little girl.*

But he could not tell them this. Virginia, he saw, had a paper cup full of water in her hand. She held it out to him, but instead of drinking it he poured it over his burning head. For a brief moment, the pain on his face subsided. But then it returned as horrible as ever. Jim looked at Nate with pleading eyes, then passed out once again.

The room grew cold suddenly, and the crystal chandelier

jangled melodically, as if unseen hands had pushed it. Behind
Nate and Virginia, the door leading into the mezzanine
slammed shut.

"Oh, my God," Nate whispered, a cold chill rushing over
him. With a trembling hand he took hold of Jim's wrist.

"I can't find a pulse!" he cried. "There's no pulse!"

"Get him on the floor!" Virginia ordered. "We'll do heart
massage on him."

Quickly, Nate and Virginia straightened out Jim's body,
opening his shirt. They took turns pressing down on his
chest, praying they were not too late.

"Come on, you big jackass," Nate said, frustrated and
terrified. "Come on and breathe, damn you!"

"Nate, let me try," Virginia said. With her strong arms she
pulled the director aside, then straddled Jim's body. From
somewhere downstairs, they heard the sound of shouting.
Nate went to the balcony and yelled.

"Up here! Hurry!"

Seconds later, two paramedics appeared. They ordered
Nate and Virginia away and went to work on Jim. But all the
modern means they had of reviving the man were useless.
Finally, one of the men looked up at Nate and shook his head.

"I'm sorry," he said. "He's gone. I can't do anything more
for him."

Nate gritted his teeth.

"What the hell do you mean?" he demanded. "Jim's my
best friend! He's like my brother! How can he be dead? You
made a mistake!"

"No, I'm sorry," he said quietly. "We'll contact the coroner's . . ."

"Try again," Nate ordered, forced calm in his voice. "Try
the heart massage thing again."

The paramedic was about to protest, but saw the look in
Virginia's eyes and with a sigh made a new effort. Nothing
happened. He looked up at the other paramedic.

"Get a stretcher."

Nate brought his hands up to his head and tugged at fistfuls
of hair, wanting to scream at this injustice. How could Jim
Orland possibly be dead? He had been Nate's strength all
these years, the brother he had never had, the man who had
loved him for himself, not because he was rich or famous or

talented. The only other person in Nate's life who had felt the same way had been Meg, but she'd died, too. Now there was no one left, no true friends.

"I don't want to be alone," Nate whispered.

"Shh," Virginia said, taking his arm as the paramedics carried Jim's body away. "Come downstairs. I'll get your chauffeur and have him take you home."

She led Nate out of the mezzanine and downstairs. As he had at his father's funeral, Nate descended into a dazed state too horrified to believe what had just happened. Virginia called George, and the chauffeur helped Nate into the back of the Rolls.

"See to it that he rests well tonight," Virginia said.

Nate looked out his window with bloodshot eyes as George switched on the ignition. Suddenly, a little girl came through the doors and stood beside Virginia and the others who'd come outside the theater. Nate knew she wasn't part of the company. What had she been doing in the theater?

"Hey!" Nate cried.

He leaned toward the window and gestured at the child. Everyone turned to find out what he was pointing at but saw nothing. A few passersby gazed at the man who tapped on the car window, wondering if he was yet another city weirdo. And then Nate, too, realized there was no one there. He slunk down into his seat and buried his face in his hands.

It had been his imagination. There was no little girl.

Nate went back to his theater the very next day, too frightened of his thoughts to stay at home alone. It had been like that after Meg's death—so bad. He tried to keep himself busy with paperwork but could only think of Jim and the crazed look that had been in his eyes before his death. It seemed so unreal now, just a day later. But Nate was forced to accept the truth when the phone rang and someone from the city coroner's office asked to speak to him.

"You'll have to come down to the office," she said. "There are some questions the medical examiner would like to ask you."

Nate sighed, knowing he had to face this sooner or later.

"I'll be there in half an hour," he said.

When he arrived, he was taken into a sterile-looking office

with metal furniture and glass walls. He sat in a metal chair and asked the coroner, "What exactly happened to my friend?"

The coroner shook his head.

"I'm afraid we don't know yet," he said. "His mother only consented this morning to an autopsy. But, since you were the last person to see Mr. Orland alive, I want to hear whatever you can tell me."

Nate swallowed and began his story.

"I was in my office doing a phone interview," he said, "while my crew was setting up for a little party. We were celebrating the end of auditions, which is a rather grueling job. When I came back to the stage, I noticed Jim wasn't there."

"Where had he gone?"

"I didn't know, at first," Nate said. "I asked about him, but everyone had been too busy to notice when he'd left. Anyway, I was about to go look for him when I heard him up at the edge of the mezzanine. I asked him what he was doing up there, but he couldn't answer me."

Nate shifted a little as the chair grew more uncomfortable.

"What do you suppose was wrong with him?" he asked. "I never saw him behave in such a way"

"What way, Mr. Dysart?"

"His face was red and covered with sweat," Nate said, waving his hand around his own face. "And all his muscles were jerking. I tried to help him, but he couldn't even tell me what was wrong. All I know is that he was in terrible, terrible pain."

"About how long did this last?"

"Four, five minutes," Nate said. "I'm not sure, exactly. And I don't know how long he'd been like that before I found him."

The coroner made some notes, then said, "Tell me what he had to eat yesterday."

"How the hell should I know?" Nate asked, not seeing the relevance of the question.

"Please cooperate with me, Mr. Dysart," the coroner said. "It's possible your friend ate something that poisoned him."

Nate thought a moment, then said, "I don't know. We didn't share lunch yesterday."

More notes went into the coroner's book.

"All right then," he said. "If anything is to be found, we'll see it in the autopsy."

He stood up and offered Nate his hand in thanks. Nate shook it, then opened the glass door.

"I suggest, Mr. Dysart," the coroner said, "that you rest for a few days. You look terribly worn out."

Nate laughed a little, without humor.

"Jim used to accuse me of the same thing," he said. "But don't ask me to rest. The only way I'll keep my sanity now is by working harder."

After speaking to the coroner, Nate returned to the theater. He walked upstairs to the mezzanine and looked around. Work would not officially begin on the production until after the funeral. The theater was deserted. Except for the glow of the ghost light, everything was dark.

It was so silent, so lonely, that Nate was unable to stop a sudden flow of emotion. He leaned forward and put his arms on the railing, covering his face as he sobbed in anger. It felt good to cry, with no one around to criticize him. As a child, he was never allowed to shed a tear, no matter how much the beatings he received hurt.

He looked down at the ghost light, his chin resting on his forearms, blinking away the last of his tears.

Something was there, something like a human figure.

Nate straightened up and stared at it for a long time, his head aching. It was a white blur, like the ones in the pictures he'd taken.

"Who's there?" he called, standing.

The white light rose about a foot, then vanished. Nate rubbed his eyes and moaned.

"God, now I'm seeing things."

A small voice with a southwestern accent answered him.

"That man was bad! He hurt me! He wanted the darkness to come!"

Nate was on his feet in a flash, looking around. The mezzanine seemed empty, but could someone be hiding in its shadows?

"Who the hell *are* you?" he cried.

No answer came. Infuriated, Nate ran through the mezzanine, demanding the stranger come out to the open. The little lights along the rows of seats seemed to wink at him, teasing him, telling him he was acting like a madman.

"I'm not crazy," Nate said out loud. "I know I heard someone!"

Finally, he was forced to admit he was all alone. That voice had only been his imagination. His mind was playing tricks on him again, as it had after his father's death. That was all it was. Imagination.

Nate shuffled wearily into his office and, burying his head in his arms at his desk, wished to God he could be sure.

According to the coroner's report, Jim Orland had died of a heart attack. When Nate protested that the man never showed any signs of a weak heart, the coroner told him these things sometimes happened without warning. And so Nate attended his second funeral in a year, comforting Jim's parents as the man was put into the ground of the same cemetery as Nate's wife, Meg, and Nate's father. A numbness held him fast all the time he mourned his friend, and he knew he would never get over this loss.

More than ever, he was determined to make his production a success. He doubled his working hours and dedicated his efforts to both Jim and Meg. With these two in mind, he contacted Sander Bernaux a few days after the funeral. He had wanted Jim to be here when the interview was held. But now he was alone, and Nate knew he had to get along without Jim's help.

Sander Bernaux entered his office in the company of his agent. Nate had one of his assistants serve coffee to everyone, then dismissed her from the office. He watched Sander take a seat on the leather couch, unable to determine by his expression what kind of mood he was in. Sander was about forty-five years old, with thick dark hair just turning gray at the temples. His tanned face was more carved than molded, with light green eyes set far behind prominent cheekbones. He had the kind of mysterious good looks that made women in the audiences squeal with delight when he came on stage. It surprised Nate that he had never tried making the transition to the screen.

"Have you read the contract?" Nate asked finally.

"Of course," Tom Selton, Sander's agent, said. "And we're quite satisfied with it."

Nate felt a wave of relief wash over him, relaxing the tension in his muscles he was feeling in the presence of this great star. But he almost lost his calmness when Tom said, "However..."

"However," Sander interrupted, "while the contract is most tempting, I'm not certain I can afford to risk working with an unknown like yourself."

"I assure you I'm well-qualified," Nate said.

Sander leaned back on the couch with his coffee cup nested between his two hands. He was wearing a diamond and gold ring fashioned in the comedy/tragedy mask design, a gift Nate knew he'd received from one of his girlfriends.

"First of all," Sander said, "what experience do you have? I understand you're able to afford this opulent palace because of your inheritance. But that doesn't qualify you as a producer/director."

"I've done a good deal of work in little theater since I was a teenager," Nate said. "In 1975 I had started my own production company, and the few performances we put on were met with excellent reviews. I can show you my scrapbook, if you'd like."

"What do you mean, 'the few performances we put on?'" Tom wanted to know. "Why did you stop?"

Nate lowered his eyes, hoping he would not be asked too many questions about Meg. Then he looked up and said quietly, "My wife died then. I decided to leave for a while, and went to California."

"What did you do there?" Sander asked.

"Started another production company," Nate said. "In fact, I'm pretty well known around the L.A. area. I would have stayed out there, but my father's funeral brought me east again. And when my inheritance came through, I knew I had the means, as well as the talent, to start my own company right here on Broadway."

Sander leaned forward and placed his coffee cup on the table before him.

"All right," he said.

Nate shook his head. "All right?"

"I'll work with you," Sander replied. "Because I can sense

when a person is sincere, and I sense that in you. But just remember, I must have star billing for this production. No other actor can be put before me."

Nate bit his lip to suppress a silly grin of joy.

"Of course," he said, extending his hand.

Sander's grip was tight when he shook it. Now Tom brought out the contract, and the three signed the last page.

When Sander had left, Nate could not help whispering to his father's spirit.

"You never thought I'd get him, did you?"

But he had gotten Sander Bernaux, and he had his company and his theater. And in about two month's time, he was going to give Broadway something to be proud of. He only wished Meg were here to share this with him.

1975

Nathaniel Dysart Sr. bumped a thin knee against the foot of Nate and Meg's four-poster bed, shaking the mattress so that Meg would wake up from her nap. He grinned with evil delight, readying himself for another confrontation with Nate's wife. Never, ever, would he call her his daughter-in-law.

Startled from a deep sleep, Meg sat up with a gasp and stared at the old man. Fear crept over her pretty face. As if it were a protective wall, she pulled up her blanket and clenched it with trembling fists.

"Are you ever going to get out of that bed, lazy bitch?" Nathaniel Sr. demanded. "Your accident happened a long time ago!"

"It's only been a few weeks," Meg said. "My doctor says I need rest. Please, stop tormenting me like this!"

"Why should I?" Nathaniel Sr. asked, his long nose wrinkling in a sneer. "This is my house that you live in. As long as your husband is too lazy to make a living of his own . . ."

"He isn't lazy!" Meg cried. "Nate works so hard—hours and hours at our theater! We'll make a name for ourselves one day!"

The old man threw back his head and let out a high-pitched laugh. Meg cringed and fought tears. How could a man be so cruel, she wondered? How could he delight so in hurting her?

"A name for yourselves?" Nathaniel Sr. said. "You're nothing but a pair of failures—in every way!"

Now it was Meg's turn to scream. She would not be comforted until Nate came home and took her in his arms to protect her from his monstrous father.

FIVE

After Sander left, Nate decided to get through some paperwork. His publicity department had put together a flyer on the progress of the theater, to be mailed to all the backers, and wanted his okay on it. Nate read it carefully, making the necessary corrections. Then he picked through the accompanying black-and-white photographs. Nate was to indicate which, in his opinion, was the best one. As he went over them, he recalled his own photographs. None of these had the strange white flaw; it must have been caused by his camera.

Still, he could not help thinking about the strange light he'd seen on the stage the other day, while standing alone on the darkened mezzanine. It had looked so much like something human, very similar to the shadow in his pictures. He laughed quietly.

"Jim thought it looked like a person himself," he said out loud.

But it really wasn't funny, and he bit his lip in anger to think of his friend. He opened his left top drawer and pulled out the red-and-white envelope of his snapshots. The glossies were lined up on his desk, and below them Nate placed his own photos. The comparison proved nothing.

He punched a button on his telephone and rang the office of the man he'd hired as his new stage manager.

"Do me a favor, Don," he said. "Find out if the design crew has a magnifying glass I can borrow."

After obtaining the magnifying glass, Nate chose one photo and began to study it. The white cloud became more discernible now, but it still did not look like anything more than a mistake made by an amateur. Most of the other pictures were the same, and Nate was almost ready to think he was imagining things. After all, none of the professional photos showed this blur. But as he neared the end of the pile, he saw something not visible in any of the other pictures.

There were dark spots at the top of the blur.

Dark spots that looked something like the features of a face.

"Oh, God," Nate said. "What are you thinking?"

There had to be a logical explanation for all this, but Nate couldn't begin to think what it might be. He decided he'd have the picture enlarged. If there was something to be seen, it would show up better then. He pushed back his chair and lifted the photographs' envelope from his desk, carefully removing the negatives. After finding the correct one, he wrote the number on the package and slid it into the back pocket of his jeans.

In the hallway outside his office he could hear the loud banging of the hammers and the buzz of saws as the building crew worked downstairs on the sets. He knocked on a door, and his chauffeur George came out of a tiny office.

"Get the car," Nate said. "I've got an errand to run."

George nodded his head once and headed for the back door. After Nate let Don know he'd be gone for a while, he headed to the back door. But just as he was about to pull it open, he heard a voice.

"Don't leave me in the dark!"

It was a childish voice with a southwestern accent. Nate's fist turned white as it clenched the doorknob. He refused to acknowledge what he was hearing.

"Please take the dark away!"

Nate jerked open the door and ran out into the chilly October rain. He slumped into the backseat of the car and gave George a destination.

What had made him hear that voice? he wondered. Was his mind playing tricks on him again? Was it brought on by the fact that he'd been going over the photographs, imagining he saw a human figure? *Was* it just in his mind?

Or was it something external, something he could not control?

When George stopped for a red light, Nate gazed at the passers-by, amused as he usually was that they all took a look at his funny car. But one face in particular caught his attention, and a moment later he had his window rolled down, calling to a red-haired woman carrying a flowered umbrella.

"Miss St. John!" he called. "Adrian!"

Adrian, who had just come out of a boutique, turned at the sound of her name and looked around in confusion. When she noticed someone waving to her from the fancy car, she took a step forward and squinted. Then, recognizing her new director, she smiled and walked over.

"Well, hello, Mr. Dysart," she said. The idea of calling a man so young "Mister" struck her as funny. But after all, he *was* her director and deserved respect. "How are you?"

"Wet," Nate replied simply. He clicked open the door and slid over.

"Come on," he said. "I'll give you a ride."

Adrian wasn't about to pass up such an offer in that nasty weather, and so she stretched over the flooded gutter and climbed in beside him. Shaking her umbrella outside before closing her door, she said, "Great day for ducks."

Nate laughed, his blue eyes brightening. Adrian felt a surge of infatuation and looked down at her lap to drive it away. She was old enough to know "love at first sight" was an impossibility.

"I shouldn't be making jokes," she said, serious now. "Not after what happened to Mr. Orland."

"Well..." Nate sighed, shrugging. He did not want to discuss Jim right now.

She looked at him, her green eyes rounding.

"It must have been horrible for you, Mr. Dysart," she said. "I read in the papers that you were with him when he died."

Her director nodded.

"Did you get the flowers I sent?" Adrian asked. "I would have attended the funeral, but I didn't have any way of getting there."

Nate smiled a little.

"The flowers were beautiful," he said. "That was very thoughtful of you. And don't worry about missing the funeral."

The rain hummed on the car roof as they rode across town.

"He was your best friend, wasn't he?" Adrian asked softly.

"Yes, he was," Nate said.

Impulsively, Adrian leaned across the seat and kissed Nate's cheek. When she pulled away, she ran her fingers through her wavy red hair, embarrassed, and said, "I hope you didn't mind."

"Why did you do that?" Nate asked, touching his cheek. It had been a long time since anyone had kissed him that way.

"You look like you need it," Adrian said. "Hey, don't worry. I'm not coming on to you. I'm not like that."

"I didn't think you were," Nate assured her. "You just—well, it kind of surprised me."

"I come from a very big family in the Midwest," Adrian said. "We're all very affectionate, and whenever anyone's down we give him a big kiss."

Nate smiled again, trying to imagine what such a home life would be like. There would be no beatings, no yelling, and no accusing and belittling. His own father had never even shook his hand.

"What part of the Midwest do you come from?" he asked, shutting off thoughts of his father.

"A little town in Ohio," Adrian said. "My parents and my nine brothers live there."

Nate whistled.

"Are you kidding?" he said with a laugh. "Nine brothers? How old are they?"

"The youngest is twelve," Adrian said, "and the oldest is two years my senior—thirty."

"Are any of them here in New York?"

Adrian shook her head.

"I was the only St. John with stars in her eyes," she said. "My parents fought like crazy to keep me home, but I was determined to come to New York and make a name for myself. And look at me, Mr. Dysart. I'm going to play the leading role in your production!"

"I think you'll be great as Daisy," Nate said.

"I can't wait until rehearsals start Monday," Adrian said. "I'll get a better feel for Daisy on the stage."

Their conversation was interrupted when George pulled the car into a side street to park.

"I just want to drop these negatives off," Nate said. "I'll have George drop you off wherever you want to go."

The man in the photographers' shop told Nate the print could not be ready for a week, but when the producer pressed a bill into his hand, he changed his tune.

"Monday," he said.

Nate walked out to the car again, where Adrian was having a discussion with George. She smiled at him when he got in.

"Your driver was telling me this car is forty years old," she said. "How do you keep it so new looking?"

"George sees to that," Nate said.

The car could not be in any other condition, he thought, considering that in most of those forty years only his father had been a passenger. Nate was never permitted in the precious vehicle.

"So, where to?" he asked Adrian.

"Macy's," Adrian said. "If it's not too far out of your way."

Nate insisted it wasn't. As they drove downtown he asked about her family and about her career and what she wanted to do in the future. By the time they reached Thirty-fourth Street, he was thinking that he hadn't met a woman so intelligent and charming and warm in a long, long time.

Rehearsals began the following Monday morning and everyone was very excited. The stage held only a few pieces of scenery, but conveyed enough of the idea for the actors to work well. While the new stage manager, Don Benson, took charge backstage, Nate found a seat in the front row. On his lap were a copy of the script and some rough sketches of the way the scenes would look with the actors in their proper groupings. He began by giving the actors an account of the first scene and what the set would look like when completed. Then he reminded them that the play would be tried out in a Connecticut theater before its Broadway opening, and ordered them to begin rehearsal. A few moments went by before he interrupted the action on stage.

"Okay, wait a minute," he said, waving his pen at the actors. "Let's see how it would look if Adrian and Denny moved left center."

The two actors shifted positions, and Nate made a note in his book. The woman beside him, his assistant stage manager, did the same. Now Nate gave orders for the action to begin again, and Adrian started to talk to Denny. Don watched from the wings, ready to cue the actors who would be walking on next. He held Cartier, the theater's mascot cat, in his arms.

"Now, Jimmy," Adrian, as Daisy, was saying to Denny,

"when your daddy points his finger at you, start moaning like you got the devil himself in your blood."

As Denny was answering her Don felt someone come to stand beside him. He turned and looked at Georgia Richmond, watching her son with a smile of pride on her face. Her bleached blonde wig seemed to glow in the shadows, and her makeup was gaudy.

"Excuse me," Don whispered as two actresses moved by him, "but you really aren't allowed back here."

Georgia turned to him, still smiling.

"Oh, I know," she said. "But it's the first time Denny's performed on Broadway, and I'm so terribly proud!"

"Well, I suppose it's okay for just this one time," Don consented.

"Thank you," Georgia replied.

A few moments later, she was brushed aside by an actor hurrying on stage. It was Sander Bernaux, and, according to his script, he climbed on top of a chair and started calling to the people on stage. Sander was playing the role of a hell-fire preacher, in reality a con artist. His speech was loud and forceful, but suddenly it was cut short. Sander fixed his eyes on one of the extras and said, "You're wearing green!"

The actor looked down at his clothes and pressed his hands on the front of his green Lacoste shirt. Then he looked up at Sander with innocent eyes.

"Don't you know what an unlucky color green is?" Sander asked.

Nate stood up and walked toward the stage, resting his hands on the railing of the orchestra pit.

"I'm sure Mr. Smith was not aware of that particular superstition," he said.

"How can I work with such amateurs?" Sander demanded. "Young man, don't you know that color is reserved for the fairies?"

Smith doubled his fists.

"Who're you callin' a fairy?"

Nate tried to explain to the confused young man what had upset Sander, though, in his mind, the actor was making a big deal out of nothing. Nate did not share the beliefs that some superstitious actors held.

"People used to believe the fairies would get jealous if they saw an actor wearing green," he said. "It was supposedly *their* official color, and reserved for their use alone."

Sander clicked his tongue.

"It isn't as unimportant as you make it sound," he said.

"Well, have a sense of humor about it," Nate said. "After all, this is a comedy we're doing."

Smith looked over at Nate, who nodded his head.

"I guess I could take it off," he said.

"Have the wardrobe mistress give you something else to wear," Nate said.

The actor hurried off the stage, cursing temperamental Sander under his breath. Now Denny walked up to the famous actor and said, "If the color green is so unlucky, Mr. Bernaux, then why do we call the place where we rest between scenes the greenroom? That's a place where it's happy!"

"Impudent brat," Sander snarled, for lack of a better answer.

They rehearsed for another two hours. When lunchtime came, everyone started talking about the morning's work, and friendships started to form. Adrian met Nate as he came up the staircase next to the stage and said, "We seemed to do all right."

"There's a lot of room for improvement," Nate said. "But yes, you did fine for a first rehearsal."

They walked along the hall together.

"I liked the faces you were making during Sander's speech," Nate went on. "You're wonderfully expressive, Adrian."

"Oh, did you think I should have exaggerated that look on my face when I drank that cheap wine?"

"You might even spit the stuff out at your husband," Nate suggested.

Adrian laughed.

"I'll bet Sander wouldn't appreciate *that* scene!"

Halfway down the hallway, they parted company—Adrian heading for her dressing room and Nate for his office. He planned to go back to that photographers' shop today. So far, this first day of rehearsals had been uneventful. Nate wondered if he might be inviting trouble if he started thinking about the pictures again.

But he had to find out if there was anything there.

As he was walking toward the front door he bumped into
an attractive young woman who was dressed in coveralls and
had her arms filled with lighting equipment and drooping
extension cords. They both began to apologize and then
started to laugh.

"This is a very pretty theater, Mr. Dysart," she said. "It
makes me think of the Palace of Versailles in France!"

"Thanks," Nate said. He brought a hand to his mouth.
"Miss, uh..."

She smiled.

"It's Mrs. Warner," she said. "Barbara Warner. I work on
the lighting crew."

"Oh, yes," Nate said, recalling her name now. "I hope you
like it here."

"Oh, I love everything about the theater," Barbara said,
her eyes lighting up.

Nate turned and walked to his car. He was happy to be
working with such good people. If only his father could see
him now!

After visiting the photographer's shop, Nate did not wait
until he got back to the theater to look at the enlargement.
Holding it toward the car window for better light, he studied
it slowly. A chill rushed over him as he realized it *was* a
human figure in the picture! In this larger print he could see
the eyes and mouth, though these were only faint, and the
suggestion of short, dark hair.

But this seemed an impossible photograph, for the figure
was faded even though everything around it was perfectly
clear. Someone was playing a trick on him. That had to be it.
But why? Who would do such a thing to him? Nate thought
he had no enemies in the world, yet he knew there were
some unscrupulous people in the business. There was a lot of
money tied up in the theatrical world, not to mention a lot of
temperamental, sometimes unstable people. Was someone
trying to drive him crazy?

All sorts of explanations ran through Nate's head. Someone
had paid to have the development of the photos tampered
with, of course. Someone who wanted to see Nate fail.
Maybe, just maybe, this was also the explanation behind the
voices he'd been hearing. There were plenty of places in the
Dysart Theater where someone could hide a tape recorder.

It wasn't difficult to imagine he might have enemies now. His father had been associated with many people, and yet had left his entire fortune to Nate. What about his cousin Vance? Nate got at least one angry phone call from him every week. The man seemed to get more irrational all the time. Nate almost felt sympathy for his cousin, who had been a loser all his life. Or could one of his father's business associates be responsible? Someone who had wanted a cut of the Dysart fortune and was getting his revenge by trying to bring Nate to ruin?

"I don't understand this," Nate whispered. "But I know one thing. My show is going to be a hit, and nothing is going to stop me!"

Angrily, he tore up the photograph and threw it on the floor of the car. He promised himself he would completely ignore the voices next time he heard them.

He would not let himself think that no one else could possibly know what the little girl in his dreams said to him.

Barbara Warner picked up her two-year-old son Alec and gave him a big bear hug. The child squealed, then wriggled out of her arms and ran back to the wooden blocks he'd piled up under the dining room table. She smiled to see him toddling about. He was such a happy, healthy, well-behaved child. Never gave them a moment's worry.

"Why're you so happy today, Mom?" her eight-year-old, Bobby, wanted to know. He stood in the doorway to the kitchen, armed with a can of soda and a handful of pretzels. She resisted the impulse to tell him not to spoil his appetite for supper.

"Your mother's always happy, Bobby," his father said. Joel Warner winked in his wife's direction, then put aside the newspaper column he was writing.

"I take it you're still enjoying this new job of yours?" he asked, putting his arms around her.

She accepted his kiss, then laughed again as Bobby made a face at their affectionate display and retreated into the kitchen. Give him a few years, Barbara thought, and he'd understand about hugging and kissing.

"I met my boss today," she said. "He's such a nice man, Joel! He doesn't keep his nose in the air like some of the producers I've worked with."

"He's a pretty young guy, isn't he?" Joel asked.

"Oh, about thirty or so and very handsome," Barbara said. She studied her husband's eyes through the wire-frame glasses he wore. "Say, you aren't jealous, are you?"

"Of course not," Joel said, hugging her close. "I know you love me."

Barbara kissed him.

"More than anything in the world," she said.

Barbara Warner, secure with a loving husband and family, thought that life would always be this wonderful.

SIX

Many actors have a mascot, some little trinket that they believe will bring them good luck. Because her son had carried his basketball to all the auditions, Georgia decided this was an appropriate amulet for him. She didn't stop to think it would have been more effective if he'd chosen it himself. To Georgia, her son was too young to make a decision like that.

Denny, on the other hand, did not believe in such things. He carried the basketball around because it was a concrete reminder of a father who had left a year ago to live in Arizona. His parents were divorced, and Denny knew there was no way they'd get back together. But still he wished they could have made up for just one day, for his birthday several months earlier. That way, his father could have given the basketball to him in person, instead of through the mail.

During the first week of rehearsals, he played with it in his dressing room, tossing it at his trash can or into an open drawer. But the room soon became too confining, and he decided the hallway would be a great place to fool around. He was dribbling it along the tile floor, back from lunch only a few minutes, when his mother came up to him and said, "Don't disturb the other actors, Denny."

"It's okay, Mom," Denny said, lifting the ball up to twirl it on his finger. "No one asked me to stop."

Georgia watched the ball go around. "My, you really do well with that, don't you?"

Denny let it drop.

"Yep," he said simply. He saw she had her purse in her hand. "Where are you going?"

"I thought I'd do some shopping," Georgia said. "And don't you be asking me to come. I may get stuck on a long line, and I don't want you to be late for this afternoon's rehearsals."

"Sure," Denny said. "Have a good time."

Georgia kissed him and left. As Denny was working around the hallway, he noticed the back door, and decided he'd check and see if there was room to play outside. The yard beyond the blue metal door was littered with wood and metal scraps left over from the theater's construction. But concrete had been poured on one corner of the yard, a place where trash cans were kept. Denny decided this would be a suitable basketball court. He kicked away the debris and moved the cans to a far corner.

Denny crouched down and dribbled the ball, bending and twisting his way around the makeshift court. Suddenly, he slammed into something he knew had not been there before. He let the ball drop and turned to see a little girl standing near him, watching him with big brown eyes. She looked vaguely familiar, yet he couldn't place her. He clicked his tongue and said, "Do you have to stand so close? I could have knocked you down!"

"You couldn't knock me down," the child said, matter-of-factly.

"Are you kidding?" Denny asked. "I'm twice as big as you." He looked at her for a moment.

"I remember you now," he said. "You're that weird kid from the preliminaries. What're you doing back here now?"

"I want to play with you," she said. "Where did you get that orange ball?"

"My dad gave it to me," Denny said. "He lives in Arizona." The child's eyes rounded.

"Arizona is forever away," she said. "Why isn't your daddy here with you?"

"He and my mom are divorced," Denny said, bouncing the basketball again.

"Divorced?" the girl said, lisping the word. "Did a man come and steal your mommy away from your daddy?"

Denny frowned at her. Sure, a man came. Lots of men came. That was what broke up Georgia and Randall Richmond—Georgia's steady stream of boyfriends. But Denny did not like to think about that.

"You didn't answer me."

"I don't have to," Denny replied. He started dribbling the basketball again, hoping she'd lose interest and go away, but the little girl skipped after him, easily keeping up with his pace.

"Hey, you might fall," Denny cautioned. "Then you'll mess up that pretty white dress of yours."

Wouldn't hurt you to get a new one, anyway, he thought. That thing looks like it's a thousand years old!

The child smacked the basketball from his hands, sending it flying into a pile of crates.

"I like my dress," she snapped. "It's from Paris, and my daddy bought it for me!"

Denny's mouth dropped open. How did she know what he was thinking? Unable to figure it out, he moved off the concrete to retrieve his basketball.

"I've got to go back inside," he said, watching the child's glaring eyes as he moved towards the back door. "I'm due on stage soon."

"No!" the child cried, racing toward him. "Stay here and be my friend!"

"I can't," Denny said, wishing she'd go away. All he needed was a little kid following him around. "I've got to rehearse. Uhm—uhm, maybe I'll see you next time I come out."

With that, he slipped into the building and shut the door. As he was heading toward his dressing room, he heard the door open and close again. But when he turned around, there was no one behind him in the hallway.

Nate was surprised to find himself a little jealous as Sander and Adrian rehearsed a love scene. He had known Adrian only a few weeks, but he had enjoyed their few conversations, and realized he was beginning to think of Adrian as more than just an employee. She had already shown genuine concern for him, the way a true friend would.

He interrupted the action on stage.

"Sander," he said, "let's see a little less tenderness in that kiss. Remember, Nigel Bertrand looks at Daisy as 'just another broad.' He doesn't have any true affection for her."

"I'm well aware of my character, Mr. Dysart," Sander said coldly.

"Fine," Nate replied, undaunted. "Okay, go on with it."

He smiled slightly when Sander eased up on the kiss and made a note in his book even as the assistant stage manager did the same. On cue, Denny walked on stage. For the next half hour, Nate watched the action, interrupting with suggestions and recording them in his book. Finally, he called an end to the rehearsal.

"Adrian, Sander, take a break," he said. "Denny, you've got another scene coming up, so stick around."

"Sure," Denny said. He thought about asking Mr. Dysart if he knew that strange little girl, but decided it didn't matter. Besides, his mother wouldn't like him bothering a busy important man like Mr. Dysart with such a silly question.

As Sander and Adrian walked toward the dressing rooms Sander turned to her.

"You did very well this time. I find it easy to work with someone as professional as you."

Adrian smiled, though she felt confident enough to do without Sander's condescending praise.

"Thank you," she said. "But I'm afraid Daisy came on a little too strong."

"Not at all," Sander told her. "She's an exaggerated character as it is, Ms. St. John."

Adrian thanked him for the encouragement, then headed for her dressing room. She thought of how excited she'd been at first to learn she'd be working with Sander Bernaux. Most actresses would give their right arm for such an opportunity. And yet, somehow, she wasn't all that impressed by him. Of course he was a fine actor. And he was handsome in a classical way, with his chiseled features and gray-tinted hair. But he wasn't her type.

"Now, that director of mine," she said to her reflection as she took her hair down to brush it. "He's a real doll. Mmm—those gorgeous blue eyes!"

She laughed at her infatuation, thinking she sounded like a teenager, and leaned over to pick up her hairbrush. As she did so, she caught the reflection of a little girl sitting in the brown armchair across the room. Adrian turned abruptly.

"Who are you?" she asked. "How did you get in here?"

The child stared at her without speaking. Adrian started brushing her hair, smiling at the little girl. With eight younger brothers, she was used to the ways of children. The child was obviously very shy.

"I don't remember you from the cast," she said. "Do you belong to someone in the crew?"

The little girl shook her head.

Adrian put her brush down and found some hairpins to roll up her red tresses. She decided to give the child a few moments to speak to her. But all the while the little girl simply stared, until Adrian finally became so bothered that she moved her chair so that she couldn't see the child's reflection.

"Well," she said, when the last hairpin was in. "I'm going to the greenroom to get some coffee. Would you like to come with me?"

She turned to the little girl.

The chair was empty.

"Hello?" Adrian called. She stood up. "Are you hiding somewhere?"

Crouching, she looked underneath the furniture, then stood up and walked over to the trunk and checked behind it. The child was not there. Nor was she in the small closet.

"Strange," Adrian said. "She must have sneaked out when I had my back turned.

Adrian passed several people on her way to the greenroom. No one saw the little girl who walked at her side.

Fishing in her pocket for change, she punched the vending machine for a cup of coffee. As she watched the liquid pour into a paper cup, she heard someone say, *You can't have him!*

She turned around and saw that no one was near her. Deciding it was not meant for her ears, she carried her drink over to a couch, where two women sat talking. They smiled up at her and said, "Taking a break, Adrian?"

"Just for a few minutes," Adrian told Barbara Warner and Judy Terrel. "How are things on the lighting crew?"

"We're putting up more fixtures in the building room," Judy

said. "The light's so damned poor in there the workers could go blind."

"Judy, don't talk that way," Barbara said, looking down at her lap.

Judy laughed. "I only said 'damn,' for crying out loud."

She said to Adrian, "Barbara's father was a minister. She doesn't like anyone to swear."

"Oh, I'm not such a prude," Barbara insisted, a bit embarrassed. She changed the subject. "How do you like working with Sander Bernaux?"

"The same way I like working with every other actor," Adrian said, sipping her coffee. "He doesn't impress me."

"Really?" Judy said. "But he's the biggest star on Broadway! I'd die if he even said 'boo' to me!"

Barbara and Adrian laughed at this. Barbara explained that she was only impressed by her husband and asked if Adrian had someone.

"If I'm not being too nosy," she added quickly.

"Not at all," Adrian said. "There was somebody a while ago, but it just didn't work out." Conscious that she sounded sad, she brightened her voice. "There isn't anyone in my life right now. I've been too busy lately."

"What kind of guy do you go for?" Judy asked, leaning forward.

Adrian thought a moment.

"Blond hair, blue eyes," she said. "A good build and not too tall. And he has to be intelligent with a gentle disposition."

Judy nudged Barbara with her elbow.

"She just described Nate Dysart perfectly," she said. "Now *there's* a good-looking man!"

"Isn't it a romantic idea?" Barbara sighed. "The director and his leading lady."

Adrian blushed a little to think they were reading her thoughts.

"How about your husband, Barbara? What does he look like?"

"You'd know if you read the papers," Barbara said. "I'm married to Joel Warner."

"Oh, yes!" Adrian said, recognizing the name. "I read his articles all the time."

Joel Warner was an investigative reporter who freelanced

for all the city's papers. Adrian considered Barbara to be lucky to have such a man for a husband. A picture of herself with Nate came unbidden to her mind, and Adrian smiled. She wondered if there was a chance for her and Nate.

Suddenly, she felt a sharp, burning pain on her arm. She dropped her paper cup, fortunately empty of coffee now.

"What happened?"

"I don't know," Adrian said, taking off her jacket. "It feels like something burned me."

But when she looked, there was no mark at all on her arm.

"That's strange," she said. "I really felt *something*."

"Maybe it was a bug-bite," Barbara suggested.

"In the middle of autumn?" Adrian wanted to know. "There must be a wire sticking out of this couch somewhere, or a pin."

"Say," Judy said with a laugh, "maybe this theater is haunted."

"Oh, that's childish!" Barbara said. "It was just an accident."

"You're probably right," Adrian said. "It's no big deal."

She stood up, moving very close to the little girl who stood unseen next to the couch.

She forgot completely about the stinging pain as soon as rehearsals began. When the day was over, she went to her dressing room and got ready to leave. The theater was still bustling with activity as others did the same. As she left, she noticed the lights were still on, and wondered if anyone was rehearsing.

When she walked on stage, Nate was busy reading his script, going over notes he'd recorded that day. Adrian's shoes clicked along the wooden floor, but he didn't hear her. For a moment, she stood admiring him, thinking how handsome he looked under the stage lights. Finally, she spoke up.

"Hi, there," she said.

Nate nearly dropped the script, and he turned quickly to look up at her.

"Adrian," he said, feeling like a fool. He had thought it was the voices again. "You startled me."

Adrian took a seat next to him on the edge of the stage and put her purse down at her side.

"You must have been working really hard," she said. "I guess you didn't hear me come in."

"I guess not," Nate said. He showed her the script. "I'm trying to decipher my notes while I still can. By this time tomorrow these scribblings will turn into a foreign language."

"You could compare with your assistants," Adrian suggested. "Why don't you take a break? You've been working nonstop since lunchtime."

"I've got a lot to do," Nate said.

In truth, he wanted to keep busy so that he would not think about the strange things that had happened in the last months. Nate was certain that the cure for the voices he had heard was hard work, total dedication to his production.

"Oh, really," Adrian said. "The work will keep! Aren't you even going to break for dinner?"

Nate's eyes widened.

"Are you inviting me out?"

"Oh, no!" Adrian cried with a laugh. "I didn't mean it that way. I guess it's the country girl in me talking again. Don't want you to miss a meal."

Nate closed his script and smacked his knees lightly with it.

"You know you're right," he said. "I could use a good dinner right now. How does seafood sound to you?"

Adrian shook her head. "Fine, I guess. But I was going home in a few minutes. I have some chicken I made the day before yesterday, and . . ."

"Forget the chicken," Nate said, standing. He offered Adrian his hand and helped her to her feet. "Let me take you out to dinner."

For a few moments, he did not let go of her hand. She gazed into his blue eyes, so caught up in them for a moment that she did not see her purse sliding into the orchestra pit.

"That would be nice," she said.

Then she realized what she was doing and pulled her hand from Nate's. She wanted him, but not this way. If she was going to have a serious relationship with the good-looking blond man, she would go about it slowly and let it develop in its own time.

"But I'll have to go home right after," she said. "I mean, I want to read the script for tomorrow's rehearsal."

"I'll have my chauffeur take you home," Nate said.

They walked off the stage together, and in the wings Nate

switched off all the lights, except for the ghost light. When he closed the doors, a small child suddenly appeared on the floor of the orchestra pit, holding Adrian's quilted purse in her hands. She unzipped it and turned it upside down to spill its contents. She did not like what that red-haired lady was doing. She would teach her a lesson.

Lipstick, a purply color. Daddy didn't like makeup. He said women looked prettier when they were natural. She had promised her daddy she would never, ever wear makeup. Not even when she was old enough to date boys. She didn't want to date boys, anyway. She just wanted to be with her daddy, for ever and ever.

And now someone was trying to spoil her plans. Her anger grew, engulfing her tiny frame and making her pretty face turn ugly. She took the lipstick and started scribbling on the polished floor. Then she threw down the empty tube.

A memory came back to her suddenly, a memory many times older than the mortal part of herself that had died so long ago. She was in a dressing room, playing with her mommy's lipstick.

"How dare you touch my things?" Mommy had yelled, smacking her hands. "A brand-new lipstick! You'll have to be punished for this, young lady."

And then her mommy had put her in a small, dark place. Was it a trunk or a closet? It didn't matter, it was frightening all the same.

The child looked around, hating the blackness that hovered just outside the beam of the ghost light, waiting to gobble her up. Mommy had brought the dark. Mommy had hurt her. But Daddy—Daddy would make it light again. He would help his little girl.

She bowed her small head.

"I want my daddy," she whimpered, like the innocent child she had once been.

After Nate had put his papers away, he and Adrian started for the car, where George was waiting to take them to dinner. But just before reaching the back door, Adrian winced and said, "Oh, I went and left my purse on the stage."

"Let's go get it, then," Nate said. "We've got plenty of time."

He and Adrian walked back to the stage, where Nate turned on the overhead lights again.

Adrian said, "I'm not usually so absentminded. I left it right over.."

She went to the place where Nate and she had been sitting, but the purse was not there. Nate came to help her look for it, and in a few moments they found it down in the orchestra pit, its contents strewn all over.

"It must have dropped down there," Adrian said. "I guess I left it open."

"Let me get it for you," Nate offered, crouching to jump into the pit.

"Oh, it's all right," Adrian said. "I can manage."

But Nate was already putting everything back into the small quilt bag. He handed it up to Adrian and started to hoist himself onto the stage again.

"Thanks," Adrian said. She looked over the contents of the purse, then said, "Oh, wait a minute. My lipstick is missing."

Nate put his feet back on the floor.

"I don't see anything else down here," he said, turning around with his eyes to the floor.

"But I know I had it," Adrian said. "I just bought it today. Oh, let it go! I'm sure I'll find it tomorrow."

Nate waved a hand at her.

"Let me look for it while I'm down here," he said.

Adrian was still making apologies when Nate found the missing lipstick. He lifted the now-empty tube from the shadows cast by the front of the stage.

"I thought this was brand-new," he said, handing it up to her.

"Maybe it broke," Adrian said. She sighed. "Well, that's a few dollars down the drain!"

"I'll buy you a new lipstick," Nate told her. "But let me find where the broken piece went before I have purple goop ruining my floor here."

He found the rest of the lipstick, smeared all over the floor at his feet. But it wasn't just a smear mark that he saw. It was something more definite than that. The smudge marks looked like letters.

"Maybe you should let the janitor do that," Adrian suggested.

Nate did not reply. He knelt down and examined the smudge marks closer. There was a message scrawled on the floor.

I AM WAITING

Quickly, he rose to his feet again. This was a trick again, just like the photography and the voices. He would not fall into their trap.

"You're right," he told Adrian. "That's what I pay him for."

He climbed back up onto the stage, and together he and Adrian left the theater. On the way to the restaurant Nate could not stop thinking of the strange words he'd seen on the floor.

SEVEN

It didn't dawn on Nate until he was at the door of Bailey's Seafood House on Manhattan's fashionable East Side that this was his first "social" outing since his arrival from California. He couldn't call it a date, really, since it was a spur-of-the-moment decision to join Adrian for dinner. He was just enjoying a night out with a woman who was already proving to be a new friend. Certainly it would not go beyond that, he thought as he held the door open for her.

They both ordered sautéed bay scallops and talked of trivial things, the way people do when they don't really know each other. But Nate's smile was a forced one; he could not get that strange message off his mind. "I AM WAITING," scrawled in lipstick. What could that mean? *Who* was waiting? And why?

"Hey, those scallops taste better hot," Adrian said, tilting her head a little so that her silver hair-clips caught the lights.

Nate shook his head abruptly and found her watching him with smiling eyes.

"Sorry, I was thinking," he said, starting on his food again.

"About what?"

He waved a hand at her.

"Oh, nothing that you need bother about," he said. "Something about the theater."

Adrian took on a mock-serious expression.

"Well, then, I certainly will worry about it," she said. "Anything to do with that affects all of us.

Nate shook his head, thinking, *It doesn't affect you at all. You don't have nightmares or hear voices.*

"Come on," Adrian pressed. "It seems to really be bothering you. Don't you think you'd feel better getting it off your chest?"

Nate chewed his mouthful of scallops and thought about that. Yes, it would feel better. Each time he'd discussed his problems with Jim, it was as if a little of his burden was lifted. But why should he discuss them with Adrian? He didn't know her very well—as yet, not even as a colleague. She'd probably think he was crazy. But he did need to talk to someone, and Adrian was so willing to listen . . .

He decided to start with the least of his problems.

"Adrian," he asked, "do you know anything about photography?"

"Photography?" she echoed, not understanding. "Well, very little. One of my brothers took a summer-school course in it, so I might know something by osmosis. Try me, anyway."

"Okay, imagine this," Nate said, holding up both hands. "You take a picture—say of a building. And there are no people in the scene. Yet when the picture is developed, someone is there—or rather, what *seems* to be a person."

"Maybe he ducked into the shot at the last minute, and you didn't notice," Adrian suggested.

"No, it's not like that," Nate said. "This figure is floating in midair. Above a girder of the theater's frame."

Adrian rubbed her lower lip with the rim of her wineglass, thinking about this. She didn't have the slightest idea what Nate was leading up to, but could tell by the tone of his voice and the serious expression on his face that it really bothered him.

"Eat some of that food," she said finally, for lack of a better response.

Nate laughed for the first time in ten minutes.

"Country girl," he said. "Did your mother equate food with comfort?"

"I suppose," Adrian said, smiling slightly. She sounded

more like an older sister now. She tried to cover herself by turning back to the photograph issue.

"This figure you're talking about," she said, "you aren't one hundred percent sure it *is* a person?"

"How can I be?" Nate said. "It's very blurry, and like I said, it's floating in midair."

"Well," Adrian said, "unless Casper the Friendly Ghost got in on the picture, it must not be a person. Probably a flaw in the film."

But, Nate thought, a flaw would not be exactly the same in almost an entire roll of film. Still, it was a possibility, considering how little he knew of photography.

"Nate, why are you asking me all this?" Adrian wanted to know.

"Oh, well," Nate said, not sure how much more to tell her, "it's just that something like that happened to a roll of film I took. I can't explain it, and it really bugs me."

Adrian finished her plate of food and pushed it away.

"Why don't you take another set of pictures, and see what happens? If it's the film, there should be nothing wrong with this roll. But if there is, I suggest you go out and buy a new camera."

"You think it might be as simple as that?" Nate asked.

There was a worried yet hopeful look in his eyes that made Adrian think something more was bothering him.

"Try and see," she said. Impulsively, as she did many things, she took his hand. "Nate, is something else on your mind? I hardly think the mistakes of an amateur photographer should make you so intense."

Nate shook his head, deciding he'd told her enough. He would not frighten this lovely woman with talk of voices and nightmares, though it seemed Adrian was not the type who was easily frightened.

"Please," she said softly, "if there's anything you want to talk about, I'm willing to listen. And I can keep a secret."

Nate smiled at her.

"I'm okay," he insisted, squeezing her hand. "I guess I'm just tired. Sorry I'm not a better dinner partner."

Adrian pulled her hand out of his, patted his wrist, then picked up her wineglass.

"No wonder you're tired," she said. "You work so hard, and such long hours!"

She wondered, though, if that was all that was bothering him. Though he *did* work hard, he seemed to enjoy himself while doing so. Was it just fatigue she was seeing right now? Or something more?

Adrian decided then that she would watch Nate closely. If he needed someone, she would be there.

When he arrived home, it was to receive yet another phone call from Vance. Nate slammed the receiver down in his usual angry way, but his cousin had upset him so much that he was unable to fall asleep that night. His mind was a boiling cauldron of thoughts and memories. The dinner with Adrian had been purely platonic—Nate hadn't even kissed her good night. But it stirred up memories of another woman, his wife, Meg, that were so clear he could almost imagine her next to him in the big brass bed. Nate rolled over onto his stomach and threw out his arm as if to embrace her, a chill running through him when he felt only the cold satin sheets.

It was all right to want to get close to someone again, wasn't it? In the six years since Meg had died, Nate had dated on occasion, but had never felt anything like he did tonight. Adrian was something special. Someone caring and warm who was willing to listen to his problems. And he so needed to talk.

"Adrian," he whispered aloud to the full moon hanging just outside the room's balcony.

He gave up trying to fall asleep and crawled out of bed, groping in the dark room for his bathrobe. It was a warm, summery night, and sitting by the pool might be relaxing. Quietly, Nate walked along the darkened hallway toward the back staircase. He passed ancient portraits of family members, staring at him with cold eyes. Nate could not help stopping at the portrait of his father that hung just outside one of the mansion's countless bedrooms.

"I spent nearly eighty dollars on dinner tonight," he whispered. "It was all your money, too."

Nathaniel Dysart Sr., dressed in a black suit with a white nandkerchief in his pocket (hand-rolled, Nate was sure), simply watched his son without response. Nate thought it seemed strange not to hear his father yelling at him. Even though the old man had been dead nearly a year, Nate had yet to get used to the blissful silence in the big house.

1975

Nate found his wife standing outside their room one night, holding on to the marble railing of the balcony and staring at the moon. He came up behind her and kissed her softly on the neck, putting his arms around her. She didn't turn around, but sighed and sniffed back a tear.

"Meg, you're crying," Nate said. "Again. What happened?"

She turned and buried her face in the soft folds of his velvet robe.

"Your father," she choked.

"I might have known," Nate said. "What did he do this time?"

"It's always the same thing, Nate," Meg said. "He says I was a clumsy fool. He says the accident was all my fault!"

Nate squeezed her and kissed her hair.

"Meg." He sighed. "My father is a cruel, vicious man. Don't even listen to him."

"I can't help it!" Meg said. "He harps at me all day long!"

She burst into tears, and choked, "He says I killed her! He says I killed our . . ."

"Meg, no," Nate said. "Don't ever talk like that! It wasn't your fault and you know it!"

He turned her around and led her from the chilly balcony to their bedroom. A soft light was burning next to the four-poster bed, and Nate switched it off after he had climbed under the covers with his wife. He put his arms around her and closed his eyes to fall asleep.

There were footsteps outside the door, thumping angrily over the old carpeting. They stopped suddenly, and as they did so Nate felt Meg stiffen a little.

"Clumsy bitch!"

Meg covered her ears to shut out the words she had heard so often as Nate held her close.

"Ignore him," he whispered. "Just ignore him."

But Nate knew better than anyone that this was impossible.

Adrian met Nate just outside his office as she walked to her dressing room the next morning. She shifted her handbag to her other shoulder and smiled at him.

"Thanks again for dinner," she said. "It was wonderful."

"I enjoyed it," Nate said. "Maybe—maybe we'll go out again soon."

"I sure hope so," Adrian answered, grinning.

She stood there until Nate had entered his office and closed the door, then whispered to herself, "Way to go, lady."

She smiled all the way to her dressing room. Adrian was completely infatuated by Nate. He was so vulnerably sweet, she thought. And yet beneath those sad eyes and that soft voice was a strong, highly professional head of a theater company already noticed by the critics. Whatever problems Nate had, he did not let them get in the way of his production. Adrian admired him for that.

EIGHT

The next week passed uneventfully, innocent of strange voices and nightmares for Nate. He was in a particularly good mood one October morning when he met Georgia and Denny in a hallway. Georgia, noticing his good mood, seized the opportunity.

"Mr. Dysart," she said, fingering a string of colored beads around her neck, "I've been wanting to ask you a favor. May I?"

Nate lifted his hands a little and dropped them.

"Sure," he said. "What can I do for you, Mrs. Richmond?"

"Well, I was thinking," Georgia said. "Do you mind if I watch Denny from the wings? Your new stage manager said I have to wait in Denny's dressing room. But it's so boring in there, and I really want to see how my son is progressing."

Nate didn't like the idea of working with stage mothers, yet despite her rather strident appearance and behavior, Georgia had never butted in. He decided he might give her a chance.

"What do you think, Denny?"

The boy's lips curled.

"I have to do whatever she wants," he said. "She's my mom."

Nate laughed and gave his consent.

Georgia stood out of the way in the wings and kept her eyes fixed on her son, who went through a dialogue now with Sander. On stage, Denny lost his faint southern accent and replaced it with a New York one so perfect no one would have guessed he was from South Carolina.

Don carried the Siamese cat, Cartier, around with him as he gave instructions to the waiting actors. He stroked the animal's head, and soon she began to purr so loudly that Sander turned to look at her. He interrupted the action on stage to say, "Be certain that animal doesn't come out here on stage."

"Would that bring more bad luck, Mr. Bernaux?" Denny asked, looking up at the tall actor.

"It certainly would," Sander replied. "A cat watching from the wings is good fortune, but he must never run onto the stage."

"All right," Nate said from his seat in the front row. "Enough about the cat. We've got a play to rehearse, remember."

As the actors continued their scene, with extras walking on or off stage as Don cued them, Cartier continued to purr. But all of a sudden, she was silent. Her eyes fixed on the floor at Don and Georgia's feet, growing so wide that the stage lights were reflected in her golden irises. She stiffened a little, her ears laid flat against the sides of her head.

Suddenly, she let out a horrible shriek and jumped from Don's arms, clawing him in her frenzy. She tore onto the stage, climbing up the nearest tall thing she could find—Sander's leg. The actor cried out as her claws dug into him and kicked her across the floor.

"Don't!" Denny cried, hurrying after the cat.

"What's wrong with that beast?" Sander roared, rubbing his leg. "Get it off the stage!"

Nate stood up and walked to the apron of the stage, telling Denny to be careful as the boy attempted to coax the animal from her hiding place behind the curtains. Finally, after she'd calmed down, she let Denny lift her into his arms.

"Poor kitty," Denny said.

"Bad luck," Sander mumbled. "It means bad luck."

"It'll be all right," Nate soothed. He looked at Georgia and Don.

"What do you suppose happened?"

"It's as if she was spooked," one of the extras said.

Georgia took the cat from Denny.

"We'll never know," she said. "But I'll take the poor thing back to the wardrobe mistress's room, to her bed and food. She'll calm down. Sometimes it's hard to understand cats; they do the darnedest things. Why, back home we had a cat..."

Nate signaled the actors on stage back into position, cutting her off.

"All right," he said, "the excitement's over. Sander, I'm sorry that happened. But let's get back to work. Previews start in Connecticut on November twenty-third, and we don't have time to waste."

Sander's jaw stiffened, but he joined in like the professional that he was. Nate returned to his seat in the first row, wishing all his problems were as minor as a cat. He tried not to imagine what might have frightened the usually well-adjusted animal.

Cartier would never be able to tell him of the strange little girl who burned him with her tiny hands.

Nate and Adrian sometimes shared lunch, but two days after the cat incident Nate backed out by saying he had an interview with someone at the *Times*. Adrian planned to eat in the greenroom and was looking forward to a leisurely hour after a busy morning. She pulled the brown paper bag containing her lunch from the drawer of her vanity, checked her purse for small change, then turned to leave the room.

A little girl was blocking the way.

"Oh!" Adrian gasped. "You startled me!" She brought a small hand up to her neck and laughed nervously.

"Who are you?" Adrian asked.

"You're a bad woman," she said. "I've seen you with him. Don't think I haven't! But you can't have him!"

"Who?" Adrian asked.

"The dark is going to come," the little girl said in reply. "The dark and the fire."

Adrian, beginning to lose patience, took her by the arm.

"Come on," she said. "I'll take you to your mommy. You can't just run around the theater by yourself."

The little girl pulled away and began to scream. Adrian

covered her ears, demanding that she stop. The child did and glared at her.

"Don't want to go to Mommy," she hissed. "Mommy makes it dark! I hate the dark! The dark hurts!"

"I don't find you amusing," Adrian said sternly. "I think you're a temperamental brat, and when I locate your mother I'm going to tell her you need a good spanking!"

With that, she reached for the doorknob. But the child grabbed her arm. Adrian gasped as a burning pain shot over her skin.

"Don't you say that to me," the child warned in a low voice.

Adrian pulled her arm away, suddenly afraid. The pain—it was like that sting she'd felt the other day in the greenroom! And yet, there was nothing on her arm.

"What is this?" she demanded.

"You can't have him," the child said. "If you try to take him away, I'll kill you."

Adrian suddenly lost her power to speak, and stared for a long time into the deep, dark eyes. And then, the sound of someone laughing in the hallway brought her to her senses. She pushed the child aside.

"Stay out of my dressing room," she said. Then, before she realized how ridiculous it sounded to speak this way to a child, she added, "And stay away from me!"

She jerked open the door and hurried to the safety of the greenroom. The little girl stared after her, angered. She would have to get rid of that woman.

Denny and Georgia were discussing Georgia's plans for the lunch hour. She wanted to do some shopping and didn't want Denny to come along. He guessed she was starting her Christmas shopping and promised to behave himself while she was gone.

Denny liked the idea of being left alone. It was unusually warm and sunny for October, so he'd play in the backyard. He hardly ever went back there. During all his breaks, his mother insisted he study his lines, and then there were the hours spent doing schoolwork with his tutor. But this was lunchtime, and his mother was gone. He was on his own—free!

"Free!" he cried, running around the cement and bouncing the ball vigorously. "No one's gonna bother me!"

Suddenly he noticed the little girl in the white dress. She was standing a few yards away, watching him with those spooky black eyes of hers. Where had she been hiding?

"Not you again," he whined. "Get lost, will you?"

But she walked right up to him and took the ball from his hands.

"I want to play with you," she said, her voice commanding. "I want you to be my friend."

"Look, why . . ."

Denny cut himself off. He wouldn't let this nutty little kid ruin his fun. He decided to go along with her, hoping she wouldn't come and pester him next time.

"I don't suppose you can play basketball," he said. "You're too little."

"I can do anything," the child said.

"Sure," Denny drawled. "Well, let's play catch, anyway. I don't want to stand around talking."

They started to toss the ball back and forth. To Denny's surprise, she caught it easily, never missing. He was about to ask her where she'd learned such coordination (Denny was proud to know a big word like "coordination") but didn't. He wouldn't show any interest in her. Then, maybe, she'd leave him alone.

"Your name is Dennis Richmond," the little girl said.

"How'd you know that?" Denny asked. "I never told you my name!"

"I know so many things," the child said. "I know because I wait and listen."

"Well, go wait and listen someplace else!"

Like many boys his age, Denny didn't like playing with little kids, boys or girls. And this child in particular was annoying to him with her fussy rich-girl's dress.

"You're not my friend," the child shouted, throwing the ball so hard at him that he stepped back a few paces with it.

She walked over to him and wrenched the ball from his grip, tossing it aside.

"Cut it out," Denny said. "Boy, what a brat!"

She didn't respond. Instead, her hands reached up to touch his face. But it wasn't a caress. Denny felt something hot against his skin, like an iron that had once burned him. But this pain was ten times worse.

"Cut it out!" he yelled.

"You have to be my friend," the child said. "You have to help me!"

The pain stopped, but Denny could not move. His mind was no longer in his control, but completely in the power of the small girl standing before him. She continued to speak in a monotone, drawing him further and further into her spell.

"You will do everything I tell you," she said. "You will help me and be my friend."

"I don't want to be your friend..." Denny's voice was pathetic and weak.

But then the horrible burning pain came back again when she touched him, and he was forced to relent.

"I'll be your friend!" he whimpered. "Stop hurting me! Please stop hurting me!"

"Just remember what I can do to you," the little girl said.

All of a sudden, Denny was standing alone in the backyard, feeling strangely dizzy. He saw his basketball over by the trash cans and wondered how it had gotten there. What had happened?

"I don't feel so good," he said softly.

His head pounding, he rubbed his eyes and went to retrieve the basketball. As he brought his thin arms up, he happened to see his watch. All the weariness of a moment ago vanished, replaced by panic. Somehow, his lunch hour was over, and he was due on stage right now!

Panicking, he raced into the theater, slamming into his mother on his way to the stage. He winced.

"Dennis Randall Richmond," Georgia hissed. "If you are ever late for another rehearsal, I'll find a hickory switch somewhere in this big city and tan your hide!"

Denny hurried onto the stage, still holding his basketball.

"Not only is he late," Sander sneered, "but he brings his toys with him!"

Denny apologized to Nate for losing track of the time.

Nate smiled at the boy, but as a producer, his words were stern.

"I'm sure it won't happen again," he said. "Give the ball to

Don and let's get started. Remember, we're opening in Connecticut in just three weeks."

Georgia stood in the wings watching, feeling sorry for yelling at him, but reasoning that he would have to learn some self-discipline if he was to make it in this tough business. She did not know that Denny's mind was preoccupied during the entire rehearsal, wondering who the little girl could be, and hoping she wouldn't come back.

After rehearsals were through, Nate took Denny aside to talk with him. He put an arm over the boy's shoulders and walked out of earshot of Georgia and the others.

"Denny, what was wrong today?" he asked gently. "Your timing was off completely and you kept forgetting to use that terrific New York accent."

Denny shrugged.

"I don't know," he said. "I—I sort of didn't feel well."

He thought about the little girl but decided not to mention her. His mother might be angry to know he'd been playing with a stranger. She'd warned him about talking to strangers in the city.

"You do look tired," Nate said. "Maybe you should stay home tomorrow. I don't want you coming down with something, and missing our premiere."

"Oh, I would never do that," Denny said, looking up at Nate. "I want to come to work tomorrow, really. I'm okay now. I promise I won't goof up again."

"Hey," Nate said, giving him a friendly hug. "We all have bad days."

"You're not mad anymore?"

Nate shook his head.

For the first time in several hours, Denny grinned. But there was one watching them who did not feel happy. She watched Nate ruffle Denny's hair, and clenched her small fists in anger. Denny was getting in the way. He'd have to be dealt with, the child thought.

With something akin to jealousy stirring in her, she decided how she would use Denny in her plans.

"Denny wasn't his usual self today," Adrian commented to Nate as they walked towards their rooms.

"He did look a little tired," Nate said. "But I think it was frustration. His mother told me he'd been playing in the back yard and I guess he got carried away with it. She was pretty upset. It isn't a pleasant thing to have a parent angry with you."

He bit his lip to think of his father, who's anger had caused him a lot of grief. Nate could almost feel the sting of the old man's cane on his shoulders.

"What's the matter, Nate?" Adrian asked.

"Nothing," Nate insisted.

She knew this wasn't true, for in the past few weeks she had gotten to know his moods fairly well. But she also knew that Nate didn't like discussing his personal affairs. She decided to let him tell her, if he wanted to, in his own time.

"Are you doing anything for dinner tonight?" Nate asked.

Adrian smiled. "I'm meeting a girl friend. But I think I can get out of it."

"Great," Nate said. "I'll get us reservations at Lutece, and . . ."

"Nate!" Adrian gasped. "We can't go there! They don't even have prices on the menu!"

"So?"

"You don't have to spend so much money," she told him.

"I'm trying to impress you," Nate said.

Adrian looked into his blue eyes and sighed. "Nathaniel Dysart, you already have."

There was a moment of silence as the two gazed at each other, suddenly lost in their own world. All the sounds of the crew and cast members faded out, the pictures on the wall did not exist, there were no doors along the hallway. There was just the two of them.

Nate pulled Adrian close to him and kissed her warmly, at first in a gentle way. But her body was comforting to him, and he found himself tightening his embrace until it seemed she'd break. He wanted her so much. And with her sighs, Adrian showed she wanted him too.

It was an impulsive kiss, exchanged because imagination would no longer suffice. But there was one who did not share their ecstasy. Nearby, a little girl watched them, her fists clenched tightly at the sides of her ruffled dress.

Suddenly, a loud cry interrupted the two lovers. Adrian

pulled away from Nate as the two of them looked around, startled.

"It's coming from the basement," Nate said, breaking into a run.

Adrian, close at his heels, followed him down the stone steps. They were halfway across the basement when they smelled smoke, coming from the building room. Nate crashed through the door and found the room in total chaos as the crew members rushed around trying to put out a fire and save what they could from the flames.

"It's one of the sets!" a carpenter shouted at Nate.

Nate grabbed a fire extinguisher. A scream rang out. One of the men had been burned. He was holding his hand up, roaring in pain.

Nate turned back to the fire, squinting against the heavy smoke. Suddenly, he saw a vision in the flames that made him drop the extinguisher in fear. It was a body. The body of a child...

"Hey, that isn't empty yet!" one of the crew shouted at Nate, pointing to the extinguisher.

When Nate didn't pick it up again, the man retrieved it and blasted at the fire. Nate continued to stare at the figure near his feet. It was curling up, blackening. And he couldn't move to save it.

"*Take the dark away!*" a child's voice screamed. "*Please take the dark away! It hurts!*"

Slowly, Nate crouched down, his arms reaching out toward the blackened little body. But all of a sudden he was wrenched back, as the carpenter roared, "Are you *nuts?!*"

And the little child became a piece of wood. Just a piece of wood.

"We can't save anything here," the carpenter said. "Let's get the fire out before it spreads to the other sets!"

Nate had to get away from the fire. His mind was playing tricks on him again.

I'm going to lose my theater, his thoughts said. *It's going to burn up again like it did...*

Nate shook his head. His theater had never burned! Why had he thought that?

Finally the flames were doused and only a few wisps of smoke remained.

"Thank God it only damaged one set," someone said.

"All that hard work ruined, and you're thanking God?"

"How did this happen?" Nate asked.

"I don't really know," the carpenter said. "We were packing things in for the night when I thought I smelled smoke. Before we could stop it, the whole damned thing went up."

Nate snapped out of the daze that had held him a moment ago and became the efficient company head that he was.

"Open some windows to air this place out," he said. "When the smoke clears, I want someone to check through that pile. God help you if I find evidence this fire was caused by carelessness."

Upstairs in the greenroom, Adrian was sitting with the crewman who'd gotten burned. He had his hand in a bowl full of ice water.

"Oh, Nate," Adrian said, looking up. "Is the fire out?"

"Yeah, it's out," Nate said. "How do you feel, Ronnie?"

"It doesn't hurt when I keep it in the water," Ronnie said.

Nate looked into the bowl. What he saw was not a man's hand, but something out of an old horror movie, like those drive-in flicks where a man is deformed after having acid thrown at him.

"Maybe you should go to a doctor," he said. "Those blisters look pretty ugly. How exactly did it happen?"

"It was kinda weird," Ronnie said. "I was running toward the extinguishers when someone grabbed me by the hand, and I felt this awful pain. But when I looked around, no one was there!"

"You might have accidently touched something heated up by the fire," Adrian suggested.

"Yeah, I guess that was it," Ronnie replied. "It was an accident, of course."

"Of course," Nate said, though he couldn't be sure.

NINE

Because the fire had delayed them, Nate and Adrian settled for a small Italian restaurant on a street near the theater, and now they sat in silence, each lost in thought. Adrian worried about Nate, watching him poke at his food without eating it. He, in turn, was trying to understand what had happened. Why had he been so frightened by a fire? And what in heaven's name had made him think that piece of wood was a child?

He put down his fork. Maybe all this wasn't rigged. Maybe he really was hearing voices and seeing things that weren't there.

Maybe the pressure of this business really was too much for him, and he was going to be a failure, like his father always insisted.

"Nate, it's going to be okay," Adrian said softly. "They'll rebuild the set in no time, you watch and see."

He managed a smile for her, but it was a false one, and she knew it. She took his hand and squeezed it.

"Nate, what's really wrong?" she asked.

"Nothing," he said.

Adrian clicked her tongue. "Damn it, I know something's bugging you. Will you please tell me about it?"

All of a sudden, Nate was blurting out everything that had happened since his arrival from California. Adrian listened quietly as he told her of the strange dream, of the voices, of the idea he'd had that someone might be trying to break him.

"The first suspect is my cousin, Vance Dysart," Nate said. "Even though he was my father's only other blood relative, he wasn't included in the will. He's damned pissed about that."

"Enough to want to hurt you?"

Nate nodded. "But he really doesn't have the brains to mastermind any of this." He sighed. "I don't know—maybe I'm just paranoid. I *did* see something in that fire, but if it had been set up, someone else would have seen it too. Maybe it *is* in my head."

"Oh, Nate," Adrian said. "I don't know what to tell you, except that I think you might be working too hard."

Nate shook his head.

"It isn't that," he said. "I worked steadily for five years in California, and for several years here in New York before that. I enjoy my work."

"Maybe it's finally caught up with you," Adrian said.

"Look, all those things you told me are tricks of an exhausted mind. Why don't you take a vacation?"

"With a show opening in New York in December?" Nate asked.

"Only for a few days," Adrian said. "Don Benson is qualified to take over."

"We've only been rehearsing for two weeks," Nate said. "I can't leave now. Well, I might have been able to if Jim were here . . ."

He shook his head.

"Nate, you've been through so much in the past year," Adrian said. "With your father dying, and then your best friend. Any man would be weakened by such experiences."

"I'm not weak," Nate insisted, almost hearing his father in her voice. "I'm a damned good director."

"And a terrific producer," Adrian agreed. "I've never worked with a better one. But all this that's on your mind is bound to affect your work sooner or later. I really think the best thing for you to do is take a few days off."

Nate knew she was right, but still he shook his head. He would keep on working, for it was only when he was busy that he wasn't haunted by morbid thoughts.

"I wouldn't be able to relax, knowing my theater was out of my hands," he said.

"Don't be so stubborn," Adrian said.

He waved a hand at her.

"I can't help it," he said. "I'm only happy when I'm working. I'm trying to achieve a goal, Adrian. Six years ago, when I had my own production company, my father used to make fun of me. He said I'd never amount to anything and would be a total failure. I have to prove him wrong."

"You already have," Adrian said, wondering why he cared what a dead man thought. "The box office has already sold out tickets for the first week of *Making Good*. Now, that doesn't sound like failure to me!"

"I won't be satisfied," Nate said, "until I see how the preview audiences react. And then I'll still worry about our Broadway opening!"

Adrian gazed over the light of a candle set in a wine bottle, wanting to throw her arms around him and kiss the sadness away from his face.

"Nate, I love you," she said softly.

It was so abrupt a statement that it took Nate by surprise, in spite of the passionate kiss they'd shared just a while earlier. Before he could respond, she reached up and brushed her fingers along the side of his face.

"I want to help you forget everything," she said. "I want to make you happy."

He caught her hand and kissed it.

"Come back to the theater with me," he said. "No one will be there but the night watchman, and we won't be disturbed."

Without a word, Adrian nodded her head in consent.

They walked onto the stage half an hour later, holding hands. Nate found the control board in the wings and switched on the overheads, beams of light washing the huge stage.

"Are you sure the guard won't bother us?" Adrian asked.

"If you're having doubts," Nate said, "it's okay."

"Oh, Nate," Adrian said, "I've never been so sure of anything."

Nate took her head in his hands and kissed her again.

"I just want to be with you tonight," he said. "I just want to hold on to you."

He turned back to the control board, dimmed the lights, and pulled the curtain across the stage, cutting them off from the theater and creating their own private cocoon.

"I could have gotten a room at the Pierre or the Plaza," he said, "but that didn't seem right, somehow." He paused to kiss her again. "I don't even need lights, the way you shine on this stage."

"I hope the critics are as flattering as you in a few weeks," Adrian said, laughing quietly.

But the smile disappeared when Nate pulled her close, kissing her. She smelled of lavender soap, so fresh and real. He wanted her so much. He loved her as he never thought he'd love a woman again.

Silently, he pulled her onto the sofa that was part of the set for the living room. Only the ghost light was left shining through the slightly parted curtain. Adrian looked like an angel in the soft light, her arms reaching up to him. She was so beautiful...

When they had given themselves to each other, Adrian laid her head on Nate's bare chest and fell asleep. For a little

while, Nate rubbed her back lazily. And then, lulled by the
steady rhythm of her breathing, he dozed off himself, smiling.

In the orchestra pit, a little girl watched the two of them,
her feelings tottering between hurt and anger. Why were
they always together? Why did they always smile when it was
so dark and lonely in here?

"Daddy, please take the dark away," she whispered.

If only she could get rid of that woman somehow things
would be right again.

Nate stirred a little as a cold breeze washed over him, and
opened his eyes. It was dark, except for the glow of the ghost
light. He squinted and tried to read his watch by it, but
looked back up again when he saw something white and filmy
moving across the stage. It hovered just outside the range of
the ghost light, then vanished.

"Damn it!" he cried, jumping to his feet so quickly that
Adrian was jerked awake.

"What?!" she yelped. She looked around in confusion, then
saw Nate hurrying towards the wings. Seconds later, the stage
was brightly illuminated and the curtain opened.

"What's wrong, Nate?" she asked, covering her eyes against
the blinding light.

"I saw something," Nate said, walking towards the apron.
He looked down into the orchestra pit, then surveyed the
shadowy room before him. It was deadly still.

"What do you mean, you saw something?" Adrian asked,
standing up.

Nate walked across the stage, looking all around himself.
He pointed towards the ghost light.

"It was a white figure," he said. "Like the one in those
photographs."

Adrian crossed the stage to him.

"Maybe you were just dreaming," she said. "I don't see
anything."

Nate was looking at the curtains covering the exits on
either side of the orchestra section. Could someone have
slipped through them?

"Whoever it was," Adrian said, playing along with him
although she had her doubts, "he's gone now. Forget about it
for tonight, darling."

Nate turned to her, ready to burst out that he could not

forget about it. But somehow, instead, these were the words that came out, "Adrian hold me? I need you."

She moved closer to him and put her arms around his shoulders, wishing she could say something to calm him down. His fears were so genuine—could they also be justified? Was there really someone spying on him? Nate seemed rational at other times, and he was, as she'd said, a completely professional director-producer.

"Nate, I have an idea," she said finally. She hadn't come to terms with the idea of someone trying to destroy Nate, but she would not deny it completely. "Why don't you spend the night at my apartment?"

"I'd like that," Nate said. Now he pulled away and threw his arms up in the air. "No I won't. Look at me! I'm acting paranoid."

Adrian took both his hands.

"Don't say that," she said. "You have every right to be frightened. This is a tough business we're in, and I'm sure there *are* people who'd like to see you fail. Jealous people. But if I were you, Nate, I wouldn't give them the satisfaction of seeing me cringe."

Nate looked into her eyes.

"When I got the enlargement of that photograph," he said, "I thought someone had paid the person who developed it to tamper with it. And then I thought the voices I'd heard were coming from a tape recorder someone had placed in the theater."

"You see?" Adrian said. "That's probably what it is. A vicious, childish prank."

"And I vowed I wouldn't let it get to me," Nate went on. He bent down and picked up his shirt.

"Could Vance have done this?"

"I don't think so," Nate said. "He couldn't have known I took the pictures, anyway. Much as I dislike the guy, I can't blame him for this. Some of my father's business partners would be smart enough to pull it off, but would it be worth all this effort?"

"Nate," Adrian said, "just keep telling yourself the only thing that matters is your play. This culprit will get tired and will eventually leave you alone."

Nate put his arms around her. He prayed she was right. In

a moment, the embrace changed to a long, warm kiss. Nate could easily forget his problems in Adrian's arms. He could forget there was anyone else in the world.

But they were not alone. The little girl who'd watched them sleeping a moment ago, her heart filled with anger, stood nearby and clenched her fists. She would get rid of that red-haired woman. She would make certain Adrian didn't interfere.

First, however, she'd let them think nothing more was going to happen. When they were least expecting it, she'd strike again.

As she turned her key in the lock on her apartment door Adrian heard the phone start to ring. Who would be calling her at this hour of the night? It had to be Nate, of course. She hoped he wasn't in trouble...

"Adrian, it's your mother."

"Mom, hi!" Adrian gasped. She hooked the receiver between her shoulder and jaw and wriggled out of her coat. "Why are you calling so late? Is something wrong?"

She thought about her father, who had had a heart attack several years earlier. A quick switch to her other ear allowed her to finish taking off her coat, but cut off her mother's first words.

"...at all," Martha was saying. "We're fine. But I've been trying to call you all night. We got our airline tickets to New York this afternoon!"

Adrian smiled. "Really? When are you coming?"

"Do you have to ask?" Martha said. "We'll be there the tenth of December, and we're staying about a week. Might as well make a trip of it, you know."

"That sounds great," Adrian said. "So you'll be here for my debut."

"Wouldn't miss it for the world," Martha said. "Oh, I've been *busting* all night to tell you. Where've you been?"

Adrian bit her lip and shifted a little, embarrassed. Then she laughed at herself. Imagine, acting coy at her age! And with her parents living five hundred miles away!

"I went out with Nate Dysart tonight," she said. "We had a lovely dinner in the city."

And an even better dessert, despite unpleasant surprises, she thought.

"That's nice," Martha said. "I'm glad to hear you get along so well with your director."

"I can't wait until you meet Nate, Mom," Adrian said. "He's really a good guy."

"Do I hear wedding bells?"

Adrian clicked her tongue.

"I'm too busy with my career right now, Mom," she said. "And speaking of that, I don't mean to cut you short, but I'm really tired."

"I understand," Martha said. "You need your rest. Call me again soon, okay?"

"Sure will, Mom," Adrian said. "See you the tenth!"

How nice it would be for her parents to see her Broadway debut, she thought as she hung up. Adrian just hoped that whoever was tormenting Nate would be long gone before her parents arrived.

"You must have been right," Nate said to Adrian, as they headed out to lunch together. "I've been too busy to worry about those voices, and nothing's happened."

"See?" Adrian said. "You're showing whoever it was that nothing will keep you from opening. They've probably given up."

Nate shook his head.

"I don't know," he said. "I've seen stretches of peace before, and then something always happens. I hope you're right this time."

Adrian put her arm through his.

"I bought a roll of film for your camera," she said, "and I want to take pictures of the theater again. I'll find out how that white flaw could be put on the negatives. It might help us locate the culprit. Any clue we get is worth the effort."

"I thought you didn't want to pay attention to this guy," Nate said.

"That doesn't mean I don't want to catch him!"

Nate was glad to have someone on his side, a confidante who didn't think this was all his imagination.

When they returned to the theater after lunch, Adrian hurried to her dressing room to get ready for the afternoon's

rehearsals, and Nate headed for his office. He passed Georgia
and Denny in the hallway. Denny's eyes refused to meet
Nate's, as if he were embarrassed to be caught carrying his
basketball again.

"I promise I won't be late this time," he said.

"You have about a half-hour," Nate told him.

Georgia nodded vigorously.

"Don't you worry, Mr. Dysart," she said. "I'll see to it that
he's early."

"I'm sure he will be," Nate said, ruffling Denny's hair.
"Right, kid?"

Denny nodded even as an unseen little girl clenched her
fists and let out a silent scream of jealousy. She wanted to feel
someone touch her hair, she wanted someone to smile at her.
She wanted to see *him* smile at her.

The time had come, she decided, to get rid of Denny.

The three parted company, Georgia walking Denny to the
backyard. When Nate reached his office, the phone was ringing.
To his anger, the voice at the other end belonged to his cousin.

"Don't hang up," Vance ordered.

"How the hell did you get this number?"

"Well," Vance said, "a big-shot producer like yourself can't
expect to hide away forever. I called Information. Decided I
haven't been getting across to you."

Nate rubbed his forehead and said impatiently, "Look, let's
get this over with once-and-for-all. What exactly do you want
from me?"

"Only my fair share of the estate," Vance said. "I think
thirty percent isn't asking too much."

"You're insane," Nate accused. "If you want help financially, just ask for it. But cut out these games, otherwise!"

"You cheat! You damned cheat!" Vance bellowed. With an exaggerated groan, Nate slammed down the receiver. By the time he
headed to the stage, he had pushed the call from his mind.

When Georgia and Denny entered the backyard, the air
was thick with the smells from a nearby restaurant. From one
of the nearby streets, the sound of a jackhammer reached
their ears, mingling with car horns and a long police siren.
Georgia frowned in disgust to see the litter covering the
ground and pulled Denny close as if afraid he'd touch it.

"Why on earth do you want to play here?" Georgia asked. "Lord only knows what diseases you could catch in this filth!"

Denny started dribbling his ball on the cement ground.

"Aw, Mom," he said. "There's no food or anything back here to attract germs. Just a few bottles and some crates."

"Don't sass me, young man," Georgia said. "I know what big cities are like! Those boxes could be hiding rats!"

"I haven't seen any," Denny said, gravely. Mothers could be funny sometimes.

Georgia shook her head and found a crate to sit on, kicking it over first to be sure there were no bugs or vermin under it. Satisfied, she settled down and watched her son. What she didn't know was that a small girl was also watching him, making plans. Denny had promised to help her. He wouldn't dare break that promise, and now the child was coming to collect. First Denny could help her get rid of that woman named Adrian, she thought.

A moment later, she was inside the theater, moving down a long hallway. There were so many hallways here, so many twists and turns. But they no longer frightened her as they did so long ago. She knew exactly where she was going.

One of the crew members was returning from his lunch shift and was heading toward the cellar. He didn't see the little girl but felt a sudden dizziness and stopped walking. Rubbing his eyes, he stood still for a few moments. Then, as if remembering something, he went to the back door and pulled it open.

"Mrs. Richmond?" he called. "Nate wants to see you."

"Me?" Georgia asked. "Not Denny?"

"No, just you," the stagehand said.

Georgia looked at her son.

"Now, what do you suppose this is about?" she asked. "Well, I'd better go see. Now, I may not be able to get back out here to remind you, so you'd better know what time it is."

"I promise I won't be late again," Denny said.

His mother left him and went inside the building. A moment later, he noticed the little girl standing at the edge of the yard. He was about to make a nasty comment to her but felt a sudden wave of fear creep over him and forced a smile.

"Hi," he said.

"Hello," the child replied, coming toward him. "I want you to help me today."

Denny nodded, somehow knowing it would be dangerous to refuse. Softly, uncertainly, he said, "I never learned what your name is."

Maybe, if she thought he liked her, she wouldn't hurt him.

"My name's Bonnie," the child said. She turned and looked at the door through which Georgia had just entered the theater. "There's someone in there that I don't like. You'll help me get rid of her."

"Who's that?"

But the child named Bonnie would not tell him. She took his hand, her tiny one feeling like a cube of ice. Denny wanted to pull away but couldn't. He let her take him back inside the building, keeping his eyes on her. What was she going to do to him?

They passed several stagehands in the hallway. They all greeted Denny, but none of them acknowledged the little girl at his side. She took him to the basement stairs, pointing down.

"They'll think she hurt you," Bonnie said.

Denny did not understand, but was too frightened not to follow her as she descended the stone steps. He couldn't understand why he should be afraid of this little kid, a girl wearing a sissy dress. In the distance, he could hear the building crew at work and wanted to cry out to them for help. As if reading his mind, the child turned and glared at him with wide black eyes. Denny looked at her, feeling sick in his stomach.

"Once when I was bad," she said, "my mommy put me in a dark place. And when my daddy found me, he was really angry. He told my mommy she was *wicked*. Now, you'll go in a dark place too. And everyone will be mad at *her*."

"What dark place?" Denny asked, his voice barely a whisper. It was deserted at this end of the basement, and he began to look around for a way out. But he knew Bonnie would never let him escape. She'd hurt him again, make him fall or burn his skin. Or something worse...

They entered the boiler room; it was small and stuffy. Though the theater was new, this room had already taken on the heavy, dusty odor of an ancient cellar. Denny rubbed his arms nervously and watched as the little girl walked across the room.

There was a steel grating on the wall, an entrance to the passages of the theater's air ductwork. The little girl lifted it out easily, as if it were weightless. Denny backed away, frightened by her strength. She set the cover on the floor and turned to him.

"Get in there," she said, pointing.

"I—I can't," Denny protested. "There's no room, with all those pipes and things!"

"I said 'get in there,'" Bonnie pressed, her tone grim. "You have to stay in there until they find you, and then they'll be mad at that woman and make her go away!"

"M-make who go away?"

"DON'T ASK QUESTIONS!"

Denny covered his ears at the sound of her scream as the floor suddenly opened up beneath him. He was falling, falling down into a big black pit! He was going to die! He was going to die!

"*Sssttoooppp!!!*" he screamed, his voice stretched out and sounded far away.

The floor was back again.

"If you don't do as I say," the child threatened, "I'll make you fall into the darkness forever!"

Fighting tears, Denny nodded. Scared as he was, he didn't want a girl to see him cry. Yet whoever, whatever this child named Bonnie was, he could not fight her. She made him crawl into the opening in the wall. Denny cringed back in the darkness, feeling a cold metal pipe against his lower back, and sat silently as Bonnie replaced the grating. She stared through it at him for a long time, ancient memories stirring up in her mind. Mommy had done this to her, too. And Daddy had been mad. Maybe he would get mad again to see this child hurt. And then he would get rid of that new lady . . .

"Who did this to you?" she asked finally.

"Y-you did," Denny choked.

The ringing of metal grated his ears as she slammed a little fist against the cover.

"No!" she cried. "Adrian did this to you! That woman named Adrian. Tell them Adrian did it, or I'll . . ."

"Adrian," Denny whispered, too weakened by her powers to argue.

TEN

Georgia Richmond fingered her plastic beads, trying to hide her embarrassment. Imagine, interrupting one of Mr. Dysart's rehearsals because some silly stagehand said Nate wanted to see her! Georgia decided she'd find the stagehand later and give him a piece of her mind. But right now she had to retrieve Denny, who was due on stage any minute.

She knocked softly on the dressing room door and entered. But it was dark and deserted, with no signs that Denny had been there at all. He always left the lights on, despite her scoldings. Putting her hands on her hips, Georgia said, "If I am shamed again today because that boy missed another rehearsal, I really will tan his hide!"

Angry, she marched toward the back exit and pushed it open. But the yard, too, was empty. Georgia felt a wave of guilt; what if he were already on stage even as she had thought about punishing him. She closed the back door and walked toward the stage. Don met her in the wings.

"Where the hell is Denny?" he asked. "He's late!"

"You mean he isn't here?"

"No," Don whispered, "and he's due on in a few minutes."

The guilt of a moment ago vanished.

"Let me look for him," Georgia said. "I promise I'll be right back!"

She checked the dressing room once again, then went to the greenroom, where she found Adrian chatting with Barbara.

"Oh, Adrian!" Georgia called. "Have you seen Denny anywhere?"

Adrian shook her head. "No, I haven't. Is he outside again?"

"I checked there," Georgia said. "And he isn't in his dressing room."

Barbara looked at both women and said, "Maybe he's in the—the—"

"Little boys' room?" Georgia said. "That's a good idea. I'll certainly check there."

"Don't worry," Adrian said. "I'm sure you'll find him."

Georgia left the room and located a lavatory in one of the hallways. Lord, this was a complicated building! Denny could be anywhere! She stood outside the door for a few minutes until someone came out, then asked, "Did you see a little boy in there?"

The stagehand shook his head and told her the men's room was empty. Now Don Benson came up to Georgia, as her fingers reached up to fidget with the beads she wore.

"Oh, dear," she said. "I can't find him!"

"Well, we've called his understudy, Johnny Hemlock," Don said. "You really should do something about your boy, Mrs. Richmond."

Georgia nodded slowly.

"Oh, I will," she said. "Believe me, when I find him, I'll take care of him!"

"Any ideas where he might be?"

"I looked everywhere I can think," Georgia said.

"The backyard?"

"Yes, and he wasn't there," Georgia replied.

"Let's check again," he said. "It's possible he accidentally threw his ball over the fence and went to get it."

Hoping he was right, Georgia followed the stage manager. Denny was not in the yard, but Don wouldn't give up. He leaned over the back fence and noticed a dead-drunk wino sleeping in the narrow strip that ran between the garage and the building behind it, but no sign of Denny. There were no footprints in the mud, indicating that he hadn't even climbed the fence.

"Then he's got to be inside," Don reasoned.

When he turned back to the yard, he noticed something orange hidden behind one of the crates. It was Denny's basketball.

"Oh, my Lord!" Georgia cried as Don went to pick it up. "Something's happened to my baby! He would never go anywhere without that thing! There are so many awful types in this area. Someone's taken him!"

"Take it easy," Don said. "He probably realized he was late for rehearsal and dropped it when he ran inside."

"Oh, dear," Georgia said. "I hope so!"

Don put his arm around her shoulder.

"Let's check the stage again," he suggested.

With a mixture of anger and worry stirring in her, Georgia followed him back inside.

Denny sucked at his knuckles, trying to drive away the pain he felt from banging so hard on the grating. He couldn't understand why someone didn't hear him. He had shouted and banged and kicked with all his might.

And then he realized something. He was in the back end of the cellar, and the building crew was making too much noise! No one could possibly hear him over it!

Was he going to be stuck in here forever?

Until he died?

Somehow, the strong boy he had always been took over for the moment. He looked around. The passageway he'd been forced into was about three feet high, big enough for him to crawl through. He'd have to snake his way around the twisting pipes, but if there was a grating here, there might be another one nearer to people. He had to take that chance, if he was going to get out of here.

Trying not to think what might be hidden in the darkness ahead, Denny got on his hands and knees and started crawling forward.

Georgia's eyes were bloodshot from crying when she and Don walked up to the front row, where Nate sat. Don leaned down and whispered into his ear, "Sorry to interrupt, but we've got a problem."

"What's that?"

"Denny's missing," Georgia said. Her tears began to flow again. "Oh, my Lord! My little boy is missing!"

Adrian hurried to the apron and looked down at Nate worriedly. She could tell by his expression that he was trying not to think something bad might have happened to the boy.

"Did you check the backyard?" Nate asked.

"Yes," Georgia said weakly.

"And his dressing room and the greenroom?"

"Yes! Yes!" Georgia cried, her voice shrill. "I looked everywhere. I can't *find* him!"

"He doesn't seem to be anywhere in this theater," Don said. "And I found his basketball in the yard. Georgia says he never goes anywhere without it."

Adrian brought a hand to her lips and saw Nate open and close his eyes briefly—an expression so subtle that only she noticed it. In seconds, Nate's voice took on the sound of authority.

"We'll postpone rehearsals until he's found," he said. "Adrian, you and I will check the lobby and balcony. Don and Georgia, the basement is yours. The rest of you check the dressing rooms. We'll find him."

"Of course we will, Georgia," Adrian assured her.

With Sander protesting that the boy was probably just hiding to avoid punishment for being late again, all the actors and crew went their separate ways.

Something light and airy brushed over Denny's face, and he backed up a little, his ankles skimming under a low length of pipe. Cobwebs. He grimaced and had to remind himself he wasn't afraid of bugs. But he was afraid of everything right at that moment, and his muscles were tensed as if in anticipation of—something. There might be roaches down here or black widows or . . .

"I'm not gonna think about that," Denny said out loud, his voice sounding hollow in the long tunnel.

Holding his hand in front of himself to brush away the cobwebs, he moved onward. Sometimes, it was necessary to flatten out and slither under pipes like a snake or to pull himself up over them. But for the skinny boy, the going wasn't that rough. It was the dark that weakened him. The dark and the close, thick air.

He had been crawling for a few minutes and guessed he should be near the building room. Surely, there would be another grating there, and one of the crew members would get him out. Encouraged by the idea, he kept moving, though his back ached and his breathing became more difficult.

And then he saw a patch of light, just a few yards away. Denny could hear the increasing volume of hammers and saws, and knew he was about to get out of here. He was so elated that the terror he'd felt a moment ago vanished completely.

"Hey, somebody!" he shouted. "Help! Help!"

No one came to investigate his cries. Denny sighed, realizing his voice could not be heard over the din of the workers. He would have to get right up to the grating.

Suddenly, the patch of light disappeared. Denny blinked, but still it did not return. What had happened to the light? And there were no sounds either. It was as if everyone else had vanished. Denny, confused and exhausted, stretched out and rested his head on a pipe, one of his legs thrown up over another pipe that ran along the wall. With his heart pounding so hard that it hurt his chest, he fell asleep.

"Let's try the hallway that runs alongside the auditorium," Adrian suggested as she and Nate descended the twisting lobby staircase.

"You do that," Nate said. "I'm going to take a look at the stage. We might cover more territory if we split up."

Adrian agreed, but before she turned toward one of the doors leading off the lobby, she took Nate's hand and said, "Nate, it's okay. Nothing's happened."

He tightened his fingers around her hand.

"Let's just find Denny," he said.

He did not know what to make of this incident. Was it just the mischievous act of a little boy? Nate hadn't heard the voices yet. There had been no visions. And yet he couldn't help feeling that something *would* happen. The theater was just too silent. The calm before the storm.

He walked slowly down the slanting floor that led to the stage, looking left and right between the rows of golden chairs. No one was there. The orchestra pit was empty, and so was the stage. Nate walked through a door and climbed a few steps, checking first the hallway to the left of the stage, then crossing it and investigating the right hallway. Empty.

"Denny?" he called. "Hey, kid, are you there?"

He listened carefully, praying for an answer. But there was only silence.

Someone was calling his name. Denny's eyes fluttered open, and for a moment he did not know where he was. He pulled his head away from the pipe it had rested on, crying out as he looked around in the darkness. Then he realized that he was still caught in the air passage. The air was so thick in here. The boy coughed for a few moments, rubbing his tearing eyes.

He heard his name again, and recognized Nate's voice from somewhere far away. Then another voice called to him—Adrian's. No! He wouldn't answer her! *She* had done this! She had hurt him and now she wanted to hurt him again!

He had to get out of here. He had to get out before she caught him.

"Mommmm," he groaned. "I want my mom!"

Nate and Adrian met the others near Nate's office and gave their reports. Georgia's face was red, and she clung fast to Don's arm. He shook his head to see Nate's questioning eyes.

"We didn't see him anywhere," he said. "And no one we asked saw him, either."

"I can assure you the boy is in none of the dressing rooms," Sander volunteered.

"And he's not in the lobby or balcony," Nate said. "Or anywhere else we looked."

Georgia choked on a sob and said, "Maybe he's been kidnapped!"

"Of course he hasn't," Adrian said quickly, though in her mind she was anticipating something far worse. To push aside her own fears, she said, "We'll find him, for sure."

For sure, Nate thought.

Denny didn't remember ever being so frightened. He tried to make a game of this, pretending he was a soldier like his dad had been in Vietnam, crawling along the ground to avoid enemy fire. He was an international spy, a space explorer, a . . .

It didn't work. The illusions would last only a moment, and then he would remember where he was. Trapped. Trapped in a dark, stuffy tunnel. And it was Adrian who had done it.

His head bumped something. He reached forward and felt the pipes with his hands, finding that they made a right angle here into a tunnel too small even for his skinny body. Panicking, Denny tried to turn around and go back, but

couldn't. Ready to burst into tears of fright, he backed against
the wall and sat up a little. His head did not touch the
ceiling. Carefully, Denny reached up and put his hand through
an opening overhead.

"Hey," he whispered.

It was a shaft leading to the next floor, where only a thin
pipe ran! Could this be a means of escape? Denny wriggled
his head and shoulders up into it, then scuffed his heels along
the floor until he was halfway into the shaft. With his elbows
pressed together in front of him, he reached forward and felt
the bottom of another passageway. He pushed his chest
against it and heaved himself up, bracing his feet along the
thin length of pipe behind him. Finally and only because he
was a thin, limber boy, he managed to get into the upper
tunnel. He collapsed on its floor and tried to catch his breath,
finding it somehow easier to breathe here than down below.
The air was fresher and cooler.

"DENNY?"

He picked up his head. That was his mother's voice! His
mother could help him!

"DENNY, BABY, WHERE ARE YOU?"

"MOM? MOM, HELP ME!"

He crawled forward, pulling himself along a pipeline.

Not too far away, Nate and the others stopped and listened.

"Where's that coming from?" Adrian asked. "It sounds
muffled."

"He's locked up somewhere," Georgia said. "I know it!"

Nate held up a hand.

"Wait," he said, "there it is again."

Denny's voice reached them from somewhere far off, but
in the complicated structure of the building it was hard to tell
where it was coming from.

"Denny!?" Adrian cried. "Keep calling, and we'll find you!"

At the sound of her voice, Denny clamped his mouth shut.
He couldn't let her get at him again! Trembling with fear, he
scurried ahead, refusing to call out even though he heard
them shouting his name.

There was another light up ahead. But Denny did not
hurry to it, certain it would disappear.

But it didn't. It grew wide and the space around him

opened out. Denny was able to stretch both arms from his sides. He moved toward the light, his heart beating wildly.

He was under the stage. Blissful fresh air hit his face as he crawled out over the orchestra pit.

There were people out there, sitting in the audience. Why was that? This wasn't a performance! Denny squinted and gazed out over the crowd. Something's wrong, he thought. Those people don't look right...

They were wearing funny clothes, not at all like the styles he saw out on the street every day. The women were wearing hats that fit close to their heads, and most of them had ear-length haircuts. Their dresses were either fringed or beaded, and some of them had feather fans. The men all wore suits that were cut in a funny way, not the tailored look Denny was used to seeing. A memory came to him, a thought of a movie he'd once seen that took place in the early nineteen-twenties. These people were dressed just like that!

"What...?"

He could say no more. The weakness in his muscles overcame him, and as he crashed to the floor the illusion of the audience dissolved.

In the hallway with the others, Adrian took Nate's hand as she heard the thud.

"That came from the stage," she said.

"Let's look there," Nate said, breaking into a run.

They found Denny lying on the floor of the orchestra pit, his hair mussed up and his clothes covered with dust. Nate jumped down into the pit and turned the boy over, taking his small wrist in his hand.

"There's a pulse," he said, looking up at Georgia.

"Oh, praise God!" Georgia cried.

"He's barely breathing," Nate said. "Don, call an ambulance."

The stage manager hurried to the nearest phone. Georgia pulled Denny's head onto her lap and brushed back his sweaty hair, rocking him as tears flowed from her eyes. Denny's cheeks were flushed, and his hair and clothes were thick with dust. Nate stared at her in silence, his fists clenched, waiting for the voices.

"Look," Adrian said. "He's coming to."

Denny opened his eyes once, closed them again, then opened them and looked up at his mother.

"Mom," he whispered. "I can't breathe..."

Georgia hugged him close.

"My baby," she said. "My baby. Mommy's here. You're safe now!"

"Mom, she—she—" Denny stopped to cough, then spat out, "She made me do it."

Nate knelt at his side, putting a hand on the boy's arm. Someone had made him crawl under the floor. Someone had tried to kill him...

"Who, Denny?" he pressed. "Who made you do this?"

Denny blinked at him, then looked over his shoulder. Nate followed his gaze, which seemed to rest on Adrian. The actress shook her head, confused. Abruptly, Denny turned and hid his face in his mother's arms.

"Adrian," he said weakly. "Adrian made me do it."

"Denny!" Adrian cried. "What are you talking about? I'd never do such a thing!"

"Denny, tell us who really made you crawl in there," Nate said.

Memories of a little girl came to the child's exhausted mind, but he could not form the words to describe her. It did not matter, though. It was Adrian who was guilty.

"Mom, she hurt me," Denny whimpered. "Adrian hurt me!"

Georgia kissed him, then turned to glare at Adrian.

"You monster," she hissed. "How *could* you?"

Nate stood up and put his arm around Adrian's waist.

"I didn't do a thing!" she cried.

"Georgia, the boy is hysterical," Nate said. "He doesn't know what he's saying."

"My son doesn't lie," Georgia snapped.

"Adrian..." Denny said before succumbing to another coughing fit.

"Where is that ambulance?" Georgia demanded.

At that moment Don returned to say the ambulance was on its way. Adrian closed her eyes and rested her head on Nate's shoulder, grateful the child had been found. But why, she wondered, had he said *she* had tried to hurt him?

ELEVEN

"Get her out of here!" Georgia screeched as Adrian and Nate entered the hospital emergency waiting room.

"Georgia," Nate said firmly, "Adrian and I have come as friends. We're very worried about Denny."

"You ought to be," Georgia said, staring at Adrian, "after what you did!"

"I didn't do anything," Adrian insisted. "I told you that earlier! Please believe me!"

Georgia seemed ready to cry out again, but instead her expression softened.

"I'm sorry," she said. "Of course I shouldn't blame anyone until the entire story is heard. It's just that I'm terribly upset."

Adrian put a hand on her arm.

"I understand," she said.

A doctor came out at that moment to tell Georgia her son had been moved to an upstairs room. He was conscious and could see his mother.

"I'd like to speak to him too," Nate requested.

"That's impossible," the doctor said. "Denny can have no outside visitors for the rest of the day. He's still quite weak."

"Is he going to be okay?" Adrian asked.

The doctor did not reply, but took Georgia's arm and led her towards the elevators. Adrian, watching them go, said, "I won't be able to rest until I learn what my connection to this is."

"You have *nothing* to do with it," Nate said. "I know something is going on at the theater, and I'm sure it involves what happened to Denny."

Adrian held up a hand.

"Maybe Denny will be able to give us a clue," she said. "I shouldn't say such a cruel thing, but maybe his ordeal is a blessing in disguise."

"You mean that it might help solve this mystery," Nate

said. He sighed. "Maybe he can give us a name. God, I hope so."

Adrian put her arms around him and together they walked to a waiting area. Finding a place to sit in the crowded room, they waited in silence for Georgia to return.

"He's a little tired," Georgia told them when she came back half an hour later. "But other than that, he seems fine. Of course, I can't be too sure. We have to wait for the test results."

Georgia seemed better herself. Her eyes were no longer bloodshot, and she had stopped twisting her necklace. Somewhere between Denny's room and here she had found a mirror, and her hair was neatly combed again.

"Did he tell you anything more?" Adrian asked.

"I'm afraid not," Georgia said. "I didn't press the poor darling for details. I think it would be too much for him right now."

"Sure," Nate said, obviously disappointed. But Georgia's next words made him feel better.

"I'd like to say how sorry I am for my earlier behavior," she told Adrian. "I should never have acted that way."

"It's no problem," Adrian said, smiling a little.

"I'm sure you're not to blame," Georgia went on, though Adrian could hear doubt in her tone. "Denny's told me on several occasions that you've always been very nice to him."

"Do you have any idea who might really have done this?" Nate asked.

Georgia thought a moment.

"No," she said. "Everyone on the cast and crew liked Denny, I believe." A slender hand found her beads again.

"Although," she said, "that Sander Bernaux was abrupt several times."

"Sander's abrupt with everyone," Adrian said. "Besides, he was on stage when Denny disappeared."

"You weren't, though," Georgia said to Adrian. The accusation filled her eyes again. "Where were you at the time, Adrian?"

The actress looked at Nate, then back at Georgia.

"In the greenroom," she said. "On my break."

Georgia's eyes thinned as the doubts of a moment ago came back.

"Can you prove that?"

"Of course I can," Adrian said. "There were other people in there!"

Georgia did not say anything, but Nate and Adrian could tell she was wondering again about Adrian. Finally, she said, "I'm dreadfully tired. I'm going home to rest so that I can be here early tomorrow."

"Don't worry," Nate said. "We'll find the culprit."

"We'll leave that to the police," Georgia said, eyeing Adrian.

After she'd left, Adrian said, "She still thinks I'm behind all this."

"Forget about her," Nate said. "You and I both know you're innocent. Come on, let's go home ourselves. We can talk in the car."

A few minutes later they were seated in the back of the Rolls-Royce.

"I still can't figure out how Denny fell off the stage like that," Adrian said.

"Neither can . . ." Nate cut himself off. "Oh, God."

"What is it?"

"I just realized something," Nate told her. "He didn't fall *off* the stage, he fell from *under* it. The theater is built with air passages running through it. He must have been crawling in them."

"That poor kid," Adrian said. "No wonder he was delirious."

"Someone must have forced him inside," Nate said.

Adrian clicked her tongue.

"And Georgia thinks that someone was me," she replied. She turned to Nate. "But I'd never do such a thing."

"No you wouldn't," Nate said.

"It all comes back to those voices you heard," Adrian said. "And your idea that someone is doing this to torment you."

She took his hand.

"You once said you thought it might be your cousin," she said.

"It's possible," Nate said. "But I still don't think Vance could pull off something like this. For one thing, he lives and works up in Connecticut. It would be hard for him to get down here that often."

"Did your father ever cheat anyone?" Adrian asked.

"Probably," Nate said. "Although I heard nothing about it.

I made certain that all his debts were paid off once the will was out of probate."

"But is there still a possibility of one of *them* doing this?"

"I have little association with my father's people," Nate said. "I let others run his businesses, and they report to me only on occasion."

"There's obviously someone who's trying to cause trouble," Adrian said. She scoffed at that. "Trying! More like succeeding!"

"I won't give in to it," Nate said defiantly.

"Good for you," Adrian said.

She rested her head on his shoulder and closed her eyes. Nate kissed her soft hair.

"Come home with me tonight?" he asked.

Adrian's curls tickled his neck as she shook her head.

"You've had a tiring day, Nate," she said. "I think we'd be better off going our separate ways."

"I wish . . ."

"Shh," Adrian said, touching his lips. "I want you to go home and rest, if we're going to get up early to see Denny in the morning."

"You're right," Nate sighed.

But he could not rest that night. Though his body was tired and the satin sheets were comforting, Nate could not relax. Sleep was not a panacea to him but poison that unlocked the horrors in his mind. When he closed his eyes, he heard a shrill laugh.

"She killed the child!" someone shouted. "She killed it!"

"Denny's alive," Nate protested. "Adrian didn't . . ."

But he was not in his bedroom anymore. He was in another room in the house, in a carved wooden bed. And his father was standing at the foot, pointing at him and yelling.

"She killed the child!" he shouted again. "You made a weak child together, and *she* killed it."

Nate felt something press against him and found Meg at his side. Her eyes were bloodshot as she stared up at him, clinging to him with trembling arms.

"Make him stop, Nate," she begged. "Please make him stop!"

Nate jumped to his feet with a cry of his own.

"You bastard!" he shouted. "You bastard! I won't listen to

you anymore! I'm going to kill you for what you did to my wife!"

He ran after the old man, but somehow Nathaniel Sr. kept ahead of him and slammed the bedroom door in his face. Nate opened it, but didn't walk into a hallway. He was on a stage again, watching the little girl singing. The nightmare of the theater repeated itself once more, coming to an abrupt end when Nate forced himself awake.

"Damn," he whispered. No matter how many times this happened, he could not get used to it. He sat up and brought his knees under his chin. He had been reliving a day when he'd finally stood up to his father, sick of the old man's ridicule. Nathaniel Sr. had tormented Meg endlessly, even invading their privacy by entering their bedroom.

Anger still tensed Nate's muscles, and he could not stop himself from getting out of bed and hurrying down to the kitchen. He found a butcher knife hanging over a counter and tore it from the wall.

Like a madman, he raced back upstairs to his father's hallway portrait.

"Bastard!" he screamed, slashing at it. "You bastard! You killed my wife!"

There were running footsteps, and suddenly Carl was wrenching the knife from him.

"Nathaniel!" he cried. "Stop this at once!"

Nate stood back and looked at the ribbons that had once been a portrait of his father. He felt satisfied at first, and then frightened. Why had he done this? Was he really going mad?

"Come back to bed, sir," Carl said. "You must have been having another nightmare."

"No," Nate said slowly. "No, it was real."

"Perhaps you should discuss this with a doctor," Carl said as he led Nate back down the hall, carefully holding the machete down at his side.

"I don't need a doctor," Nate insisted. "I'm *not* crazy!"

But after tonight, he was no longer sure of that.

When Nate met Adrian in the hallway the next morning, he crushed her to him and held her for a long time. Feeling the tension in his muscles, Adrian rubbed his arms and said, "Did something else happen?"

"Last night," Nate said. "I had the worst nightmare, ever."

"It's no wonder," Adrian said, thinking of what had happened to Denny. She took Nate's hand. "Come on, let's go inside your office and you can tell me about it."

She called to one of the director's assistants and ordered two cups of coffee, then followed Nate into his room. He sank down onto the leather couch, holding an arm out to take her and pull her close to him.

"I'm glad it's daylight," he said. "Isn't that sick? Thirty-two years old, and I'm glad it's daylight."

"What kind of dream did you have?" Adrian asked. "The little girl in the burning theater again?"

Nate nodded yes.

"But it started differently," he said. "I was in my bed—in the bed I used to sleep in when my father was alive. And he was standing at the foot of the bed, pointing his finger, yelling something about . . ."

He rubbed his eyes, unable to remember all the details. Adrian watched him, feeling anger grow inside herself to see this dear, loving man hurt so much. Why did he have to suffer? Wasn't the work he did at the theater demanding enough?

Now more than ever Adrian thought that she'd always be there to help him.

"I—I don't remember very much," Nate said. He wouldn't tell her about Meg. He couldn't do that. "Uhm, I remember jumping from the bed and running after him."

He breathed deeply.

"Next thing I knew, the butler was yelling at me," he went on. "I'd gotten hold of a knife, and I was slashing up my father's portrait." His hands clenched into fists. "God, I was acting like a maniac!"

"Oh, Nate!" Adrian cried, throwing her arms around him. "Don't say that! Never say that!"

"Adrian, I hear voices, I see things that aren't there," Nate said, running his fingers through his hair. "Why else would that be happening?"

"You thought someone was causing it," Adrian reminded. "Someone who doesn't want to see you succeed."

"But how could they control my dreams?" Nate asked. "That's the one aspect of all this that I have no explanation for whatsoever."

"I don't know, Nate," Adrian said.

There was silence for a moment while Adrian sat staring at the calendar, circled in red on November twenty-third, the date of the previews, and Nate tried desperately to understand what was happening to him. All of a sudden, he pulled away from Adrian and leaned forward, burying his head in his arms.

"Damn it," he growled. "I am *scared*. And I don't know what it is that frightens me!"

"Nate," Adrian said, "you've been through so much. I think..."

He sat up and looked at her, his eyes glassy.

"Don't suggest seeing a psychiatrist," he said. "My butler suggested the same last night. But I *know* I'm not crazy. And nothing will make me leave this production."

He slammed his fist on the coffee table, sending a rattling vibration throughout the room.

"This is my life," he said forcefully, "and no one can take it from me!"

"Of course not," Adrian said. She took his hand. "Everything's going to be all right, Nate. Denny's going to be out of the hospital before we know it, and..."

But Nate, unable to stop himself, had turned away from her with tears in his eyes. They were tears of frustration, of a man who wondered what he had done to deserve such torment.

Of a man who felt himself being driven to the brink of madness with no outlet in sight.

"Help me, Adrian," he pleaded.

She took his shoulders and rested her head on his back.

"Nate, my love," she said, "I will help you in any way I can. I won't let anyone hurt you."

He turned again to look at her and she kissed him softly.

"I promise," she whispered.

Nate was his usual professional self at rehearsals and even felt a little ashamed of the scene in his office. He knew Adrian would never ridicule him. But if his father were alive...

Someone tapped him on the shoulder, and his father's image vanished into the darkness of the auditorium.

"There's a policeman in your office," Don Benson whispered. "He says Georgia Richmond sent him here."

Nate didn't like the interruption but knew it was inevitable he'd be questioned. He ordered those on stage to take five, then left for his office. He found the cop sitting on the leather sofa and was greeted with a firm handshake and the presentation of an ID.

"Sounds like you had some trouble here yesterday," the policeman said. "The boy's mother requested that I ask you some questions."

"I'd be glad to help," Nate said, taking a seat behind his desk.

"According to Mrs. Richmond," the cop began, "Denny was last seen playing in the backyard of this theater."

"He likes it out there," Nate said.

"But when she went to look for him," the cop went on, "he was gone. And he didn't seem to be anywhere you looked. I understand you formed a search party."

"Yes, I did," Nate said. "And we combed every inch of the theater. I suppose Georgia told you he'd somehow gotten into the air passages?"

The policeman nodded.

"But I don't get it," he said, "how could he move so freely if the building is run through with pipes and such?"

"Have you seen Denny?" Nate asked. "He's a skinny little kid. You know how limber they are at that age."

"That's true," was the reply. "Now, Mrs. Richmond also said a woman named Adrian may be involved with this. Can I talk to her?"

"Adrian has nothing to do with it," Nate insisted, wishing he did not have to drag her into this mess. But Adrian had vowed to share this all with him, and she did have a right to defend herself. He punched a button on his phone and asked an assistant to locate her. After he'd hung up, he said, "Denny did accuse her of forcing him into those air passages, but I know Adrian would do no such thing."

When Adrian opened the door, she frowned momentarily on seeing the cop.

"Georgia sent him," Nate explained as she sat down.

"What can I tell you?" Adrian asked.

The cop opened his small notebook and readied his pencil.

"Everything you were doing yesterday afternoon," he said.

For the most part, Adrian's story coincided with Nate's and Georgia's, but there was one opening the cop didn't like.

"You took your break the same time as Denny disappeared," he said.

"Yes, I suppose I did." Adrian sighed. "But I have witnesses to prove I was nowhere near Denny in that time."

"Can you get someone to come in here?" Nate asked

Adrian turned to him.

"Barbara Warner was with me," she said. "I was with her in the greenroom the entire time."

Again, Nate punched a button on his telephone and sent word that he wanted to see Barbara. She entered the office a few minutes later, dressed in coveralls and adjusting the ribbon that held back her long hair. She could sense there was something wrong and, embarrassed, slowly lowered her hands.

"Sit down over there, Babs," Adrian said. "The police officer just wants to talk to you."

"You were with Ms. St. John yesterday, weren't you?"

"For about a half hour," Barbara said. "We took our breaks yesterday after she came off the stage."

"And what time was this?"

Barbara shrugged, then finally recalled the hour. The cop put this down in his notebook.

"You say others can prove you were in this—what did you call it?"

"Greenroom," Nate said. "It's the place where actors take their breaks."

"Greenroom, yes," the cop replied.

"I can prove I was there," Adrian said.

Barbara's eyes grew wide

"Why does she have to prove anything?" she demanded. "Are you accusing Adrian of hurting Denny?"

"I just want . . ."

Barbara interrupted the cop.

"This is awful," she said. "I know Adrian, and I can tell you she'd never hurt anyone!"

Across the room, a small statue suddenly crashed to the floor. Everyone in the room turned abruptly to see the shattered pieces.

"Vibrations from the building crew," Adrian said quickly, seeing Nate's eyes glaze over. He blinked and looked at her.

"I'll have it cleaned up later," he said quietly.

Bonnie stared at the woman named Barbara and thought that now there were *two* to be gotten rid of. Two women who interfered.

They would both pay.

TWELVE

Denny was in such good spirits when Nate and Adrian entered his hospital room that it seemed the terror of the previous day had never happened. There were no frightened looks in Adrian's direction, no accusations. He was sitting up in a sterile-looking bed reading a copy of *Sports Illustrated*. There was a tube connected to him that seemed hardly bigger than his thin arm. He smiled and pointed to the suspended bottle over his shoulder.

"That's an IV," he said. "It means I'm being fed inter-inter—*in-tra-venously*. In my veins."

"That's great," Nate said, relieved to see Denny was his old self again.

He offered a chair next to Denny's bed to Adrian, then took one himself.

"How do you feel, kid?" he asked.

"Kinda tired," Denny said. "My neck aches, and so do my legs. The doctor says it's cause I was stuck in that air passage."

Adrian leaned forward and got to the point of the visit.

"Denny," she asked, "what do you remember about that?"

"I crawled through an opening in the wall near the boiler," Denny said.

"But why would you do such a dangerous thing?"

Denny looked at her, then at Nate. He lowered his head and started to fidget with his plastic ID tag, his lips turning down. From somewhere out in the hall, he could hear the squeaking of a metal cart. Someone else was ringing for a nurse.

"I didn't want to do it," he said softly. "She made me."

The voice was pained, not the cheerful one of a moment ago.

"Who did?" Nate asked.

Denny's expression went blank, and he said in monotone, "Adrian made me."

"Denny," Adrian said calmly. "I was with several other people when you disappeared. Please tell us the truth."

Denny wriggled a bit and whined, "It is the truth! Why is everyone mad at me?"

Nate patted his leg. "No one's mad at you. We just want to know the truth so we can help you."

"She did it!" Denny cried loudly, the brown of his eyes wavering behind tears. "She did! She made me do it!"

He was pointing at Adrian, who in turn was watching Nate with worry and confusion in her eyes.

"Easy, Denny," Nate said. "We don't have to talk about this now if..."

Denny's lips curled and his eyes thinned as if to squeeze out his tears, but for the moment he had calmed down. He refused to look at Nate, afraid of the hurt in the director's eyes. Something was wrong here, Denny sensed. He wasn't saying the right thing. Adrian didn't...

"Denny," Nate said in a gentle tone, "I know you're scared. But Adrian and I are your friends."

"Adrian..."

"Shh," Nate said. "Listen to me. I think someone else made you climb into the air passages. Someone who frightened you so terribly that you are afraid now to tell us who it was. Denny, did someone tell you to use Adrian's name?"

Silence. Denny continued to twist his ID bracelet. He wanted to tell the truth, but he didn't know what the truth was! A memory was trying to emerge, something about another child. Denny closed his eyes tightly and tried to bring it into focus.

"Bonnie," he whispered.

"I didn't hear you, Denny," Nate said. "What was that?"

But the word wouldn't come out again. Denny's lips would not form to say it. He was frozen, his hands opened stiffly on his lap, his head hung. And then the trembling began.

Suddenly, he began to feel hotter and hotter. From some-where far away he heard Adrian's voice.

"Pull his covers up, Nate. He's cold."

Not cold. Hot. Terribly hot.

Denny's two legs began to kick spasmodically, and all sensation of the bed beneath him was gone. There was no bed, no floor, no ground. He was falling! Falling into the darkness!

"MMMMMAAAA!!!!"

"Denny?!"

Falling! Falling!

"Adrian, get a nurse!"

"MMMMMMMAAAA!!!!"

There was darkness everywhere. His bones had no sub-stance, his arms and legs refused to hold him. He was going to go splat all over the ground! He was going to die!

Someone was touching his shoulders.

"Denny, snap out of it!"

Adrian was back with a doctor and a nurse.

Falling! Gonna smash up like a water balloon!

"Denny, wake up!"

A face came into view, floating in the darkness above him as he fell. A woman's face. Adrian. She had hurt him.

"NNNOOOO!!!"

Denny's arm lashed out and caught her across the bridge of her nose. He screamed with such terror that tears came to Adrian's eyes as she brought the back of her hand to her bleeding nose.

The nurse ordered them from the room as the doctor readied a needle. Nate took Adrian's arm and walked out into the hall. They held each other and listened as Denny's pitiful screams filled the air. Then, after a few long minutes, silence.

"The sedative's taken effect," Nate said.

"My God, Nate," Adrian said, dabbing with a tissue at her bloody nose. "What was going on in there?"

Nate shook his head.

"I don't know," he whispered. "It's like everything else. I just don't know."

The door to Denny's room swung open and both the doctor and nurse came out. The doctor, a sad-eyed Indian, looked at Adrian and asked.

"Are you the boy's mother?"

"No, I work with him in Nate's—in Mr. Dysart's production company," she said nodding her head toward Nate.

"You're Nate Dysart?" he asked, recognizing the name.

"Yes, I am," Nate said. "Can you tell us what's wrong with Denny?"

"That's one terrified little boy," the doctor replied. "But since he's a minor I can only discuss his condition with his parents."

Nate waved a hand.

"Then maybe you can answer a nonmedical question," he said. "Did he mention any names? Did he accuse anyone of hurting him?"

"He said 'Adrian,' once." The doctor paused, as if considering. "There was one other name. I couldn't quite make it out, but it sounded like Tommy, or Bonnie, or . . ."

He gestured to indicate the array of similar-sounding names. Nate felt his heart jump as the name Bonnie conjured up some sort of elusive memory.

"Bonnie?" he repeated.

"Does that name mean something to you?" Adrian asked.

"No," he said. "I thought it sounded familiar, but I guess it doesn't."

"If you'll excuse me," the doctor said, "I have other patients to see."

Nate thanked him for his time, then put his arm around Adrian's shoulder. Together they walked from the hospital. There was nothing more they could do here today.

The afternoon's rehearsal went smoothly. John Hemlock, Denny's understudy worked well, pleased to be on stage. At the end of the day Adrian and Nate were approached by Judy and Barbara.

"How's Denny?" Barbara wanted to know.

Nate assured her the boy was doing fine. He deliberately didn't mention Denny's outburst.

"You know what this one did?" Barbara asked, pointing to Judy.

"What's that?" Nate asked.

Barbara looked away, as if embarrassed.

"On our lunch hour," Judy said, "she got everyone who was in the greenroom with Adrian the other day to come with her to the police station. And she insisted the sergeant there take a statement from each one."

"I thought it might help Adrian," Barbara said. "Georgia Richmond insists you hurt Denny, but we all know better."

Adrian threw her arms around Barbara.

"What a sweet thing to do!"

It made her happy to know she had such good friends.

The police were finally convinced of Adrian's innocence after comparing all the statements. Adrian had ample witnesses to prove she was nowhere near Denny at the time of his disappearance. And when Georgia returned to the theater a few days later, she was also made to see the truth.

"I refuse to believe Denny did it on his own," she insisted, however. "He's mischievous, yes. But not malicious! He wouldn't tell lies!"

"We think someone made him give Adrian's name," Nate said. "Georgia, do you know anyone named Bonnie?"

The southern woman shook her head.

"Not a soul," she said. "Why?"

"Just asking."

"Did someone named Bonnie hurt my son?"

"I don't know," Nate said. "Possibly. He mentioned the name when we visited him the other day."

"Well, whoever it is," Adrian said, "we're going to find him or her."

"And when you do," Georgia drawled, "I'd like to see him tarred and feathered!"

THIRTEEN

The boy's accident became the primary topic at the theater, even edging out the fast-approaching previews in Connecticut. Everyone was glad to hear Denny had been released from the hospital and was planning to return to work as soon as possible. Nonetheless, they all wanted to see his tormentor found. Everyone liked Denny and couldn't understand how anyone could be so cruel. No one said much, but they all wondered, if someone among them was a traitor, some kind of psychopath who could lash out at any moment.

"Just look at Son of Sam," Judy told Barbara as they returned from lunch together. "Everyone thought he was a nice guy, and he turned out to be a murderer."

Barbara shuddered, thinking of her own kids. "I hate to think someone like that is in this theater, right now."

"I just hope they find the bastard," Judy said.

"Judy!"

Barbara's best friend widened her eyes in amusement.

"You are such a little girl!" she cried. "I only said 'bastard,' and that's exactly what he is!"

"I still don't like to hear swear words," Barbara said.

It grew suddenly cold in the hallway, and just then the lights began to flicker. Judy laughed and patted Barbara's arm.

"I guess you're right," she said. "That must be a sign from above."

"Don't make fun of me," Barbara said, though she laughed herself.

When the lights came on again, the two stopped their giggling, and found themselves looking at a small child. She stood in the middle of the hallway, staring up at them with solemn black eyes, her hands clenched into tiny fists at the sides of her ruffled dress.

"Where'd you come from?" Judy asked.

The child said nothing. Barbara, comfortable with children because she had two of her own, asked, "Are you waiting for someone, honey?"

"I'm waiting for you," the child said. Her pretty face was expressionless.

Barbara held out a hand.

"Come on," she said. "I'll take you to your mommy."

"NO!" the child snapped.

Barbara felt something twist inside of her to see the pretty child's eyes grow cold. She took a step toward her but was suddenly pushed aside when the little girl broke into a run and sped past the two women. Before Barbara could move, Judy had her by the arm.

"Let her go," Judy said. "She isn't your worry."

But Barbara could not stop thinking about the child. After what had happened to Denny, a little kid shouldn't be allowed to wander alone in that big theater. She could be the next victim! Barbara decided to find the child's mother, whoever she was, and warn her.

Judy headed straight for the stage, where the lighting crew would be working this afternoon, but Barbara went downstairs to the basement lockers to drop off her jacket. At the other end of the huge basement, the sounds of the building crew started up again, and Barbara wondered what the new scenery would look like. In all her years as a lighting technician, she had never tired of the magic of the theater. Next to her beautiful family, it was the best part of her life.

She opened her locker. It had been empty earlier, but now something small and yellow sat in it: a stuffed dog, one of those autograph hounds from years back. Barbara took it out and examined it, wondering if Judy might have put it in here. And yet Barbara had a feeling Judy *hadn't* done this. Something was wrong. A yellow dog meant something, but what?

Suddenly, Barbara dropped the toy as if it had burned her. She knew what a yellow dog meant! There was an old theatrical superstition that said a yellow dog found in the theater meant someone was going to die!

"Oh, no," she whispered.

Could the maniac who had hurt Denny have left this here? Was she going to be his next victim? She looked around. She was completely alone. Anything or anyone could be hiding behind the long rows of lockers. Nervously, she tried to unzip her jacket, but the zipper stuck.

"Damn!" she hissed, hardly noticing the curse word.

She fumbled with it; her hands began to tremble. Was someone watching her now, waiting?

It was no use. She decided to pull the jacket off over her head. It had an elastic waist, and she crossed her arms to pull it up. Suddenly, she was tangled up inside the thing. She couldn't see. Struggling to escape, she felt something touch her knee.

Barbara's startled cry was muffled by the sound of a buzz saw from the far end of the basement. She jerked the jacket back down and found herself staring at the little girl.

"You scared me," she said, suddenly relieved and ashamed of her fear.

No reply.

"Can you help me get out of this thing?" Barbara asked. "I don't want to wear it under the hot stage lights, but I can't seem to get it off."

The child made no move.

"It gets so hot on that stage," Barbara said.

"Terribly hot," the child agreed, walking slowly toward her.

Without warning, she pushed at Barbara with all her might, slamming the woman's body against the metal lockers. A resounding bang echoed down the row as Barbara's eyes widened in shock.

"Hey!" she cried. "Don't . . ."

But the little girl had her by the front of her jacket, pulling her down to the floor. Barbara struggled to resist, not understanding the child's incredible strength. Her hand felt the yellow dog. *Someone in the company was going to die . . .*

"What do you want?" She choked out the words.

"To punish you," the child said. "You are a *bad* lady."

Barbara shook her head and tried to break away from the child's grip. Instead, she was slammed back against the locker. The child pressed close to her, bringing her hands up to Barbara's face. The woman froze, wanting to cry out in pain but unable. A horrible burning sensation filled her entire head, a pain worse than any she had ever known. When she looked into the little girl's eyes, she could see the reflection of flames.

"You have to suffer the way I did." The child's voice had a demonic tone to it, hollow and unemotional. Barbara stared at the flames in her eyes, until suddenly the darkness came. It was not the darkness of a fusebox giving in to the strain of power drills and chain saws, but the dark that comes when evil overtakes the mind.

Barbara began to fall, tumbling head over heels, like Alice down the rabbit hole. Now she was in an unfamiliar hallway, with rows of glass-knobbed doors and a black-and-white tile floor. At the far end stood an enormous door, larger than any of the others, beckoning her like a gateway to safety. By the light of some unseen bulb that flickered nearby, Barbara tried to read the white letters painted on it. But the door was edged in shadow and too far away. Shadows and light wavered like apparitions, giving the hallway a pulsating life of its own. Barbara tried to open her mouth to cry out, but could not make a sound.

"You have to pay!"

She looked around at the sound of the child's voice. Her head moved slowly and felt terribly light; her joints were numb. And the hallway was empty.

Someone in the company was going to die . . .

She broke into a run, heading toward that big door. But there was no door at the hallway's end. Barbara slammed into a solid wall that teasingly said FIRE EXIT. But there was no exit. No way out.

Something crashed behind her, sending vibrations up from the floor and through her body. Barbara turned with a gasp and saw that one of the ceiling beams had fallen to the floor. All around her, flames were shooting along the walls and ceiling like so many red and orange party streamers. A two-by-four fell and barely missed her head. Barbara tried to scream, but all that escaped was a pathetic mouse-like squeak.

"You have to pay for bringing the dark!"

The little girl was standing before her, screaming. The ruffles of her fancy dress glowed orange and yellow, changing colors as the flames waxed and waned. She tilted her head to one side, her black tresses brushing over a small shoulder.

"It's too late," she said. *"You ruined my plans, and you're going to die!"*

As the child stepped forward Barbara stiffened, anticipating the horrible pain she'd feel at the touch of those small hands.

But there was no pain. The fire disappeared, the little girl faded away, and suddenly Barbara was standing before her locker, her head pounding. A few moments passed before she was fully conscious. Everything was ominously silent. Barbara's eyes darted around her like those of a frightened animal. She knew she had to get out of the basement, and it terrified her that she didn't know why.

Leaving her jacket on, Barbara quickly locked her locker and ran for the stairs. Each time her foot struck the ground, a pain swelled up inside her head. By the time she reached the stage she was ready to scream.

But she didn't scream. She held her fears inside, afraid the others would think she was hysterical. After all, nothing had happened—nothing she could recall. She just had a sense that time had passed in the cellar, time that was lost to her.

"I must have had a dizzy spell," she rationalized to herself. "Maybe I ate something that disagreed with me." Vaguely she wondered if she could perhaps be pregnant. She remembered the dizzy spells she'd suffered before her youngest was born. No, that wasn't likely, still...

As she walked onto the stage Judy Terrel came over and looked at her with concern. Any other time, Barbara would have assured her that everything was fine. But now, somehow, she only wanted to poke out Judy's pretty blue eyes.

"God," Judy said, "you look awful. Maybe you ought to take the day off—you look like you've seen a ghost!"

"I'm okay," Barbara insisted.

"Your face is pale," Judy pointed out. "And why are you still wearing that jacket? It's warm in here! Babs, you really should..."

"I said I was okay," Barbara snapped. "What the fuck do you care what I look like, anyway?"

"Well, aren't you the bitch?" Judy shot back. "And where did you learn to swear, minister's daughter?"

Barbara ignored the remark and walked over to Mike Woodson, the chief electrician. "I want the mediums put up over the striplights today," Mike was saying as Barbara joined the group. "Three of you have to get up on the scaffolding."

Several hands went up. Mike picked two of the men and was about to choose a third when he noticed Barbara's hand. She had experience at this type of work, so Mike chose her. She picked up a toolbox and climbed the steel ladder that led up to the scaffolding.

"Mike," Judy said softly, "I don't think she belongs up there."

"And why not?" Mike said, looking over a lighting plan that was rolled open like a scroll between his hands.

"She's not...Oh, heck, I don't know. But I think..."

"There's a lot of work to do, Miss Terrel," Mike said, abruptly.

Judy turned away and went to her own work, looking up at Barbara. She wanted to call to her, to apologize for the senseless words, but Barbara was too far away and probably wouldn't hear her, anyway. She sighed and walked away.

Up above, Barbara was reading a diagram that told her in what order to place the mediums—colored pieces of glass in metal frames. "RED, BLUE, AMBER, RED..." She picked up a red piece and started for the first light. Her hands trembled as she worked, and her head ached. But this was the job she loved, and maybe if she concentrated on it, the uneasy feelings she had would go away.

Still, she couldn't help looking over her shoulder every once in a while.

Barbara moved along the scaffolding, fitting the lights with color frames in the right sequence. Unconsciously she chewed her lips to fight the headache that pounded at her brain. Maybe she should have listened to Judy. Maybe she really shouldn't be working this afternoon.

But she was afraid to stop, to leave here. As long as she was with the other stagehands, she felt safe. From what, though, she didn't know.

Barbara noticed that a lamp in front of her was cracked and decided to replace it. She unscrewed it, but her hands were shaking so that it slipped from her grip and crashed to the floor some thirty feet below. Barbara froze. A sensation of falling came over her, and her knees locked as if to prevent her own body from tumbling off the scaffolding. Mike Woodson's voice carried up to her a moment later, breaking the spell.

"Careful!" he yelled. "That's a helluva drop!"

"It—it slipped," Barbara called back.

Judy turned away from her work to look up at Barbara. She noticed the windbreaker Barbara still wore, and wondered about it. But her friend did not seem as upset as before, and Judy returned to the panel she was wiring.

While waiting for a new bulb to be sent up, Barbara continued to work down the line. The next color was amber, wasn't it? No, red. Barbara rechecked her diagram and confirmed the latter. She had never lost track like this before. But it was the headache, of course.

Suddenly she heard a hissing noise very close to her ear. She looked around for steam escaping a pipe but could find none. It was growing terribly hot there, though, and she wished she could take off her jacket. She was about to ask one of the men to help her with the zipper when she felt something burn her skin. She jumped, gasping.

"Hey, hold still," one of the men working with her called as the lightweight platform shook.

But Barbara didn't even hear him. She was looking down from the scaffolding, out into the theater. It was filled with people, but not the actors, actresses, and stagehands she had been working with. These were women dressed in fringed and beaded shifts and satin gowns, and men with slicked down hair and straight-cut evening jackets! Hundreds of them. They were running toward the doors, pushing and screaming in panic, and yet there were no sounds coming from their lips. Just as suddenly as it had come, the illusion disappeared, and once again the theater was empty.

"Hey, you look like you've seen a ghost," the man down the platform called.

Barbara didn't answer him. She was staring at something he could not see—the little girl in a white dress. The child was frowning at her in such a way that Barbara's blood ran cold despite the intense heat she felt.

"You shouldn't have interfered," the child was saying. "You have to pay now. You have to *die*."

Barbara shook her head, backing away as the child advanced slowly upon her. Down the scaffolding, her partner noticed her wild eyes and perspiring skin and called, "Hey, Babs, are you okay?"

"You have to die," the little girl said again, her voice audible only to Barbara.

Suddenly, she lunged forward, pushing the woman with all her might. All those who were watching thought Barbara had somehow lost her balance. Her thoughts filled with visions of fire and crashing timber, she tried desperately to grab for something, but there was nothing within her reach. Barbara Warner hit the floor so hard on impact that she never felt a thing.

"Barbara!"

Judy's scream broke the silence.

The two men above leaned over the railing and looked down in horror. Someone shouted orders to get a doctor, and someone else ran to find Nate. He was in his office, holding a cast meeting with Adrian and the others. Without a word, he hurried to the stage.

"What happened?" he demanded.

"She—she f-fell from the scaffolding," Judy stammered. "I don't know how, but she fell!"

Nate knelt down beside Barbara and gently touched her. Then he looked up at Adrian, something souring in the pit of his stomach.

"Her neck is broken," he told her in a whisper.

"Oh, my God," Adrian replied, bringing a hand to her mouth. She looked around at the people on the stage. "Did someone call an ambulance?"

"I did," Mike Woodson said.

No sooner had they spoken when they heard sirens. Someone ran to let the paramedics in, and they immediately went to work. But after a futile effort to revive Barbara, one man shook his head sadly.

"No need to rush with this one," he said.

No one else spoke. They all backed away, standing en masse and watching in silence as the paramedics lifted Barbara onto a stretcher. Two of the women were crying. Judy stood expressionless, too stunned to cry.

Nate held on to Adrian's hand, squeezing it until she was certain he'd break her fingers. She winced, and he loosened his grip. But Adrian understood. He was thinking about Jim Orland. Two people in his company had died. Two innocent people. Now Adrian saw Nate's eyes widen, but she did not hear the voice that came to his ears alone.

"*She had to be punished!*" a child cried. "*She ruined everything and she had to pay!*"

Nate turned to the groups of crew members, his eyes weary.

"Who said that?" he asked softly.

"No one said anything, Mr. Dysart," Mike told him.

"Damn it, I know I heard someone!" Nate cried.

He waved a hand angrily, realizing the voices had returned. In a fury, he rushed off the stage, Adrian close at his heels. He stormed into his office and sat down at his desk, weaving his fingers through his hair.

"What's happening here?" he demanded. "What the hell is happening?"

"Nate, it was an accident," Adrian said, standing behind him so that she could massage his shoulders. "All those people saw Barbara fall."

"No, no," Nate said. "It was meant to happen."

Adrian kissed the top of his head.

"Nate, I understand why you'd think that," she said, "but this time, it's obvious there's nothing sinister involved. Too many people are witnesses!"

Nate heard tension in her voice and knew she was frightened too. He wanted to tell her about the voice he'd heard but instead backed up his chair and stood up.

"I have to go back on stage," he said. "I'm in charge here. I should take responsibility."

"They expect it of you," Adrian said.

Together, they returned. The paramedics were gone, and the place was thick with stunned silence. Nate sucked in his breath, forcing himself to remain calm. Another outburst and he'd lose the respect of his cast and crew.

"Where's Judy?" he asked, noticing the woman wasn't here.

"She went to contact Joel Warner," Mike said. "Barbara's husband."

Adrian mumbled something to hear the name. Joel Warner was an investigative reporter—would he try to learn what exactly had happened to Barbara? She decided not to think about it. Instead, she moved closer to Nate.

"Look, God only knows why this happened. It shouldn't have. Barbara Warner was a wonderful human being. She shouldn't have..."

Mike cut Nate off.

"That scaffolding was checked earlier today," he said.

"But still Barbara fell," Nate said. "And damn it, I want to know why!"

Judy returned now, walking onto the stage with red rims around her eyes. She looked at Nate and said softly, "I've told Joel."

"Thank you," Nate said.

Judy came closer to the group on stage.

"Barbara had two little boys," she said. "Alec and Bobby. Alec is just two years old."

Her lips curled now, and she began to sob.

"They're just babies," she choked, covering her face.

Adrian hurried over to her and put her arms around the
woman. Nate watched the scene with anger growing in him.
Someone would pay for this.

"Go home, everyone," he said. "Take tomorrow off. I'll let
you know about Barbara's..."

He waved a hand to dismiss them. He did not want to
think he was about to attend his third funeral in one year.

1975

*Nate stood out in the rain, watching red lights of an
ambulance whirl around, coloring the portico of Dysart
Manor. Behind him, his father stood in the doorway, openly
cursing the attendants as they carried out a stretcher.*

*"Damned blockheads!" he cried. "What's taking so blasted
long? I want that maniacal bitch out of my house!"*

*Nate heard a weak voice call out his name. His hands,
shoved into his pockets, balled into fists. Didn't his father
have even a drop of pity for a sick person?*

*Slowly, he turned around. He saw Meg lying on the
stretcher, strapped down like some unruly animal. That had
been his father's doing. Nate felt a lump in his throat to recall
what had happened just half an hour earlier. Meg, fed up
with Nathaniel Sr.'s constant torment, had flown at the old
man in a rage. It didn't seem possible that the pale, tiny
woman on that stretcher could have been capable of such
fury.*

*Nate glanced back at his father again, who waved an
impatient hand and closed the door. Then he stopped the
attendants and knelt down to take Meg's hand.*

"I don't want to go, Nate," Meg whimpered.

Nate kissed her.

*"It's only for a few days," he said. "You know you haven't
been getting better since the accident, and the doctors want
to do some tests."*

*"I didn't mean it," Meg said softly. "I didn't mean to hurt
our..."*

*Nate hushed her with a gentle kiss, stopping the words he
did not want to hear.*

FOURTEEN

Adrian turned over in the brass bed and ran the back of her hand along Nate's face, enjoying the feel of the roughness of razor stubble. He sighed and moved closer to her, burying his face in her neck. She was here tonight because he hadn't wanted to be alone. Like some little kid, he was afraid of what his dreams might be.

Two people were dead at the theater. Two deaths that on the surface did not seem to involve foul play. But Jim Orland had died of a heart attack, in horrible pain, though he had never had a heart condition and was strong as an ox. Barbara Warner had fallen from a scaffolding—with ten years of experience at that kind of work behind her and no record of carelessness. What had happened that had caused her to lose her balance and fall?

Had she lost her balance?

Nate pulled away from Adrian and lay on his back, staring up through the darkness. His hand found hers, and she squeezed his fingers.

"Thanks," he said.

"For what?"

"For coming here tonight."

Adrian propped herself up on an elbow and leaned down to kiss Nate in the darkness. He put his arms around her and held her until they both fell asleep. For Adrian, it was a sleep edged with worries about Nate. But for Nate, it was something far, far worse.

The nightmares came back again.

He opened his eyes, and saw a dark-haired woman beside him. She turned over and smiled—Meg's smile. The bed was no longer brass, but wood, and the sheets were cotton, not satin. Nate smiled back at Meg. But soon her expression changed, her eyes growing big with fear. Silent tears dripped over her cheeks.

"I didn't kill her," she whispered. *"I didn't kill our ..."*

"Meg, don't!" Nate cried, pulling her close to him. *"Don't!"*

There was laughter from somewhere. High-pitched, insane laughter. And suddenly Nate's father was at the foot of the bed, invading their privacy, mocking them as they held fast to each other.

"Failures! Failures! Couldn't even keep a baby!"

Nate broke away from Meg and leaped from the bed, running after the old man. But when he pushed through the door, it was not to enter the hallway. He was in the wings of that stage again. The stage where the little girl was singing. The stage of fire and darkness and falling...

"NNNNNOOOOO!!!"

Someone was shaking him as he fell into the darkness of the orchestra pit.

"NNNOOOO!!!"

"Nate, honey!" Adrian said. "Wake up! You're dreaming!"

His eyes snapped open and he stared at her, but what he saw was his wife.

"Oh, Meg," he groaned, throwing his arms around her.

Adrian stiffened. Meg? Who was Meg? She hugged Nate, feeling his body heave as his breathing slowed. He looked so terribly vulnerable then that she could not help lifting a hand to rub his back. There was certainly an explanation for the name he'd called her.

Finally, he moved away and settled down on his pillow.

"God," he said.

"Another nightmare?"

He nodded.

"I don't know when they'll stop," he said.

A few moments passed, and then Adrian said quietly, "You called me Meg."

"I..."

Nate cut himself off.

"Meg was my wife," he told her.

"I didn't know you were married."

She heard his hair brush the pillow as he shook his head.

"She died a few years ago," he said. "I—I guess I was dreaming about her."

"Tell me about her, Nate."

Nate was silent. He at first did not want to talk about Meg, but the encouraging feeling of Adrian's arms as they went around him shattered his inhibitions. For years, he had kept

the truth bottled up inside, yet now he was telling the new
woman in his life everything he could.

"We had a little production company," he said. "Jim, Meg,
and I. Jim used to say it was so far off Broadway that it might
fall into the East River."

He sighed to remember how they'd laughed at that little
joke.

"Meg was always helping out," Nate said. "She did more
work than any of us, even though she was very frail and
should never have tried to strain herself. But she had a hell of
a mind. She was terrific at scenic design and costuming. When
you don't have a lot of money, you double up on your jobs."

"But I thought you were very wealthy," Adrian protested.

"My father was," Nate said. "But he didn't share that
wealth with anyone. Whatever we put into that company, we
did on our own. My father thought the theater was a waste of
time. He used to say we were overgrown children playing
make-believe."

Adrian began to rub his stomach.

"Tell me about Meg."

"Well, she always did more than her share of work," Nate
continued. "One day, she was up on a scaffolding. She—she
slipped and fell from it. When I saw Barbara lying on the
stage, I could only think of Meg."

"Oh, Nate," Adrian said.

Nate paused to deal with the wave of anger that was
rushing over him. When he had calmed again, he went on
with his story.

"It turned out Meg was several months pregnant," he said.
"I didn't know it. She didn't tell me yet. I guess it was because we were so busy with the theater. She lost the baby—a
little girl."

He bit his lip.

"But she was more ill than we realized," he said. "She
should have survived that miscarriage. She should have lived
to have a family with me."

"What happened to her afterward?"

Nate shook his head.

"She died," he said simply. He turned away. "I don't want
to talk about it anymore."

There was still a part of the story he could not discuss. A memory so terrible that Nate had not thought of it in all the years since Meg's death.

1975

Meg Dysart stroked the hair of the doll in her arms and rocked herself back and forth on a cushioned floor. She knew she was supposed to be in her bed, but she didn't like that bed. It was so cold, with its metal fixtures and white sheets. She wanted the big wooden four-poster again. She wanted to be home again, with Nate.

There was a vague memory of leaving home in her mind. She knew she had become very, very angered at someone. She had started screaming and had gone completely hysterical— so hysterical that an ambulance was brought to the big house. It took her to this hospital, where she was told she would be able to relax. A nice woman had given her this doll when Meg had said how she loved babies.

She wished this dolly was a real baby.

She wished Nate were here with her.

"I want to go home," she whispered.

But she couldn't go home until she remembered why she had come to this hospital in the first place.

That Thursday, just four days before the Connecticut previews were scheduled, everyone from the Dysart Theater company attended Barbara's funeral. The old church was beautiful, thick with the scent of incense and illuminated only by wooden chandeliers. Nate could see Judy Terrel at the front, holding on to the hands of two little boys.

When the service was over, Nate made his way to Joel Warner and offered his condolences. He didn't know quite what to say—everything sounded clichéd.

"If there's anything I can do . . ."

"You can't bring Barbara back again," Joel said. "She shouldn't have died, Mr. Dysart."

Nate shook his head and stared at the doors to the church.

"I want to ask you some questions," Joel said. "When the time is right. But at the moment my children need me."

With that he hurried toward the car that waited to take him

home. Nate felt Adrian's hand reach for his, and together they walked to the car.

"He suspects something," Nate said as George opened Adrian's door.

"He's just upset, I'm sure," Adrian said.

"But he has a right to be," Nate answered. "Barbara shouldn't have died. There shouldn't have been an accident."

"That's just what it was too," Adrian said. "An accident, no matter how awful. And no matter what else had gone on in that theater!"

The engine started and the car rolled onto the street, bumping over a pothole. Nate looked out the window at the group in front of the church, some of whom were staring after the huge Rolls-Royce. Then he said, without turning, "I heard voices on the stage."

"When?" Adrian asked, her tone concerned.

"After we found Barbara," Nate replied. "I heard someone say she deserved to die."

Adrian took his hand. "But darling," she said, "no one else heard anything."

She kissed him.

"I believe you heard something, though," she said quickly, soothing him. "When we go back to work tomorrow, we can ask if anyone else remembers something."

Most of the crew who'd been on stage that afternoon hadn't paid attention to Barbara until they heard her scream. Mike Woodson did remember that he had thought it was strange that she wore a jacket, but since she didn't complain about being ill, he didn't give the matter much thought. Only Judy Terrel had more to say.

"After lunch Barbara went down to her locker by herself to hang up her jacket," she said. "But she was still wearing it when she came back upstairs. I asked her about it and she snapped at me."

Judy looked down at her hands.

"She said 'fuck,' Nate," she went on. "That was from a woman who blushed at the sound of 'darn.'"

"What happened during lunch?" Nate asked. "Anything that might have upset her?"

"Not really," Judy said. "Well, she did seem to be preoccupied. But Barbara tells me everything that's on her mind, so since she didn't say anything, I assumed she was okay."

"Then it's possible something happened to her in the cellar," Adrian said.

Nate looked at her.

"Yes, it is," he said. "Judy, can you tell us anything more?"

"No," Judy said apologetically. "She was in a foul mood when she came back to work. And I've never heard her swear in my life."

She stood up.

"Do you mind if I clean out her locker?" she asked. "There might be something in there Joel should have."

"Please do," Nate said. "And when you see Mr. Warner, tell him I want to help in any way I can."

Judy headed down to the cellar. Barbara's locker was next to her own. It was locked and except for a stuffed yellow dog, it was empty. Judy pulled the toy out, guessing it was a Christmas present for Bobby or Alec.

As she was coming up the stairs a thought occurred to her. Something seemed familiar about the yellow dog. But before she could figure out what it was, she bumped into Sander Bernaux.

"Where did you get that thing?" he demanded, something like panic in his voice.

"It was in Barbara's locker," Judy said. "I guess she bought it for one of the children."

Sander breathed in deeply through his long nose to calm himself.

"Ah, yes, Barbara," he said. "It was a shame what happened to her."

The yellow dog had already brought bad luck, the superstitious actor thought. It had already killed one member of the company. And if it were removed from the premises quickly, all would be well again.

"You say that as if you were talking about an animal hit by a car," Judy said. "Barbara was a dear, sweet woman who shouldn't have died."

"I'm sure it could have been prevented," Sander replied. "Dysart may be a good producer, but he isn't worth much when it comes to fine details, is he?"

"What do you mean?"

Sander shrugged.

"Oh well, there have been a number of tragedies here, haven't there?"

"That isn't Nate's fault."

"I would say it is," Sander told her, tilting his head back a little. "He's responsible for everything that goes on in this theater. And if you ask me, the man is incompetent and..."

"That's nonsense," Judy retorted. "Nate had nothing to do with Barbara's accident. Mike Woodson himself checked the scaffolding! Nate can't be everywhere at once!"

Sander sniffed haughtily, thinking of the emotional way Nate had reacted when he saw Barbara's prone form on the stage. A weakling!

"If you'll excuse me," Judy said, "I'd like to go home. It's been a difficult time for some of us."

She sidled past the actor and hurried down the hall. Sander watched her, chilled. A yellow dog in the theater! Someone in this company was going to die...

But then, someone *had* died. Sander couldn't help a smug grin, thinking how often people made fun of his superstitions. This time, he was right.

In spite of tragedy, "the show must go on," and that old adage applied to Nate's production. The following Monday, the twenty-third of November, he brought his entire company up to a theater in Connecticut, where they put on the previews of *Making Good*. The first showings of a play were always done outside New York. It gave the director a chance to see where more corrections could be made, so that it would be perfect for his Broadway opening. Nate sat in the back row of the audience and kept notes. He watched the audiences' reactions and felt happier than he had in a long time. They applauded and laughed and cheered—they seemed to love *Making Good*.

And it was the same every night—the theater was even packed on Thursday, Thanksgiving Day. To Nate's surprise, his cousin Vance showed up at the last performance. Nate tried to ignore Vance when he came backstage, but his cousin persisted, until Nate finally threatened to take his head off if he so much as mentioned the will.

"Did I say anything about the will?" Vance asked innocently.

"I just came back here to tell you you've got a fine show. Maybe not Broadway material, but..."

"Thanks," Nate said, cutting him off. One of the extras walked by him, smiling. "You did great, Mike."

"Thanks, Mr. Dysart."

Nate walked along the small hallway, reading his notes. To his dismay, Vance kept at his heels.

"I've got something else to tell you," he said. "Pearl and I are heading out to Montana next week. You know, I've got sabbatical coming up."

Nate stopped and looked at him.

"Why?"

"Pearl wants to visit her folks," Vance said, dismissing it with a shrug. "We'll be gone for a few months so you can have a little vacation from me—if you know what I mean."

"I'm very busy, Vance," Nate said.

He hurried away from Vance, dwelling on his cousin's words for only a moment before the elated mood of his company brought a smile to his face again.

It was obvious Nate had a hit. When the company returned to New York the following Monday, for two weeks of rehearsals before the Broadway opening, everyone was elated. Even Nate, who smiled at everyone who walked on stage for rehearsal.

"I'm so proud of all of you," he said, not for the first time. "Have you seen the reviews? Here's one that says, 'Broadway's got a treat coming up!' And the *Times* is overflowing with praise."

On stage the actors applauded happily. Only Sander remained still. It was bad luck to get too sure of one's self. And he knew that New York critics were tougher than anyone.

But this did not matter to Nate. In spite of all that had happened, he hadn't been destroyed. People would know now what a good director he was. And maybe, somehow, his doubting father would know it too.

"All right," he said. "You were terrific in Connecticut, but there's room for improvement before we're good enough for Broadway. Places, everyone!"

The morning passed quickly. Everyone worked well. Good feelings were in the air. Then just before lunchtime, Joel Warner walked onto the stage. The cast all watched in stunned, embarrassed silence.

"Take five, everyone," Nate said.

Adrian wanted to stay, but something in Joel's eyes told her she was not welcome.

"What can I do for you?" Nate asked. It was a stupid question, and Nate wished he could retract it. But the sandy-haired, mustached reporter seemed not to hear him. He was staring at the scaffolding overhead, the colored lights making little stars on his wire-rimmed glasses.

"It's a long way down from there, isn't it?" he asked.

"About thirty feet," Nate said, following the man's gaze upward.

Joel took a few steps, his shoes making echoing sounds on the wood floor. He studied the ropes, pulleys, and lead weights at either side of the stage. The gold curtains sparkled, and rainbows shot out from the crystal chandelier. Joel found it was wrong that the sight of his wife's death should be so opulent.

"Was that thing checked before work began?" he asked.

"It's checked every morning," Nate said, "at my insistance. And it was checked again after Bar—after the accident. My insurance people told me there was nothing wrong with it."

Joel stopped pacing and turned to Nate.

"Barbara worked on lighting crews for ten years," he said. "I can't bring myself to believe she slipped and fell thirty feet by her own carelessness."

Nate wanted to say that he did not believe it, either, but he kept silent. He would not involve this man, an outsider, in the tragedies befalling his theater. He would let Joel think it was an accident.

"I don't know what you want me to tell you," he said finally.

"What really happened."

"Barbara had an accident," Nate said, wishing he could believe it himself. "According to everyone who saw, she slipped and fell."

"I spoke to Judy Terrel last night," Joel said. "She said Barbara was in a terrible mood that afternoon, and even swore at her. In all the years we've been married, I never heard her use one off-color word. She used to have fits if I said 'damn,' for God's sake. And Judy tells me she used the word 'fuck'?"

"Everyone has their bad days," Nate said uneasily. "What are you thinking?"

"That Barbara was driven to that accident," Joel said. "Something upset her—something so terrible that she lost control and fell from that damned thing up there. I'm going to find out who's responsible."

Nate sighed. "I really couldn't tell you, Mr. Warner. But it *was* an accident. It wasn't anyone's fault."

Joel glared at him.

"It's never anyone's fault, is it?" he asked bitterly.

He turned and left the stage. Nate watched him, his suspicions about the accident stronger than ever. Even an outsider sensed something was wrong.

"I've got to find out what it is," he said out loud.

From behind him, a little girl took a step forward but stopped. Her outstretched arms dropped to her sides. It wasn't time yet.

After rehearsal Adrian took a seat next to Nate.

"I was right," Nate said. "He does suspect something about Barbara's death."

"Do you think he'll do an investigation?" Adrian asked.

"He said he would," Nate replied.

"We don't have to tell him anything," Adrian said. "We can declare this theater off limits to outsiders."

Nate shook his head.

"Oh, no," he said. "Then Joel will believe we really have something to hide. The only way we can convince him Barbara's death was completely accidental is by being cooperative."

"It's bound to cause a lot of bad publicity anyhow. I just hope to God he doesn't cause us to miss our opening."

"Nothing," Nate said, "could ever do that."

Adrian took his hand.

"We know the crew members won't tell him anything," she said. "Nor the cast."

"But wait a minute," Nate said. "What about Denny? And Georgia is quite the blabbermouth. Maybe we ought to go there and talk to them."

"Good idea," Adrian said.

Nate closed his black book.

"Well, one thing's for sure," he said. "Denny's safe at home now. Nothing can happen to him."

But Denny was not safe. At that very moment he was grasping the edges of his dinner tray, looking into the eyes of the little girl who stood before him. She was angry, and her anger terrified him.

"He went away for a whole week," she said. "They all went away, and when they came back, they were happy. I don't want them to be happy!"

There was a malevolence in her voice that made Denny stiffen. Was he going to start falling again?

"But they're back now," Bonnie said. "And pretty soon they're going to pay. *She's* going to pay. That stupid lady named Adrian!"

"Adrian?" Denny choked uncertainly.

"She interferes," Bonnie snapped. "I don't want her to have him!"

"Who?"

Bonnie simply shook her head.

"You're all going to die," she said. "Even you, Denny. I thought you were my friend, but you aren't."

"Yes, I am!" Denny insisted, panicking.

"Liar!"

She heard footsteps and her eyes darted towards the door. Denny leaned back against his pillow, grateful his mother was coming. When she opened the door, Bonnie disappeared.

"Who were you talking to?" she asked.

"No one, Mom," the boy said.

Georgia looked around the room, then at the still full dinner tray.

"Well, eat your supper, darling," she said. "You need your strength."

She started to leave, but Denny called, "Mom, could you stay a while?"

"Why, darling?"

Denny shrugged, unable to answer that. He knew his mother, who fussed over him endlessly, would stay if he wanted. But he couldn't tell her. Finally, he picked up his fork and started eating.

"It's okay," he said.

"Well, all right," Georgia said. "You call if you need anything."

"Yes, ma'am."

Georgia's eyebrows went up. He hadn't called her "ma'am" since they had left South Carolina. Still, she didn't think anything was wrong. Denny was eating hungrily—a good sign. He'd be back on stage soon enough, for sure.

After she'd left again, Bonnie reappeared, and pulled the fork from Denny's hand.

"Listen to me," she said. "You are going to forget what happened. When they ask you about the air passages, you are going to say you did it yourself!"

"But I didn't," Denny protested.

"Shut up! You listen, or I'll make the dark come again, and I'll make you fall."

Denny cringed.

"You lied," Bonnie said. "You went into the air passage by yourself and lied so your mommy wouldn't put you in a dark closet! Say you lied, or I'll make you fall again!"

Denny swallowed and said softly, "I lied."

Suddenly, the child was gone, and Denny was left staring at his tray in total confusion. He felt disoriented, as if some of the last moments had been lost. But that happened a lot since his stay at the hospital. And that was why he hadn't returned to work yet. Rubbing his eyes, he looked around for his fork to start eating again.

For some reason, it was on the floor. Had it dropped there? Denny let it go and picked up a spoon.

His mother opened the door. She smiled and said, "You have visitors, Denny."

"Who, Mom?"

"Why, it's Nate and Adrian," Georgia said. "Come on, darling. Put on your robe and come into the living room."

She took the tray away, noting he'd only eaten half his food. Well, she'd see to it that he had more a little later. Right now, she thought he might be happy to see his director. Denny adored Nate. But for some reason he seemed afraid to leave his bed.

"Denny?"

"Mom, I don't feel very good."

"What's wrong, darling?"

"My—my stomach."

"You're hungry," Georgia said with a nod. "You can finish this nice piece of cornbread in the living room."

Finally, the little boy got up and pulled on the grown-up looking red velour robe the cast had sent him. He shuffled into the living room. Adrian watched him carefully, afraid of another outburst.

"How do you feel?" she asked as the boy climbed into a lounge chair.

"Okay," Denny lied. His mother came over to him and kissed his forehead.

"He's so happy to be home again," Georgia said, smiling at him. "Home and safe."

Somehow, Denny didn't feel very safe. But he didn't tell the adults this. They'd only fuss over him and say it was part of his illness.

Nate looked at Georgia and said, "You heard about Barbara Warner, didn't you?"

"Oh, yes," Georgia said. "How awful!"

"Well," Adrian said, "her husband is asking the cast and crew a lot of questions about the accident. We want to make sure Denny is very careful in answering him."

"I won't have anyone questioning my little boy," Georgia said firmly, putting her arm around Denny's shoulder.

"Good," Nate said. "I doubt Joel will get to Denny, anyway. But we wanted to be certain."

Adrian smiled at the small figure curled up in the massive lounge chair.

"Denny, we missed you during the previews."

"We sure did," Nate said. "Your understudy did just fine, but you would have done better."

Denny's eyes lit up.

"Really?"

"Really," Nate said. "And I want you to get well quickly so that you can come back to the theater."

Denny looked down, suddenly grim. For a moment, Nate and Adrian tensed, afraid he was about to go into another attack. But the room stayed silent except for the clicking of an ornate clock on the mantel.

"I don't think you're going to let me back," he said.

"Yes, we are," Nate said.

Denny shook his head and swallowed.

"No, you don't understand," he said. "I did a terrible thing. I—I . . ."

He chewed at his lips, then blurted out, "I crawled into that air passage by myself! I just blamed Adrian so I wouldn't get in trouble!"

Georgia gasped, and Nate and Adrian exchanged looks. Nate was surprised at the outburst but kept an even tone when he asked Denny to go on.

"I—I don't remember very well," Denny said. "I think I was exploring. I wanted to see where the passage led, and I . . ."

He could not recall climbing into the opening but somehow knew that he had. There was only a vague memory of crawling in darkness, and nothing more.

But he had to tell what he knew as the truth.

"I knew I did a stupid thing," he said. "I knew my mom would really give it to me, so I lied and said Adrian made me do it."

"Why?" Adrian asked, hurt. "Haven't I always been your friend?"

Denny looked up at her, tears in his eyes.

"Sure," he said. "You're really nice, Adrian. I don't know why I did that!"

Georgia brushed his hair back and said in a gentle tone, "It's all right now, darling," she said. "Adrian will forgive you, I'm sure."

"There's nothing to forgive," the actress said.

Nate wasn't buying any of this. Nate knew what it was like to be a frightened child. How often had he been so terrified of a beating that he made up stories to save himself? This child was frightened too. But not of punishment at the hands of his mother. He was afraid of someone else. Someone who had put him up to this.

"Denny," he said finally, "does the name Bonnie mean anything to you?"

Adrian looked at Nate, then back at the small boy who sat cuddled in his robe across the room.

"No," Denny said.

"You don't have any friends named Bonnie?"

He insisted that he didn't.

"Who's Bonnie?" Georgia wanted to know.

"A name he mentioned once at the hospital," Nate said. "It may be a clue as to who made him do all this."

"I did it myself!" Denny cried.

"I don't believe that," Nate said. "You aren't foolish, Denny. You would never have done this on your own."

"But I . . ."

Georgia put her arms around him.

"Easy, darling," she said. "Maybe you ought to go to bed now. It's getting late, and you're upset."

"It's only eight o'clock," Denny said.

"Never mind," Georgia replied, though her tone was not as scolding as usual.

Denny obeyed her, and silently the three adults watched him slink toward his room, his head hanging. He opened the door, then turned and said, "I did it myself."

"We'll talk about it another time," Nate said.

When Denny had shut his door, Nate turned to Adrian and Georgia.

"Someone made Denny tell us this new lie," he said.

"But how?" Georgia asked. "Denny's been alone all night."

Nate shrugged. "I don't know."

"Do you think someone named Bonnie is involved?"

"Maybe," Nate said. "I'm going to start asking around the theater. See if anyone knows someone by that name."

"Oh, please do," Georgia said. "I don't want some maniac running around when my Denny returns to the theater!"

"I promise I will," Nate said.

But he couldn't be certain how he'd go about doing that. How do you catch someone you can't see?

FIFTEEN

No one at the Dysart Theater knew anyone named Bonnie, and Nate found himself at another dead end. He had an important clue—a name—but couldn't seem to go anywhere with it. It was the first of December and his play was opening in less than two weeks, so he had no choice but to let the matter go and concentrate on the morning's rehearsals. He wanted to discuss the next step with Adrian, but at lunchtime Don announced that Joel Warner was waiting in his office.

"Already?" Nate sighed. "All right, tell him I'll be there in a minute."

He wanted Adrian with him, since she was as much a part of all this as he, but she'd made a date to eat with Judy. And, Nate reasoned, Joel probably wouldn't appreciate her being around.

"Mr. Warner," he said as he entered his office. "Have you thought of any new questions since yesterday?"

Nate locked his copy of the script in his desk, then walked over to the office bar. He offered Joel a drink and, as he fixed a scotch on the rocks, listened to his new line of questions.

"Some things have been bothering me," Joel said, taking the drink and making himself comfortable on the leather couch.

"Like what?"

"First, can you tell me how many people are working here?"

Nate sat down behind his desk and propped his elbows on its glass top. He pulled his hands away from each other and shrugged.

"Oh, about forty-two," he said. "Including both the cast and crew. I can look up the exact number, if you'd like."

"That won't be necessary," Joel said. "Have they all been with you since this company opened?"

Nate said that was true.

"You trust them all?"

That was a question the director could not answer immediately. When he'd chosen his staff, he picked them because they had had experience elsewhere. How much did he really know about any of them? He had trusted each one of them to do his or her professional best for the Dysart Theater Company. Yet now he had to face the fact that one of them might be a killer who was trying to destroy him and his life's work.

"Of course I do," he said, finally.

"Then why did it take you so long to answer me?" Joel demanded.

"Look, I don't need to justify..."

Joel picked up his scotch and waved his hand at Nate.

"Never mind," he said. He twirled the ice in his drink. "Let me ask you this—have you ever fired anyone?"

Nate shook his head.

"All my staff have been with me since day one," he told Joel. "With the exception of Don Benson, my new stage manager."

"You had to have the other one replaced after he died," Joel said.

Nate felt a sudden flash of anger. "The other one" had been his best friend! He sat back in his chair with his lips set hard.

"Jim died of a heart attack," he said grimly. "And as far as Don Benson goes, he's a fine man. I *do* trust him."

"What about the people who built this theater?" Joel went on. "Were any of them ever fired?"

"Possibly," Nate said. "I didn't have control over the contracting company."

Joel leaned forward, holding his drink in two hands.

"But if someone had been fired," he said, "for whatever reason, it's possible he could hold a grudge against this theater, isn't it?"

Nate bit his lip, wondering if this might be a new clue.

But he dropped that hope very quickly. The nightmares and voices had started long before the theater was even designed.

"People get fired every day," he said at last. "That doesn't mean they try to get even with their employers by causing trouble."

"This city is full of nuts," Joel said. "In my work, I find them all the time. And some nut might have killed my wife."

"Barbara's death was an accident," Nate said perfunctorily.

Joel's eyes widened.

"The way your wife's death was an accident?"

"How did you know about that?" Nate asked softly.

"I did some research."

"You leave her out of this," Nate warned. "She has nothing to do with it."

"Not directly, no," Joel said. "But I read about her in a back issue of your hometown paper. Said she fell from a scaffolding. Just like Barbara."

"I don't want to talk about that," Nate said forcefully, standing.

But Joel would not relent. If he hit below the belt like this, maybe he could shatter Nate's cool, protective shell. And then he'd learn the truth.

"It's strange how accidents keep happening around you," he taunted. "You were right there when Meg was hurt, too, weren't you?"

A red film came down over Nate's vision, and he lost control of himself. Lunging forward with a terrible roar, he knocked Joel from the couch. His hands wrapped around Joel's neck, the fingers tightening as his rage increased.

"You bastard!" Nate cried, his face reddening.

Joel's fist came up from under Nate's jaw, stunning him momentarily. It was time enough for Joel to pull away from him and hurry toward the door.

"You *are* hiding something!" he said, adjusting his glasses as he gasped for air. "And believe me, I'll be back again to find out what it is!"

Adrian who had been outside the door, jumped out of the way as the reporter hurried down the hall. She turned and saw Nate pick himself up off the floor. His jaw was bruised purple, and he was fingering it gently. Adrian ran and pulled his hand away.

She winced. "What happened?"

When Nate simply shook his head, she pressed on.

"Look, I can't help you deal with these things if you aren't totally honest with me. What did he do that made you so angry?"

Nate rubbed his eyes.

"He started talking about Meg," he said finally. "About how she died."

Hating the memory, he busied himself with picking up ice cubes from the floor.

"Sit down, Nate," Adrian said. "Let me do that."

"I feel okay," Nate said, though his jaw was sore. Still, he could move it, so it wasn't broken.

Adrian went to the bar and opened the ice bucket. With a hand towel, she made an ice pack and carried it back to Nate.

"Don't put it right on the bruise," she said. "There, hold it there. It'll help a little."

"Thanks," Nate said. "What happened to your lunch date?"

"Believe it or don't," Adrian said, smiling, "it's for tomorrow. We got our dates mixed up. And a good thing for that! You look like you need a friend right now."

Nate closed his eyes and nodded.

"It scares the hell out of me when I get that angry," he said.

"That's because you're usually so patient," Adrian said. "It's so out of character for you to get really infuriated that it's frightening."

"I wanted to kill Joel Warner," Nate said. "When he mentioned Meg, I wanted to tear his throat open."

"He shouldn't have touched such a sore spot," Adrian said, rubbing his thigh a little. "Don't worry about him."

"But I do," Nate said. "My father used to fly off the handle like that all the time. I vowed I would never be like that."

"And you aren't," Adrian reassured.

"I was just like my father a few minutes ago," he said. "I was just like the man I hate!"

Adrian put her arms around him.

"Don't even think about that old SOB," she said. "He's dead and gone. And Joel Warner deserved worse from you."

"Sometimes," Nate said softly, playing with Adrian's hair, "I wish my father were alive. He said I'd never make it in show business, but I want to prove he was wrong."

He sighed.

"But, maybe he wasn't."

Adrian pulled away and looked into Nate's blue eyes.

"Don't even talk like that," she said. "This show is going to be a hit, and you know it!"

"But..."

"Just look how well we did in Connecticut," Adrian pointed out. "Now, don't start worrying just because Joel Warner is harassing you! You're going to be all right!"

Nate pulled her close and held her tightly, wishing he shared her confidence.

1975

Nate walked down a long, cold hallway, his eyes fixed on a door straight ahead of him. The walls and ceiling and floor were all stark white and unsettling, and overhead, pale green lights shone down on him with chilling beams. He hated this

*place. He hated coming here. And yet he couldn't bear to
imagine never seeing Meg again.*

*"She's gotten worse since your last visit, Mr. Dysart," the
nurse beside him said. "She clings to the doll I gave her as if
she were a real baby."*

*Why did you give her a doll? Nate wondered. Why torment
her?*

*But he said nothing. He stopped at the door to his wife's
room and put his hand on the knob. Before he could think
that he didn't want to see what was inside, he turned it
quickly and opened the door onto a small room.*

*Meg turned and stared up at him with wide, dark-rimmed
eyes. Her hair, once so beautiful, hung like straw. Her lips
were cracked and pale. But still she smiled, recognizing him.*

"Our baby," she sing-songed, holding up the doll.

SIXTEEN

The next afternoon, Adrian asked Nate's chauffeur to take
her to F.A.O. Schwartz. She had decided Nate needed something to get his mind off his worries, if only for a little while.
He'd been very distant all morning, his eyes filled with a
sadness he refused to discuss with her. She decided he ought
to have something to amuse himself. It wouldn't solve any
problems, but maybe it would make him smile.

George let her off on the corner where the toy store sat,
half-hidden behind a cluster of window-shoppers dreaming
about being able to afford the magnificent dollhouses and
huge stuffed toys on display in the windows. Adrian was
caught up in a knot of children as she pushed through the
doors, fighting the rush of Christmas shoppers.

George pulled his double-parked car onto Fifth Avenue
and circled the block on the slim chance he'd find a parking
space. In the rearview mirror, he noticed a familiar-looking
man walking toward the toy store. After a moment he realized it was the reporter, Joel Warner. He decided he'd park
the car as quickly as possible and follow the man into the
store, to make certain he didn't bother Adrian.

Joel had spotted Nate's distinctive Rolls, and after a moment's thought he had turned around and walked toward it. To his surprise, only Adrian St. John got out of the car.

Well, she might be easier to talk to, he decided, remembering Nate's angered outburst as a hand went to his throat.

It took some time to find her amongst the crowds in the store, but at last he spotted Adrian admiring a set of electric trains. Coming up beside her, he said, "I had a set of those when I was a kid. But who can afford them these days?"

Adrian turned around to make a friendly comment, the way anyone would in a cheerful place like a toy store. But when she recognized Joel her smile faded.

"Mr. Warner," she said simply.

"I'd like to speak with you, Ms. St. John," Joel replied.

She shook her head.

"I'm in a hurry," she said. "And I don't want to talk to you. You've caused enough trouble, hurting Nate the way you did!"

Joel's expression turned angry.

"He nearly strangled me," he said. "The man is..."

"Under a lot of pressure these days," Adrian said. "And how could you have been so insensitive—bringing up his dead wife?"

Joel followed closely behind her as she moved away from the display.

"I'm not insensitive," Joel said. "I know what he feels like."

Adrian turned to him.

"I'm sorry." She sighed. "I understand how angry you are. But please realize you're pursuing something you'll never find. Barbara died accidentally. Why do you torture yourself?"

"Because I can't believe it," Joel said. "I know that Barbara was not herself before the—what *you* call—the accident, according to Judy Terrel. Judy was her best friend. She'd never lie!"

"I'm sure she wouldn't," Adrian said. "Look, I'm in a hurry. I've got to get back to rehearsals..."

Joel grabbed her arm and held it fast.

"I'm not through," he said. "There's also the parallel between Barbara's death and Meg Dysart's accident that..."

But now someone placed a large hand on Joel's shoulder.

"However," George said, "the young lady *is* through."

"Oh, George," Adrian said. She glanced at Joel, who

removed his hand from her arm. "This is Nate's chauffeur. If you'll excuse me, I really do have to get back to work. We do want to cooperate with you, Mr. Warner. But please don't harass us. You can reach me at the theater."

When Adrian and George reached the car, George opened the door and let her in. As they headed down Fifth Avenue, Adrian looked out the window and debated about stopping elsewhere to get something for Nate anyway. But suddenly, the car started making strange noises. She leaned forward.

"What's that noise?"

"I'm sure I don't know," George said worriedly. "Perhaps I should pull over and . . ."

But there was no chance to pull over. A city bus cut in front of them at an intersection, and George's foot automatically slammed onto the brakes.

They didn't work.

"George!"

In a flash, George jerked the wheel to one side, hearing the front bumper scrape over the side of the bus. As dozens of people watched in horror the big old car flipped over and skidded on its roof into a newspaper stand. It all happened in a matter of seconds, and for a moment there was stunned silence on the street. Then a mob of people were running toward the car. Adrian, completely dazed, saw a dozen faces looking in the upside-down window.

"Are you—are you all right?" George asked weakly.

"I don't know," Adrian answered in a small voice.

Sirens screamed through the air, and a few moments later someone was trying to pry the door open. A woman poked her head in and said, "I'm a doctor. Do you hurt anywhere? Any dizziness? Nausea?"

"I—I don't think so," Adrian said, hardly believing it.

Two policemen came into the picture.

"We're going to help you out of there," one said. "If anything hurts, you tell us."

When at last she was pulled out, Adrian was made to sit on the curb next to the ruined newsstand. Her head dropped between her knees as a wave of nausea came over her. Nearby, the owner of the stand was ranting about suing someone or other for the damage done to his property.

Adrian was vaguely aware of George being laid on a stretcher, then of someone poking at her.

"Does this hurt?"

Adrian shook her head.

"This? Or this?"

"Nothing hurts," Adrian said.

"You might easily have been killed," a cop said. "They sure don't build cars like this old baby any longer. It was that strong frame that saved you."

"How did it happen?" his partner inquired.

"I—I don't know," Adrian said.

The doctor put her hand on Adrian's shoulder.

"I'd like you to be taken to the hospital for observation," she said. "You don't appear to be hurt, but..."

"No, no, I'm fine," Adrian insisted. She got to her feet, though her knees were trembling. "I'd like to go back to work."

"I don't think you..."

"Please!" Adrian cried, needing to be with Nate. "Can someone take me to the Dysart Theater?"

"Sure," one of the cops said. "That's near here. But you'll have to give us a statement, first."

Adrian nodded, then turned to the news dealer and said, "Please contact Nathaniel Dysart at the Dysart Theater. He'll pay for this."

Even as she told what little she remembered to the cop, a tow truck came and pulled the huge black car off the curb, working busily to turn it over. She was given a card telling where she'd find it and was promised it would be fixed within a week's time. At last, holding on to the young policeman's arm, she walked to his car. She said nothing as they drove, feeling too weakened to discuss the accident further. Thank God, she thought, as she entered the theater, there wasn't even a scratch on her.

And when she saw this, the little girl named Bonnie let out a silent scream of rage and knocked over a lamp on the stage.

As the actors looked at each other in wonder Adrian came down the main aisle of the theater.

Nate put his script aside and rushed to her side. All the actors on stage turned, amazed to see her disheveled hair and dirty clothes.

"What happened to you?" Sander demanded.

Adrian ignored him and threw her arms around Nate. In his embrace, the reality of the accident finally hit her, and she began to cry. Nate looked up at Don Benson, busy picking up the lamp, and said, "Take over here."

He led Adrian to his big office and sat her down on the couch, propping a pillow behind her back to make her comfortable. Gradually, between sobs, she told him what had happened.

Nate put his arms around her, thinking it was ironic that for once he was comforting her. But another thought overshadowed this one. He could not help a feeling that this was no accident, the way Barbara's fall had been no accident. He couldn't help a feeling that someone had just tried to kill Adrian too.

The next morning all the newspapers carried stories about the accident. Adrian's name was prominent, and it was mentioned that she was an actress at the Dysart Theater, where a new show would soon be opening. What worried Nate, though, was that all the newspapers chose to mention the other accidents that had been happening to the people in his company—Barbara's fall, Denny's misadventure in the air passages, even the stagehand who had been burned in that fire.

"They even include Jim Orland," Nate said, as he sat next to George's hospital bed.

"You're in the public eye now, sir," George said. "You have to expect this sort of thing. Besides, it may bring in more box-office sales. You know how curious people can be."

"I don't want tickets sold because of other people's misfortunes," Nate snapped. "I want them to come because *Making Good* is worth seeing."

He turned to the inside of the newspaper for the continuation of the story. His eyes scanned the article, then finally he shook his head and said, "Listen to this: 'In light of all the tragedies befalling Nathaniel Dysart's production of the original comedy *Making Good,* one is inclined to wonder if the theater is cursed. What malevolent specter is casting its evil eye over the cast of *Making Good?*'"

Nate crumbled up the paper and tossed it into a metal trash can.

"Damned sensationalism," he growled. "They can't leave people alone, can they? I know there's an explanation for the things that have happened at my theater, but it will be a mortal one when I find it." He waved at the trash can. "That idiot would have you think the damned place is haunted!"

"There are no such things as ghosts, sir," George agreed.

Nate managed a smile for the chauffeur, and changed the subject.

"What did the doctors tell you? Are you going to get out of this place today?"

"I have a slight concussion," George said. "And my wrist is broken. I imagine I did that when I turned the wheel of the car, sir."

"I called the repair shop," Nate said. "They say they can't find anything wrong with the brakes system."

"That's odd, sir," George said. "It was working perfectly earlier in the day, and after a half-century of driving, I ought to know how to use a brake pedal!"

"I certainly don't hold you responsible," Nate assured him. "But I still wish I knew exactly what happened."

"It is frightening, isn't it, sir?" George asked.

Nate did not say anything. It was more frightening, he thought, than George realized.

To look at her, one would never have realized Adrian had been in an accident just the day before. Her hair was neatly pinned up again, and her white wool suit was fresh and clean. Still, there was a weariness in the way she moved. It had been a sleepless night for her. She knew she should have her understudy work today, but since she'd never before missed a rehearsal (until yesterday), she refused to consider the matter. Still, the armchair across her dressing room looked very comfortable. But she knew she must keep going. Her parents were arriving soon, and she didn't want them to know about the accident. Her mother would worry too much.

Adrian glanced at the clock on her vanity. Rehearsals would not start for another ten minutes. Perhaps she could rest a while in that chair.

The dark! The dark hurts!

Adrian looked up. The voice had sounded nearby, yet her room was empty. She sat up a little.

"Is someone there?"

I don't like the dark. You're going to pay for bringing the dark!

Adrian jumped to her feet and hurried to Nate's office. He wasn't there, nor was he on the stage. At last, she found him talking to Mike Woodson about the upcoming opening night. Adrian took his arm, and when he saw the urgency in her manner, he excused himself.

"I just heard a strange voice," Adrian whispered as they walked down the hall. "Talking about the dark, just like that voice you hear."

Nate's eyes widened. "Show me where," he said.

A minute later they entered Adrian's dressing room. She pointed to her vanity chair.

"I was sitting there," she said, "when I heard someone say 'The dark, the dark hurts,' and some other things I can't remember."

"What kind of voice was it?"

Adrian thought a moment, bringing the voice back into her mind.

"Very young," she said. "Like a small child. And she had sort of an accent. Southern, I think, but not as thick as Georgia's."

Nate bit his lip. Quietly, he asked, "Could it have been a southwestern accent?"

"Well, yes," Adrian said, "that's exactly what it was like. She spoke the way people do in western movies."

Nate turned from her and walked across the room, folding his arms. Adrian came up behind him and put her own arms around his shoulders, resting her head against his back.

"It was frightening," she said, "but it was also a kind of relief. If I'm hearing voices, it means you can't be imagining the ones you hear."

"The accent is the same," Nate said. "And the childish voice."

He broke away from Adrian and threw his arms up.

"But where does that lead us? Who the hell is doing this?"

"It's got to be someone in the company," Adrian said. "You know we haven't allowed anyone in the theater since our return from Connecticut, with the exception of Joel Warner. Security is tight. No one could have wandered in off the street."

"But Joel wasn't here when I heard the first voices," Nate said.

"Look, let's put our facts together," Adrian suggested. "We have a person with a childish voice and southwestern accent. Anyone in the company like that?"

Nate shook his head.

"Not that I can recall. But don't forget—someone with acting experience might easily be able to imitate any sort of voice they wanted."

He put his arm around her and started to walk with her from the dressing room. For a moment, the fatigue Adrian had felt earlier caught up with her, and she swayed a little.

"Are you all right?" Nate asked with alarm, steadying her.

"Oh, Nate, I'm fine," Adrian said. "Just a little tired."

"Maybe you ought to rest this morning," Nate said. "That accident yesterday..."

"Nate Dysart," Adrian said with a small laugh, "you aren't the only one who can use work as a means of escape. I don't want to spend the morning moping around, thinking about that voice I heard!"

But she did think about it, all during the rehearsal. A vague memory was stirring in her mind, something connected to the horrible words she had heard that morning. And the more she thought of them, the more she was certain she'd heard that voice somewhere before.

"Adrian!"

She looked up, startled, and realized she had lost her place.

"I'm sorry," she said. "Where were we?"

"Nigel was just asking Daisy to play up to the local millionaire," Sander said. "Really, Ms. St. John. If your head was that badly injured in that accident, you shouldn't be here!"

"Thanks for your concern," Adrian said sarcastically. "But I'll be all right."

Suddenly, it had come to her. Several weeks earlier, there had been a strange little girl in her dressing room. A child who had spoken fearfully of the dark, then had seemingly vanished into thin air. At the time she'd assumed she was the daughter of one of the company or crew but now...

SEVENTEEN

At the end of the rehearsal Adrian took hold of Nate's arm and held fast to him until everyone had left the stage. Then she said, quietly, "I might have another clue."

"Is that where your mind was during rehearsal?" Nate asked, as they started to walk together down the hall. "You've never missed a cue before, Adrian."

"I'm sorry," she said. "But I couldn't help it."

Nate kissed her lightly.

"I'm not angry," he said. He was speaking partly as her director, partly as the man who loved her. "I'm just concerned. Are you sure you're all right?"

"I'm fine," Adrian said. "It's just that I can't stop thinking about that voice I heard. Nate, I think I might have an idea who it belongs to."

Nate stopped walking and turned to look at her. Was it possible? Quietly, Nate took her hand and said, "Let's go into my office."

But they never reached it. Suddenly, from back in the wings, there was a strange crackling noise, and a split second later the entire upstairs of the theater went dark.

"Oh, no," Adrian groaned, annoyed by the interruption.

Nate turned his head around, though he couldn't see anything, and listened to the sounds of others in the hallway. Recognizing Judy's voice, he called, "Get Mike Woodson, Judy, will you?"

"Sure, Nate," Judy said. "If I can find the stairs!"

Adrian found Nate and put her arms around him. As they stood waiting for the electrician, Nate could not resist searching for Adrian's lips in the darkness to place a warm kiss upon them. She sighed softly, her hand coming up behind his head. His hair felt soft to the touch, and Adrian kneaded it between her fingers for a moment before sliding her hand down to his back. She was massaging his muscles when suddenly a sharp, burning pain ran along her arm. With a cry, she pulled away.

"Something burned me!"

"What?" Nate asked. Without waiting for an answer, he demanded impatiently, "Where the hell is Mike?"

Adrian twisted her arm up to her mouth and blew on the sore spot. It felt something like the sting of a hot iron, and yet what had touched her hadn't been hard like that. It had been soft, almost like a human hand.

Bonnie could see in the dark what the others couldn't, and what she saw next enraged her so that she let out a long, silent scream. Nate was pulling Adrian back into his arms, cooing over her as if she were a child. But in a moment, the little girl collected her senses. She would be stronger than this Adrian. She would win in the end no matter what the woman did—and the end was not far away. Quietly, she disappeared into a blackness even deeper than the one that held Nate and Adrian captive.

When all the lights came up a moment later, Nate could hear cheers throughout the building. He turned to Adrian with concern in his eyes and lifted her arm gently. But there was no sign of a burn.

"Nate, something did burn me," Adrian said, her eyes wide.

"You know I believe you," Nate said. "The important thing is that you aren't seriously hurt. Do you still feel anything?"

"Not at all," Adrian said. "Forget it—or add it to the list of unexplained phenomena that we have. Let's go to your office."

"Somehow we managed," Mike Woodson said, as he way-laid them in the hall, "to blow out a third of all the fuses downstairs. Were you running too many lights at once up here?"

"No more than usual," Nate said. He shrugged perfunctorily, for the benefit of those in the hall watching him. "I guess it was just one of those things."

"Yeah," Mike said. "I'm going to check the control board. There may be something wrong there."

"If you need me," Nate said, "I'll be in my office."

A few minutes later they were interrupted by an urgent knocking. A stagehand reported that Mike had to see Nate. They found Mike in the wings, poking at the control panel— or what was left of it. All the insulation had melted, and the plastic hung like globs of old bubblegum. The bare wires

were twisted and mangled, as if someone of unnatural strength
had reached in and wrenched them from the unit.

"This could only have been done with intense heat," Mike
said.

"A fire?" Nate asked, almost in a panic.

"No, no," Mike assured him. "If I thought there was any
danger of that I would have cleared the building. But the
walls around here aren't even warm."

Nate felt a cold chill as a feeling of déjà vu ran through
him. Intense heat. Fire. A burning theater...

"Maybe someone with a blowtorch," Mike was saying when
Nate came out of the daze that had momentarily claimed
him. "That's the only thing I could think of."

"Who could do such a thing?" Adrian asked.

Nate was about to ask who could have hurt Barbara or
Denny, but he stopped.

"Just do what you can to fix it. I'll expect a progress report
tomorrow."

"Someone is trying to ruin me. I've got the building crew
working overtime, and now the damned lighting crew. I'm
going to have a strike on my hands if this keeps up!" Nate
said.

"Don't even think about that," Adrian said. "Let's talk
about what we started earlier. Listen, I might have a clue
about that voice." Adrian set a drink on the glass top
of his desk. She took a sip of her own and let the alcohol
warm her. "A few weeks ago, I was in my dressing room,
when I noticed a little girl sitting in my armchair. She kept
staring at me, so I thought she might be too shy to speak.
Anyway, I asked what she was doing there, and she started
saying all these strange things about the dark coming."

Nate leaned forward.

"Did she have the accent?"

"I don't recall," Adrian said. "Maybe, since the voice I just
heard said the same things."

"What did she look like?"

"Very pretty," Adrian said. She brushed back her hair.
"Her hair was pulled to the side with a big white bow—black
hair, I recall. And she was wearing a white dress with tiers of

ruffles. I remember it so clearly because it was such an unusual..."

She saw that Nate wasn't listening. He stared into his glass, a frown turning his lips, trying to recapture the picture that had flashed in his mind when she described the little girl. He could see a child in a white dress, standing near the theater. No, near the empty lot. He had seen that same child before the theater was built.

But in a moment, a more terrifying thought occurred to him. Nate had also seen the little girl in another place.

In his dreams.

"Adrian," he said, his voice in monotone. "You can't dream about something you've never seen before, can you?"

"I don't think so," Adrian replied. "Why?"

"The little girl in the white ruffled dress is the one I see in my nightmares," he said.

Adrian's eyes widened, but then she shook her head. At first she was a little stunned by the coincidence, but in her way she found a logical explanation.

"Look, you must have seen her somewhere before," she said.

"No," he said. "I swear I never saw her before the dreams."

"Then how do you know it's the same child?"

He spread his hands. "All of this is so bizarre that I'm beginning to think the newspapers were right the other day. Maybe there really is something supernatural going on here."

"Nate, that's impossible, and you know it," Adrian said. "Whether you can remember or not, you surely must have seen the little girl before your dreams."

"I know I didn't," Nate said.

Adrian sighed, not knowing how to comfort him. Finally, she decided to take a businesslike approach. She stood up and walked over to Nate's file cabinet.

"We were going to look up the names of people from the Southwest," she said. "Let's just concentrate on that for now."

Nate put down his glass and came to unlock the files. Though he was aching for an explanation about the little girl, he decided to follow Adrian's advice. He pulled out a folder and carried it to the coffee table. For the next ten minutes he and Adrian skimmed through résumés. At one point, Nate interrupted and said, "How could a child do all this?"

"Maybe it isn't just a child," Adrian said. "Maybe the voices belong to a child—someone small enough to duck away before being caught. But the really bad stuff is the work of a sick-minded adult."

She tossed her last sheet on top of the pile, and Nate returned them to the folder. They had gotten nowhere.

"For a minute there"—Adrian sighed—"I had the idea that we might find an adult from the Southwest, someone who sneaks his or her kid into the theater."

Nate snapped his fingers.

"But," he said, "he could have lied about his origin. We're just going to have to ask around if anyone knows about a little girl wandering through the theater."

"Oh, we can't do that," Adrian said quickly. "We'd upset everybody—and right before opening night. You know how superstitious we actors are. Besides that, we'd give ourselves away. If this monster is to be caught, he must have no warning."

"You're right," Nate said. "But I don't like being left at a dead end like this. Isn't there anyone we can talk to?"

Adrian thought a moment.

"Denny," she said. "Maybe he's thinking more clearly now, and he'll be able to tell us something."

When they arrived at Georgia's apartment, a grandmotherly-looking baby-sitter let them in. Georgia had explained she had a date, and Nate was glad they would have a chance to talk to Denny alone. Like most kids, there were probably things he didn't want his mother to know.

Denny, already in his plush robe and pajamas, hurried to the door to greet them. His eyes lit up when they handed him the present they'd bought, a big book on basketball.

"I'll be in the kitchen if you need me," the sitter said.

Denny carried the book to the couch and sat down with it, flipping through the photographs with delight.

"It's got all my favorite players in it," he said.

"We thought it might make you happy," Nate replied. It was partly a gift, partly a bribe he hoped would help the boy open up to them.

Denny smiled at him. "My mom says I can go back to work, soon."

"Wonderful!" Adrian cried. "We really miss you, Denny."

"Really?" Denny asked. "I thought you'd still be mad at me."

"Denny," Nate said, taking a seat, "we cleared that up last time we were here. We are definitely not mad at you."

Adrian crossed the room and sat beside Denny. Watching her with big eyes, he closed the book and placed it on the coffee table.

"There's something we didn't clear up, though," she said. She looked over at Nate, who picked up her signal and took over.

"Do you remember how we asked if you knew anyone named Bonnie?"

"Uh-huh," Denny said with a nod. "And I still don't."

"Denny, think really hard about that," Nate said. "See, we think someone named Bonnie has been causing—causing trouble at the theater. You may be able to help us."

He knew that children were more likely to be responsive if treated on an equal level with adults. Maybe Denny would think himself privileged to share in the problems facing the theater, instead of being left out just because he was a kid.

But Denny shook his head adamantly.

"I don't know anyone named Bonnie," he insisted.

"Maybe you just don't know her by name," Adrian said. "She's a very little girl with black hair. She wears a white dress with ruffles all over it."

Something was coming back to him, a shadowy picture. The little girl Adrian was describing did sound familiar, but Denny couldn't place her. He closed his eyes and thought deeply. A picture of the backyard came to his mind, with its crates and litter. He was playing basketball. He bumped into someone.

"Bonnie," he said, softly.

"Do you remember now?" Nate asked.

Denny nodded his head slowly. He pictured the little girl in his mind and knew she had come to play with him. He opened his eyes to tell Nate this, but almost immediately his expression went blank, and he fixed a stare on something across the room. Nate and Adrian turned that way, but saw only the darkened television set and an empty chair.

"Denny?"

Adrian went unheard. Denny was only aware of the little girl sitting in the chair next to the TV, her small hands curled around its arms. She was shaking her head at him, and when she spoke her words were for his ears alone.

"She's interfering again," she said. "I have to stop her!"

And then she was gone.

As Nate and Adrian watched in horror Denny's head fell back, and his eyes rolled back until only the whites showed. Then he collapsed across the plaid couch.

"Denny!" Adrian cried.

Nate went to the boy and put a hand on his forehead.

"He's burning up," he said. "Get the sitter and have her call a doctor."

Adrian hurried towards the kitchen. Nate, not knowing what else to do, straightened the boy out on the couch. What had he seen a moment ago? What had frightened him?

Suddenly, Denny began to shiver violently. Nate looked around and found an afghan, which he laid over the child's quaking body as Adrian and the sitter entered the room. Words began to pour from Denny's mouth, at first slurred and unintelligible, then horribly clear.

"The dark, Daddy! Take away the dark!"

Nate felt a chill run over him. It was not Denny's voice, but a little girl's. A little girl with a southwestern accent.

"Take the dark away, Daddy!" Denny screamed. "The fire! The fire! Stop, it hurts!"

Denny sat up abruptly, his eyes wide and glistening, his body stiff. Strange choking noises began to escape from the back of his throat. Then, suddenly, strings of a muslinlike substance began to gush from his mouth. Adrian screamed and backed away. The sitter turned and closed her eyes in horror.

"My God," Nate whispered, unable to move.

The strange matter began to pour from Denny's nostrils, from his ears, and even began to darken the seat of his pajamas. Whatever it was, it seemed to be escaping from every orifice of the child's body.

"What the hell is that?"

An eternity later, yet only a few seconds after the seizure had started, Denny collapsed again.

The room was silent except for the baby-sitter's sobs. Nate and Adrian stared at the mess that covered the plaid couch, a mess that somehow resembled torn-up pieces of cloth soaked in gelatin. A moment passed, then Adrian screamed.

"Nate, look!"

Nate followed the line of her finger. There in the white

mess, a face was looking up at them, a portrait of a small child somehow imprinted on the strange substance. But in the blink of an eye, it was gone.

"That was her," Adrian whispered, tears pouring from her eyes. "That was the little girl!"

Nate could not say anything. He didn't even put his arms around Adrian when she moved closer to him. He just kept staring at Denny, unable to comprehend what had just happened.

Finally, it was the sitter who broke the spell. She walked toward the couch and gingerly touched Denny's neck.

"We have to get him to a hospital," she said quietly.

She looked up at Nate and Adrian.

"Why must little ones suffer?" she asked. "Why must they be tormented?"

"Tormented?" Adrian asked.

The sitter pointed a bony finger at the mess on the couch.

"Ectoplasm," she said. "That horrible stuff is called ectoplasm."

"I—I don't know what that means," Nate said, his voice hollow.

The sitter glared at him.

"Ectoplasm," she said, "is physical evidence of a ghost."

EIGHTEEN

After bringing Denny to the hospital and notifying Georgia, Nate ordered George to take him back to the theater. He and Adrian sat in silence in the back of a Lincoln Continental, and though Adrian desired only to go home and comfort him, she did not argue with his plans. She did not tell him these things were best figured out after a good night's sleep. She did not tell him there must be some logical explanation for what they had seen. Instead, she simply took his hand to let him know she was there.

They entered the theater through the front door, crossing the dimly lit lobby where crystal chandeliers glowed in dreamlike silence. The auditorium was dark but for the ghost light burning center stage. Nate let go of Adrian's hand and

walked slowly toward it as she stood behind the back row.
Then he began to run, his anger mounting, nearly crashing
into the railing that surrounded the orchestra pit. He grabbed
hold of it and tossed his head back.

"Who the hell are you?" he cried. *"Who the hell are you?"*
Silence.

Nate tightened his fists on the railing, fury emanating from
every pore of his body. Someone was trying to ruin him.
Someone did not want his life's dream to come true.

"WHO THE HELL ARE YOU? WHAT DO YOU WANT
FROM ME? YOU WON'T DESTROY MY WORK! YOU
WON'T!"

He screamed and screamed like this until his voice was so
hoarse that he began to choke. Yet still the theater was silent.
Though she knew he was screaming for her to answer, Bonnie
simply stared at Nate, confused by his anger. Why was he
angry? He never got angry! Only Mommy did, and then
she'd be locked in a dark place until Daddy came to get her
out. Daddy was always happy.

"Don't be sad, Daddy."

But Nate did not hear her this time.

"WHY DON'T YOU ANSWER ME?"

Adrian had seen enough. She ran down the center aisle
and threw her arms around him, bursting into tears.

"For God's sake, Nate, stop it!" she cried.

Nate groaned and brought his hands up to his face. With a
heavy sigh he quieted down and dropped his head to bury it
in her soft hair. The two held each other in silence, not
knowing what to say to each other, not knowing that they
were being watched.

The Dysart Theater was busy the next morning, and no
one would have guessed what had taken place there during
the night. Nate seemed as calm and professional as ever,
interrupting with suggestions and taking notes the way he
always did. Only Adrian, who had spent the night comforting
him, knew there was something wrong. His no-nonsense
voice had an edge to it, and there were times when he
seemed not to be paying attention to the action on stage.

"Maybe you ought to let Don take over," she suggested
quietly.

Nate merely stared blankly at her and turned back to his script. Adrian decided she'd discuss this with Nate at lunch, but when noon came around, Mike Woodson got to him first and asked to discuss the blackout. Adrian expected to stay there with Nate, but to her surprise, he said, "I'll probably be a while. Why don't you eat without me?"

Adrian considered telling him she would wait, but there was something in his tone that indicated he preferred to be alone. At first she was hurt by his coldness, but then she realized he probably wanted time to think things out for himself.

As she readied herself to go out, she could not help an occasional glance at the armchair of her dressingroom. It remained innocently empty.

Deciding she would bring lunch back and eat in the greenroom, Adrian remembered she had a takeout menu in her vanity drawer. She pulled it open, pushing aside curlers and makeup and souvenirs from old shows. Something small and yellow revealed itself, as a *Playbill* slipped to one side. Adrian reached for it and pulled out a roll of film.

"I can't believe I forgot about this," she whispered.

It was the roll she and Nate had taken of the theater, to see if the strange white flaw would show up again. But then Denny's accident had happened, and in the confusion that followed the film had been forgotten. Adrian recalled the first set of photos that Nate had showed her. The blur had almost resembled a human figure, a ghostlike image.

"Ghostlike image," she said aloud. The words of Denny's sitter came back to her. *Ectoplasm. Physical evidence of a ghost.*

Had the old woman been right? Adrian shook her head. No, she would not believe that. The sitter had been hysterical, a crazy old lady. Of course there was a logical explanation for what had happened to Denny. Perhaps something not even connected to the horror at the theater. The doctors would be able to explain it and give Danny the proper medicines to make him well again.

But she and Nate had both seen that face.

We were upset, she insisted to herself.

Instead of sitting there frightening herself, she would do something constructive. It took half an hour to find a photography store that would develop the film within a day, but to Adrian it would be worth the effort if any clues were found in the new set of photos.

Nate hardly spoke to her when she returned to rehearsal. While she and Sander were waiting backstage at one point, the actor pulled her aside and whispered, "Perhaps you should tell our director to leave his problems at home. Whatever they are, they're interfering with the show."

Adrian glowered at him. Of all the people in the company, superstitious Sander was the last person she wanted to have know about what had been happening. When she heard her cue, she hurried on the stage, then remembered she was supposed to be walking lazily and slowed herself. For the rest of the afternoon she concentrated on her work. But when it was over, she walked downstairs to Nate and said carefully, "Do you want me to come home with you?"

"I have a lot of work to do," Nate said. "I really should be alone."

He hates being alone, Adrian thought.

"Nate, I . . ."

"Adrian, the show is opening in barely a week's time," Nate said. "I'm going to be very busy."

Adrian did not say anything more. Nate ducked his head back down to read his script, almost as if dismissing her. Sadly, she left. She did not see him again before going home.

Nate sat alone in his office, listlessly flipping through a copy of *Variety*. He had tried to keep himself busy all day, had even avoided Adrian, so that he would not have to think about what had happened the night before. But all day long it haunted him, and now, alone this way, he could not turn his thoughts elsewhere. The deaths, the voices, the accidents all added up to one thing:

Someone wanted him to lose his theater.

"I won't let that happen," he whispered. "Damn whoever you are, you won't do this to me!"

He ran his hands through his blond hair and leaned back with a sigh, closing his eyes, letting a memory appear in his mind. He was in his father's office, and he was wearing a black suit, though he hated dark clothes. It was just after Meg's death.

"You've won, Father," he said. "My production company is closing. I can't do it without Meg."

"You could never do anything right," the old man sneered. "Not even making a healthy baby."

Nate's eyes snapped open, and he stood up abruptly.

"This time, I will succeed," he said. "I'll show you how wrong you were, Daddy. No one will destroy me!"

He was standing, locking his briefcase to take it home, when a knock sounded at his door. Before Nate could answer, it opened, and Georgia Richmond strode into his office. Her eyes were bloodshot, and her cheeks splotchy.

"What the devil happened last night?" she demanded, her voice strained as she stared coldly at him.

"I don't..."

Georgia cut him off.

"Denny was perfectly fine yesterday," she said. "Now he's back in the hospital, indefinitely!"

"He had another attack," Nate said quietly. "I—I really don't know why."

"He was so happy yesterday," Georgia blubbered. "My poor Denny!"

Nate watched her for a few moments in silence. She cried openly, making no attempt to control her sobs.

"What exactly did they tell you at the hospital?" he asked finally.

"That Denny became so upset during your visit that he began to throw up," Georgia said. "I don't know what you said to him, but I'm going to tell you one thing. You are forbidden to go anywhere near my child! He's out of the show, and that's *final*!"

Nate didn't argue with her. Quietly, he said, "We'll have to make it official, then."

Georgia sniffled and opened her purse. Pulling out a folder of white papers, she said, "Then let's do it. I've brought my copy of the contract."

"Uh, let me get ours from my files," Nate said. He crossed the room and pulled open a drawer, fishing through it for Denny's contract. But after a moment he stopped and closed his eyes. Then he said, "Are you sure you want to do this? Denny was so happy here—and I'm sure he wants to come back in spite of everything."

"I'm quite sure," Georgia said. "My son's *health* is most important."

"But he worked so hard," Nate protested futilely.

"Oh, my son will have his chance," Georgia said. "I am going to set up some auditions for him as soon as he's better."

"Maybe you shouldn't rush things," Nate said.

He started through the file again.

"Of course Denny will have as much time as he needs to get better," Georgia said. "We're going back to South Carolina. But we'll be back here in New York—or maybe we'll go to California and try for a movie."

Nate turned with the contract and brought it to the coffee table.

"We'll need to make this official," he said. "I'll call my lawyer tomorrow. But our signatures will do for now."

After they were finished, Georgia stood up and said, "I'm sorry it worked out this way. My boy was so happy here."

Nate did not respond but watched her move toward the door and out of the office. He was sorry too. My God, he was sorry. He'd lost three people in his company—Jim, Barbara, and now Denny. But Denny was alive, thank God. Maybe it was all for the best if the child never came back.

The next day, Adrian did not bother asking to share lunch with Nate. She went directly to the photography store, then bought a sandwich at a deli. In her dressing room her lunch remained uneaten as she shuffled through the photographs. They were clear, with no mysterious flaws. She began to relax, but then she turned over the last photograph. It was a picture of the building's front, and a white blur seemed to float above the cornerstone. Adrian studied it for a long time, trying to make something human of the shape. But her eyes kept wandering, as if drawn to something else in the picture. It took a minute for Adrian to realize what it was. The date on the cornerstone was wrong.

It read "1902."

"How can that be?" she demanded of the empty room.

Someone had tampered with the pictures, of course. Nervously, Adrian skimmed through the negatives until she found this one. It also said "1902." There was no indication it had been tampered with. She swept all the photos back into the envelope and went outside to check the cornerstone. It read, quite clearly, "1981."

"Someone *did* manage to change it," she said to herself.

There were about twenty people on line at the ticket office as she reentered the theater through the front door. Adrian knew they were all staring at her, asking each other if that was the actress who'd been in the car crash a few days earlier. But Adrian ignored them. She was in a hurry to get the photos and show them to Nate.

To her surprise, he barely looked at them. He had been so adamant about finding an answer, yet now he didn't seem to even care.

"I'm not surprised to see this," he said.

"How can you say that?" Adrian demanded. "In light of all that's been happening, how can you suddenly be so nonchalant?"

Nate looked up at her.

"Only one thing matters to me," he said, "and that's to see my show open on time without any trouble."

"Of course the show is your main concern," Adrian said. "But you can't pretend none of this is happening!"

"You used to say that," Nate said. "You used to say the voices and nightmares were all products of a tired mind. Well, maybe you were right."

Adrian put her arms around him.

"Oh, no, Nate," she said. "I was wrong, terribly wrong! I heard the voices too. I saw what happened to Den..."

Nate pulled away from her.

"I have to get back to the stage," he said, almost impatiently. "Rehearsal is about to begin."

Adrian watched him leave his office, aching to run after him and yet unable. She was shocked by his complete turnaround. But in a way, she understood. This play meant the world to Nate, and he was terrified it was all going to be taken away from him. Nate could not let that happen, and so he threw himself into his work while trying to push away the truth about what had been happening at the theater. Adrian realized he wanted this play to open at any cost.

"And it will open," she said. "I promise it will."

She left the pictures on Nate's desk and went to the rehearsal. As she waited for her cues she pondered the next step. Finally, she decided she might as well start at the beginning and visit Fred Johnson, the architect who, Nate had told her, had designed the theater.

Adrian called ahead to be certain he hadn't left for the day, then fought the crush of an uptown subway. She was so deep in thought that she didn't notice the sandy-haired, mustached man who walked behind her. Joel Warner had followed her from the theater.

When the subway stopped, Joel walked off, a few paces behind Adrian, and followed her into a steel-and-glass sky-scraper. Hidden in the rush of people in the lobby, he heard her ask someone which elevator bank went to the fiftieth floor. Then he followed her, taking a different elevator.

Adrian rode up, trying to decide what questions she'd ask. She didn't want to reveal anything, yet she also didn't want to sound ridiculous. She suddenly found herself before the receptionist's desk. The woman was getting ready to go home, and she looked up at Adrian without smiling.

"I'm looking for Fred Johnson," Adrian said.

The woman pointed and gave her an office number down the hall. Adrian thanked her and headed that way. In the meantime, Joel had walked off his own elevator. The recep-tionist considered her work over for the day, and she did not question his presence.

Adrian was greeted by a thin, dark-haired man.

"Adrian St. John," Fred said as he backed away to let her enter. "I don't like using clichés, but you're prettier than your pictures."

"Thank you," Adrian said, politely. "And thanks for staying late just to see me."

"No problem," Fred assured her.

He indicated a chair for her, and she took it, resting an arm on the bookshelf filled with art volumes next to her.

"I was sorry to hear about your accident," Fred said. "But you seem to be all right. You are, aren't you?"

"I'm fine," Adrian said, though that wasn't entirely true. But for now she straightened herself and got to the point of her visit. "Mr. Johnson, I'd like to ask you some questions about the Dysart Theater."

Fred shrugged. "Go ahead, although I can't imagine what information you'd want from me."

"When you were designing this theater," Adrian began, "do you recall anything strange happening?"

Fred thought a moment, but it had been so long ago that the memory of the design process was a vague one. He finally shook his head.

"Nothing at all," he said. "Why?"

Adrian didn't answer his question. She stood up and walked over to a wall-unit sectioned into deep cubbyholes. Each one contained a half dozen cardboard tubes filled with blueprints. Adrian looked over her shoulder at the architect and said, "Could I see the prints of the theater?"

"Don't see why not," Fred replied, crossing the room.

Adrian hoped there might be a clue in the blueprints. Perhaps she'd find a hidden room or passageway where a small child could hide and call out in the voice she and Nate had heard. But when Fred unrolled them on the drafting table, there was nothing like that to be seen.

"Maybe I could help if I knew what you were looking for," Fred said.

"I'm not sure, exactly," Adrian replied.

She moved the top sheet and studied the next drawing. Somehow, the layout of the basement didn't seem right. Adrian quickly realized no room had been left for the lockers, and that the staircase was on the wrong side.

"Wait a minute," Fred said, taking it from her. "That's an old one. I had done another version of the theater before—using the plans you see there."

"Nate didn't like the original?"

Fred shook his head.

"He was quite happy with it, actually."

"Then why did you bother changing it?"

"I don't really know," Fred answered. He scratched his head. "Actually, I've often tried to figure that out for myself. I suppose the new ideas just came to me, and I decided I preferred them."

"The theater's design—" Adrian said, "that's Art Nouveau, isn't it?"

"Yes, it is," Fred replied. "I thought it was a rather old-fashioned theme for a young man like Mr. Dysart to choose."

Adrian looked up at him.

"Where do you get your ideas?"

"Oh, initially from books," Fred said, pointing to the case of art volumes. "Then I adapt them into my own."

"What book did you use for Nate's theater?"

Fred could not answer that. He hadn't used any books at all, but somehow had gotten every detail of his design from his own head. And yet he had a feeling that, as talented as he was, something was missing here. He had never felt the design was truly his. But of course that was a ridiculous idea, certainly nothing he wanted to mention. He looked at Adrian and made up a lie to satisfy both of them.

"I often visit the library at Lincoln Center," he said. "They have a good deal of theatrical literature. If you are interested in the Art Nouveau style of Mr. Dysart's theater, perhaps they can help you there."

"Thank you," Adrian said. "I'll do that."

She knew he was avoiding telling her something, but she sensed somehow that if he were able to, he would. Could Fred Johnson be controlled by the same person who had Denny in his clutches? Could he, too, have been threatened into silence?

She picked up her purse and smiled a little.

"Thank you for your time," she said, and walked to the door.

"I hope I was of some assistance," Fred said, though he had no idea what this had all been about.

Adrian nodded once and turned the doorknob. Seeing her silhouette through the translucent glass, Joel ducked into the nearby men's room. As he waited for Adrian to leave he thought about what he had just heard. The design of the theater had been changed, for no apparent reason. And Adrian had seemed very upset about this. Joel decided he would confront her again. He opened his small notebook and wrote "Lincoln Center."

The next day, Nate asked Adrian to share lunch with him. He did not seem as cold as previously, and it hurt Adrian to refuse him, but she wanted to get over to the library. That, in the long run, was more important than a lunch date.

"I'm sorry if I was mean to you," Nate said. "I shouldn't

have made you the brunt of my anger. My father did things like that, and I don't ever want to be like him."

Adrian kissed him.

"I understand," she said. "After what happened to Denny..."

Nate cut her off. "I don't want to talk about Denny."

"That's just it," Adrian said. "You don't want to talk. Your attitude has completely turned around since we visited him the other night. Nate, darling, your problems won't go away if you ignore them!"

"Yes, they will," Nate said. "Whoever is tormenting me will stop when he sees I'm not affected by it. Adrian, my show is opening December twelfth. I can't be involved with anything but thoughts of that. It's the most important thing in my life."

"Of course it is, Nate," Adrian said. "But how can..."

"Please," Nate interrupted. "Let's not talk about it, okay? I just thought we'd have a nice, pleasant lunch together."

Adrian shook her head.

"I'm really sorry, Nate," she said. "But I've already made other plans."

She kissed him again.

"I'll see you later."

She walked out of his office, leaving Nate to watch her sadly. At that moment Sander Bernaux came by and noticed they were not together.

"You've missed lunch again," he said. "That's three days in a row—has she lost interest in you?"

Nate turned to him, his expression grim.

"Shut up," he said. "Just shut up."

He slipped back into his office, slamming the door so hard that an echo reverberated down the hallway. Sander shook his head and walked away.

Adrian hesitated in the alley that ran alongside the theater, fidgeting with a bracelet that she wore. The hurt in Nate's eyes had upset her so much that she was tempted to run back and apologize. She understood that his distance had been caused by fear—it was easier to deny trouble than to face it. But she also understood that he needed her, and she was leaving him alone.

"Oh, Nate," she whispered.

She turned around and put her hand on the latch of the

door leading back inside. But then she drew it away and hurried down the alley, carefully avoiding a pile of trash. She was going out to help Nate, and putting off this trip would only delay her plans.

Adrian stood out from the curb with her arm raised, but three taxis in a row ignored her signal. Finally, when she had almost decided to walk, one pulled over. She climbed in and gave the driver her destination. Keeping his eyes on the street for an opening in the lunch-hour traffic, he said, "Cute kid you got there, lady."

Adrian shook her head, confused.

"Excuse me?"

"I said you got a cute . . ."

The driver glanced over his shoulder and noticed she was alone in the backseat.

"There was a little girl standing next to you in the street," he said. "I just thought she was yours."

Adrian grew cold suddenly. She turned to look at the theater as the car pulled away. There were lots of pedestrians: people were reading posters for *Making Good,* and one or two were entering the theater to buy tickets. But no children.

"This child," Adrian said, turning frontward again. "What did she look like?"

"Hey, kids are kids to me," the cabbie said. "Oh, well, I guess she had kinda dark, shoulder-length hair and a white dress."

She was with me, Adrian thought. *She was with me and I didn't even know it.*

"No," she said f nally. "No, that wasn't my child."

She paid the cabbie at Lincoln Center, and got out, walking up a short flight of stairs and crossing the courtyard. The Metropolitan Opera House sat regally at its back, its arched windows revealing an opulent lobby. Adrian thought about Nate's theater and wondered what she hoped to find here. Another piece to fit the puzzle, she supposed, no matter how insignificant.

The librarian directed her toward the books on theatrical architecture. Adrian skimmed over the titles but could not find one covering the proper era. From the corner of her eye she saw a tall man reach for a book on the next shelf. He heaved down the thick volume, nearly staggering under the weight of it.

"This is what you're looking for," Joel Warner told her.

Adrian turned and gaped at him with wide green eyes. She made no attempt to take the book he was holding out to her.

"You again," she said. "Why do you keep following me? There's a law against it, you know."

"It's my job," Joel said, the general answer he gave uncooperative people.

"Your job, Mr. Warner," Adrian said, folding her arms, "is to report the news. I am not someone you can question to the breaking point, the way you do those big businessmen and landlords."

"My job," Joel shot back, "is to find the truth. I know my wife's death was no accident, and I . . ."

Adrian sighed. "Oh, God. We have been through this repeatedly. Nearly a dozen people *saw* her fall. The police, insurance people, everyone involved, said it was most assuredly an accident."

"The fall, perhaps," Joel said. "But my wife wasn't herself before that. Something upset her. Something may even have frightened her to death."

Adrian was going to tell him he was ridiculous, but she decided that was too callous a statement. He was under an enormous emotional stress. Instead she took the book from him.

"What are you doing here, anyway?" Joel asked, as if he had not heard yesterday's conversation with Fred Johnson.

"Reading up on the type of architecture used in the theater," Adrian said.

"Why would an actress care about architecture?"

Adrian looked him in the eye and said quietly, "That's none of your business, Mr. Warner."

She wheeled around and hurried off toward the most occupied section of the library, hoping that Joel would stop bothering her if people were around.

It seemed to work, and as she looked carefully around she could not find the reporter. Soon she was so engrossed in the book that she didn't see Joel take a seat across the room. He sat pretending to browse through a book he'd chosen randomly, watching her.

Adrian's book contained old photographs as well as drawings and paintings of the numerous theaters built in New York in the decades surrounding 1900. There were floor plans, enlarged details, and a lot of text. Adrian recognized familiar-sounding names but could find nothing in particular of interest to her. She sighed wearily and flipped through a few more pages. She didn't want to be late for rehearsal.

Maybe I'm just wasting my time, she thought.

She turned over one more page, and what she saw there made her eyes widen. Across the room, Joel Warner noticed the change in her expression and leaned forward. He saw Adrian run her finger down the page and made out something like "Oh, my God" on her lips.

There were three pictures in front of Adrian. A photograph of a theater's front, a sketch from an old newspaper article, and a print of an oil painting of a stage. Adrian skimmed over the article, which ran under the subtitle "Winston Theater—1902." She felt a chill run over her and forgot completely about the time.

The facade of the theater featured swirling designs. There were three crystal chandeliers in the lobby, a winding staircase, and etched glass doors. But the stage was what hit Adrian hardest of all. Its curtains were of a swirling, gold-and-white design.

It looked exactly like Nate's theater.

What she read at the end of the chapter made her gasp in horror. According to the author, the Winston Theater had burned to the ground on December 12, 1921.

Exactly sixty years to the day before the opening night of Nate's production.

Because his doctors had been unable to find anything wrong with him, Denny was sent home soon after his visit to the hospital. He sat on the living room couch now, cuddling inside his velour robe, a newspaper opened on his lap. Georgia dusted one of the knickknacks she kept on the TV set and watched him sadly. Words like "mental exhaustion," "therapy," and "psychiatric help" haunted her thoughts. Denny's physician had told Georgia that his illness might have been in his head—a reaction to the hectic life of the theater, perhaps. Georgia decided that she was glad she had broken Denny's contract. Her son's health was more important than *any* job in the theater!

And he did seem healthier these days. Georgia marveled at the resilience that was so natural in children, grateful that Denny had recovered so quickly. To look at him reading there on the couch, no one would ever guess how sick he had been.

"Mom, can I have some hot chocolate?" Denny asked now.

"Sure, honey," Georgia said, putting her dust rag down. "I'll make some for both of us."

While she was in the kitchen Denny turned to the next page of his newspaper in search of the comics and instead found the entertainment page. There was a publicity shot from *Making Good* at the top of the page, in the middle of a long article. Adrian and Sander stood to either side of Nate Dysart. Denny felt a twinge of jealousy to see Nate's hand on the shoulder of his understudy, Johnny Hemlock. Denny was aware that his mother had had a few unkind words to say to Nate after Denny's second visit to the hospital. Maybe Nate was being nice to Johnny because he thought Denny didn't like him anymore! Worried about this, Denny showed the article to his mother.

"I miss everybody," he said.

"I know," Georgia said, sitting beside him. "But I've told you before that you mustn't even think about the theater. I don't want you to get sick again!"

Denny took a sip of his chocolate.

"I feel okay," he insisted. His eyes lit up then, and he asked, "Could I call Nate up on the phone?"

"I don't want you talking to Mr. Dysart," Georgia said.

"But why?"

"Don't argue with me, Denny," Georgia said. "I just don't approve of you talking to that man—after what happened the last time you did!"

"Nate's my friend," Denny protested. "He didn't hurt me."

Georgia's voice took on a shrill quality. "Denny, the subject is closed!"

Forgetting her chocolate, she hurried into the kitchen, unable to deal with her son's innocent questions. Denny gazed at the kitchen door over the rim of his mug, unable to understand why his mother suddenly hated Nate so much. Well, he would find some way to get to his friend. Nate would be happy to know that Denny still liked him.

NINETEEN

"I don't like to be kept waiting, Ms. St. John," Sander said coldly as Adrian raced on stage five minutes late. "Do you realize we're opening in one week?"

"I'm sorry," she gasped, her face red.

She had run all the way from the library, and now it took her a moment to calm down. She shook her head at Nate, who stood off to one side of the stage, talking with Denny's understudy.

"I really have to talk with you," she said, hoping he'd tell the others to "take five."

"We're losing time, Adrian," he said, sounding more like her director at that moment than ever before.

"But I..."

Nate walked off the stage to his seat in the front row and called for action. It was as if he hadn't even heard Adrian. Frustrated, she nonetheless played her part, reciting lines that had been drummed into her head for the past five-and-a-half weeks. It was only her "show must go on" training that kept her from crying out her news.

By the time the day ended she was so full of anxiety that she felt ready to burst. Sander came up to her and said, "If you're this nervous for rehearsals, how will you be on opening night?"

Adrian was about to tell him it wasn't stage fright that made her so edgy, but quickly thought the better of it. She smiled bravely.

"I'm just upset because I was late," she said. "I've never done that before."

"And never do it again," Sander said. "It's the sign of an amateur."

"Yes, sir," Adrian said, resisting the urge to salute him. Instead, she walked down to Nate.

"Can we talk now?"

"Well, I wanted to discuss..."

"Please, Nate!"

182

He read the desperation in her eyes and consented finally. They walked together to his office, where he fixed a drink for Adrian.

"You look like you need this," he said. "What was wrong with you today?"

"Oh, Nate," Adrian said, taking the glass from him. "I just learned something that terrifies me."

Nate took a seat behind his desk, not sure he wanted to hear it. But Adrian was already talking.

"I was doing some research in the library this noon," she said. "I found a book on old theaters and I was trying to find out something about the architecture of this one."

"Why would you do that?"

"Because I went to Fred Johnson," she said, "and he couldn't give me a solid reason for building the theater just the way he did. That really bothered me, and I..."

Nate leaned forward, resting his arms on the glass top of his desk.

"You went to my architect," he said, "and I didn't know it?"

Adrian dropped her shoulders a bit.

"Nate, I tried to tell you," she said, "but you weren't willing to listen. I understand it was because you were upset by what we saw at Denny's apartment the other night. But I couldn't start denying this theater was in trouble, the way you did. I had to take matters into my own hands!"

Nate shook his head.

"I never denied there was trouble," he said. "I just feel it's best not to give in!"

Adrian took a sip of her drink, then set it down on the coffee table.

"Does the name Winston Theater mean anything to you?" she asked now.

"Should it?"

Adrian nodded. "You're damned right it should. I found a chapter on the Winston Theater in the book I was reading. I understand it was a pretty spiffy place in its day—and it was built in 1902. Remember the photograph?"

"Coincidence," Nate said. "Lots of theaters were built around that time."

"No, darling," Adrian said. "There were three pictures with the article: the building's front, the lobby, and the stage.

Nate, the Dysart Theater is an exact replica of the Winston Theater."

"You can't be sure of that with only three pictures," Nate said. "Fred might have used that particular theater as a model."

Adrian shook her head.

"For God's sake," she said. "All the pieces are falling together and you're acting as if it's no big deal!"

"My opening night is the only big deal I care about," Nate said.

"Nate," Adrian said, "the Winston Theater burned down in 1921. On December twelfth—the same date as our first performance here. Is *that* coincidence? And I learned something else. The address of this theater is exactly the same as the Winston Theater's had been. Is that *another* coincidence?"

Her eyes were wide as she looked at him for an answer. But Nate simply looked behind himself then back at her again and said, "I don't know what to tell you."

"Listen to me," Adrian said. "Something is going to happen here on December twelfth. Everything I've learned points to that conclusion."

"You sound like that sitter the other night," Nate replied. "Are you going to tell me my theater is haunted?"

"It could be!" Adrian cried. "Stranger things have happened in this world. But listen—let's stick to your theory that someone is trying to destroy you. That person could have persuaded Fred Johnson to rebuild the Winston Theater as part of some sick plan. It all fits into place, Nate. I'm telling you this theater can't be occupied that night."

"Adrian," Nate said, "you are talking about something that's going to happen in a matter of days. I can't do anything about it now."

"Yes, you can," Adrian said. "Shows are often closed for a night or two."

"And thousands of dollars are lost," Nate said. "Be realistic, will you? I have backers to pay, not to mention the cast and crew here. I am not going to close the show for even one night, and that's final!"

Adrian opened her mouth to make a reply, but instead, her eyes went wide and her hand flew to her lips.

"Nate, I just thought of something," she said. "My parents will be here that night."

Nate shook his head.

"That's something you'll have to deal with, then," he said.

"How can you be so stubborn?" Adrian cried. "Don't you see the danger we're facing?"

"I won't close my show!"

Their discussion had turned into a shouting match, and out in the hall, Sander Bernaux stood listening. What was going on, he wondered? Why was Adrian so terrified to have the show open on schedule? All Sander's fears about bad luck rushed to his brain, and he began chewing at his fingernails.

"She's making him sad."

Sander turned to see a little girl.

"I beg your pardon?"

"She's making him sad," the child said again. "Make her stop!"

Sander threw his shoulders back.

"I'll do no such thing," he said. "How dare you order me about like that?"

"I don't like you," the child said. "You're going to die, just like the rest of them."

"Impudent brat," Sander growled. He wanted to listen to more of the conversation in Nate's office but couldn't bear having this child staring at him. With a grunt, he walked swiftly away.

Bonnie was inside Nate's office in a second's time, standing near the door unseen. She wanted to kill Adrian right now but didn't make a move. The time was coming quickly enough, and then Adrian would pay with the others.

"Look, Adrian," Nate said finally, his voice lowered considerably. "If it'll make you happy, I'll post security guards all over this theater on opening night. People will wonder about them, and I'll sound pretty ridiculous when I can't explain why they're there."

Adrian wasn't quite sure she liked the idea. So much had happened right under their noses that the idea of security guards seemed a waste of time. And yet she realized Nate was trying to compromise.

"You're my leading lady," Nate said. "In more ways than one. But as far as this theater goes, I call all the shots."

"Nate," Adrian said. "I love you, and you know that. But I'm frightened!"

Nate stood up and crossed the room. Adrian rose from her own seat and held her arms open to accept him into them. He kissed her softly, wanting to chase away her fears and yet so full of his own. Finally, he said, "I will never, ever let anyone hurt you."

He tightened his arms around her, and whispered, without really hearing himself, "I won't lose you the way I lost Meg."

Adrian sighed.

"You won't lose me, Nate," she said. "Not ever."

As frightened as she was by the things she'd learned, she knew she would never leave Nate alone to face them.

Joel walked from the skyscraper where he'd just interviewed a union boss, thinking not of the upcoming strike (the subject of his latest column) but of the things he'd learned in the library earlier. He had taken Adrian's seat after she left and, after reading the opened pages, knew what had frightened her.

The question that seemed to drum most loudly in his mind was why sixty years had passed before the theater was rebuilt. Anyone old enough to remember it would have to be over seventy. And, Joel wondered, what other buildings had stood there in the past six decades. Surely it hadn't remained an empty lot, considering its prime location and property value.

As he headed towards the Fifty-ninth Street subway station he asked himself if there were answers to be found in the history of the land. The Winston Theater was rebuilt for some reason—an evil one, Joel was certain, because no one had ever publicized that the Dysart Theater was its replica. And that meant no one was supposed to know. Obviously, Adrian hadn't, or she wouldn't have been so shocked by the information.

Joel descended a long flight of stairs into the subway. He always thought of Barbara when he rode the underground trains. She had hated them, with their stale smells and graffiti-covered walls. Barbara wanted everything in life to be happy and beautiful, and she often succeeded in making others as cheerful as she was.

But now she was dead, killed not by an accident, as her

colleagues insisted, but by something that was as malevolent as she had been good.

Adrian was sitting at her kitchen table, eating a store-bought quiche and trying to figure out what to do about her parents. She could hardly tell them not to come to New York for her opening, and if she gave them the real reason, they'd think she was crazy. Nutty things like this just didn't happen in small Ohio towns. Suddenly the shrill ring of the phone interrupted her thoughts. To her surprise, it was her mother's voice that she heard. But Martha didn't sound as animated as usual. Adrian prayed nothing had happened at home to add to her worries.

"I have some bad news, darling," Martha said.

"Mom, what's wrong?"

"Well, I'm afraid your father and I won't be able to make it to New York after all," Martha said.

Adrian felt something like relief wash over her, but she kept the emotion out of her voice and asked with concern, "Why not?"

"Well," Martha said, "you know your father's been having some heart trouble these past few years, and . . ."

"Oh, my God," Adrian said. "Dad didn't have a heart attack, did he?"

She heard her mother click her tongue a few times.

"Just a very mild one," she said. "He's out of the hospital. In fact, they only kept him in overnight."

"Why didn't you call me?"

"Well, I know how busy you've been," Martha said apologetically. "I didn't want to upset you. But I wanted to let you know we had to cancel our reservations. The doctor said your father shouldn't be traveling right now."

"He's right," Adrian agreed, unable to believe this coincidence. Now at least she didn't have to worry about them. She continued the conversation by asking more about her father's health and inquiring after her brothers. Her youngest brother came on the line, excited about being chosen for the grade school basketball team. She had to hear all the details. Her baby brother was growing up. By the time she hung up, she felt as if a burden had been lifted from her. Now, if only she could solve the mystery of Nate's tormentor. But that was impossible.

Much as Adrian wanted to research the theater's history even further, she couldn't. There were so many things to do for the play coming up the next Saturday night that she simply did not have the time. Nate didn't take any leisurely lunch breaks, so it was rare that they could sit down and talk. Maybe Nate was right—the best defense against whoever it was that tormented them was denial.

The day before opening night a mixture of tension and excitement filled the air. Actors could be seen embracing each other in the hallways or on the stage, silently wishing each other good luck. A week had passed since Adrian had learned of the Winston Theater, and nothing bad had happened. Everything on stage and off was going smoothly.

"You see?" Nate said. "After all this time, maybe whoever it was gave up."

"Or maybe you've been too busy to notice anything," Adrian said. "And because of that, he got bored."

Nate grinned at her, the first time he'd done that in days.

"One of the extras tore her dress during a fitting," he said. "And the cat chewed up Don Benson's script."

Adrian laughed, and Nate threw up his arms.

"Problems!" Nate cried. "Everyday, innocent, ordinary problems!" He looked up at the ceiling. "God, I hope this good luck lasts."

"Sander would tell you it's a bad idea to get too cocky before the show goes on," Adrian said.

"I can't help it," Nate said. "This isn't eight weeks of rehearsals behind me, Adrian. It's thirty-two years of dreaming."

He came over to her and put his arms around her. As she held him close and pressed her lips to his Adrian prayed nothing would happen to shatter this happiness.

Bobby and Alec Warner were staring in awe at the bustling sidewalk activity to either side of the bus and eating the big salty pretzels their father had bought for them. Alec was holding the yellow dog Judy had brought home from Barbara's locker. He was really too young to understand it was his mommy's last present to him, but it had become a symbol of security for him, and he never let it out of his sight.

The two boys were with Joel today because their sitter had canceled at the last minute. There had been no time to find a substitute, and so Bobby and Alec had accompanied Joel to his newspaper office.

Joel tried to answer his sons' questions in as animated a voice as possible and hoped they did not figure out that there was something wrong. But he couldn't stop thinking of the Winston Theater and the information he found in back issues of *The New York Times*. His destination now was the Dysart Theater, and he could feel his muscles stiffen with anger in anticipation of his meeting with Nate.

He was holding on to both his sons' hands when they entered the vestibule of the building.

"Bobby," Joel said, "you sit right here and wait for me. When I get back we'll go to the Museum of Natural History."

"Mr. Warner," Nate said simply when he entered the office. Adrian, sitting next to him on the couch, put an arm over his shoulder.

"I haven't come to cause trouble," Joel said, reading the distrust in their eyes. "I just want to ask you some questions."

"All right," Nate said. "Sit down over there, will you? Adrian told me you followed her to the library."

"I had a right to do that," Joel said defensively. "And you will definitely want to hear what I have to tell you—provided you don't know it already."

Adrian leaned forward, entwining her fingers together, and asked quietly, "Did you read about the Winston Theater?"

Joel nodded. "The book you left open on the table," he said. "But that passage wasn't half the story. I went to the archives at the *Times* and read up on the history of the place."

"I know about the fire in 1921," Nate said. "And if you've come to tell me I should close my show..."

"You may want to," Joel interrupted, "after you've heard what I have to say."

Nate looked at Adrian as if asking for support. He'd been so happy a moment ago! But maybe it had been too much to ask for that happiness to last.

"As you know," Joel began, looking at Adrian, "the Winston

Theater, which stood on this very ground, burned down in 1921. According to an article dated December thirteenth—the day after the fire—it was of a mysterious origin. No later article solved the mystery, so I guess it remains an open case to this day. Anyway, it happened at night, after the evening's performance, and for some reason there were several people still in the theater."

"Did they die?" Adrian asked. "Who were they?"

"Only one name was given," Joel said. "And that was of the fire's only victim—a five-year-old child named Bonnie Jackson."

Adrian gasped, and Nate closed his eyes to mutter a swearword.

"The name means something to you?"

"No, no," Adrian said quickly. "How could it?"

Their initial reactions told Joel she was lying. He watched Nate carefully as he spoke; the man was chewing his lips as if to bite clear through them.

"Anyway," he went on, "another theater was built about a year after that one went down. It never had a successful run and finally closed down, bankrupt, in 1934. Now, according to the microfilms I was reading, a restaurant was established there. It, too, burned in a mysterious fire."

"The realtors never told me any of this," Nate said quietly, refusing to believe what he was hearing.

"A hotel was built next," Joel said. "By 1968, the place was a haven for addicts and prostitutes. One day, a hooker opened a fifth-story window and started screaming something about the dark. Next thing people knew, she jumped to her death."

The dark, Nate thought. *My God, she was talking about the dark*.

But still he stared at his hands, listening intently, on the surface not seeming to react.

"They did an investigation and found nothing. The girl hadn't even been on drugs," Joel said. "Finally, the place was torn down two years later. And that property sat barren for over ten years. After a hell of an effort I located the realtor and asked why. But they couldn't tell me."

He stood up and walked to Nate, looking down at him.

"Didn't you ask?" he inquired. "Didn't it seem strange to you that a lot in a prime location like this remained unsold for a decade? Didn't you worry that there was some reason for that?"

"Why would he think to do such a thing?" Adrian demanded. "He's had enough on his mind without worrying about the history of a piece of land!"

"Well, he damned well should have worried about it," Joel snapped. "Every damned building erected here since that fire in 'twenty-one has met with tragedy! He should have known more would happen! He could have prevented my wife's death!"

Nate stood up abruptly now, the blank expression leaving his face. With widened eyes he grabbed hold of Joel's collar and hissed, "I did not murder your wife! I didn't want that to happen to her! I didn't want anything to happen to anyone!"

Joel forced Nate's fingers from his neck and said quietly, "What do you mean you didn't want anything to happen to anyone?"

Adrian came closer to them and put her arms around Nate. "He's upset," she said. "The play is opening tomorrow, and he's got too much in his mind."

But Nate shook his head and stared at his shoes. "Adrian," he said, "the man knows more than we do. There's no use denying that."

Adrian led him back to the couch and forced him to sit down before he spoke again. He looked up at Joel, feeling every nerve ending tingle, wanting to scream and yet forcing himself to remain calm. Joel was already looking at him as if he were a madman, and Nate couldn't risk that. He couldn't have this reporter telling his colleagues that the director/producer of *Making Good* was out of his mind.

"You're right," he said finally. "Something is going on at this theater. I didn't tell you about it because I didn't believe it myself, but now I do."

"You don't have to tell him anything, Nate," Adrian interrupted.

Joel sank into a chair. "He'd better," he said. "I want full cooperation or I'll spread this story over every paper in the city."

"You're very cruel," Adrian said.

"No," Joel answered. "I'm just a man who wants to know the truth. I'm listening, Mr. Dysart."

For the next twenty minutes, Nate found himself telling
Joel everything that had happened at the theater. The reporter learned about the voices, about Denny, about the little
girl.

"Her name was Bonnie," Nate said. He rubbed his eyes
and looked wearily at Joel. "The little girl who died in that
fire was also named Bonnie."

"Coincidence," Adrian said.

"I don't know," Nate replied. He wanted to agree with
Adrian, but her doubting answer had come out too quickly. "I
mean, there may be a connection. It—it isn't the same little
girl, of course."

Joel pointed a finger at him.

"But it could be a relative," he said. "Look, the kid's
parents survived that fire. If her mother were alive today,
she'd be about ninety years old."

"A woman that age couldn't do what's been done here,"
Nate said.

"No," Joel said, "but her children could."

"Presuming she went on to have other children," Adrian
put in.

"Women those days had a baby every year," Joel said.
"Now let's take that theory. The woman is about ninety-five.
If she had another child at, say, age thirty, that child would be
sixty-five right now."

"Still too old," Nate said. "This isn't working."

"But you said it was a child's voice you heard," Joel
answered. "And a child you've seen. This new Bonnie could
be the original Bonnie's descendant."

Adrian left Nate's side to walk across the room. She paced
the floor for a few moments, then threw up her arms.

"This is so impossible," she protested. "You're talking
about four generations! How could a need for vengeance last
so long?"

"Considering all the things that have happened in this
theater," Joel said, "it doesn't surprise me. Look, let's start
with Bonnie's mother. She has another child, and she tells
this child about Bonnie's death. Her child tells the grand-
child, then *that* one tells her own little girl. Crazier things
have happened in the world—especially in this big city.

Maybe the family has never been able to avenge the child's death until now."

Nate began shaking his head.

"But why me?" he asked. "Why do they pick on me? Why did they choose me to rebuild this theater?"

"You were in the right place at the wrong time, I guess," Joel suggested. "They heard you wanted to build a new theater and saw to it that you built this one. How they did it doesn't matter right now. The only important thing is that they're planning to avenge the first Bonnie's death on your opening night."

"But why," Adrian asked, "would anyone want revenge? Surely the first fire must have been an accident."

Joel could only shake his head.

Adrian hurried back to the couch and put her arms around Nate.

"I can't believe this," Nate said. "It can't be possible."

"You'd better believe it," Joel said coldly. "Because if anything happens tomorrow night, your hands will be so soaked in blood that you'll never be able to wash them clean."

Denny played basketball with Mikey Smith and Paul Kasson for the first time in weeks, racing around the street outside his apartment building, shooting baskets.

"So, anyway," he said, stopping for a moment as Paul tried to reach the hoop over their heads, "I want to go into the city to see my director so he'll know that I still like him. My mother thinks it was Nate's fault that I got sick when he came here last time. But I know it wasn't!"

"Denny, that's a crazy idea," Mikey said as he knocked the ball from Paul's hands. "This is the first day your mom let you outside, and you think she's gonna let you go all the way into Manhattan tomorrow night?"

"She won't know about it," Denny replied. "My mother never wakes up once she goes to sleep at night—and she's been going to bed around eight-thirty these days. I don't know why. But as long as she's asleep when I sneak out tomorrow night, that's okay by me. I'll be back before she knows it."

The ball dropped from Mikey's hand and rolled to the curb, where it was forgotten.

"So, what do you want from us?" he asked. "I can't sneak out like that."

"Yeah, and I'd probably get caught," Paul added. "I don't want to be grounded over Christmas vacation!"

"Oh, you guys are just chicken!" Denny accused. "Now I know where my real friends are—at the theater!"

He grabbed up his ball from the curb and began to walk home, determined to go into Manhattan the next night even if Mikey and Paul didn't. He really didn't want to go inside just yet—not after it had taken so long to convince his mother that he felt good enough to leave the apartment. But he was mad at his two friends; he had thought they would be with him all the way. He hadn't been wrong—in a moment, Mikey and Paul were at his sides.

"Okay, we'll go," Mikey said. "I'll tell my mother we're going to the movies. But we have to be back home by midnight!"

It amazed Denny that anyone his age would be allowed out that late, but he was delighted. Now he would have someone to share his adventure!

"Thanks," he said. "C'mon, let's play some more basketball."

Denny played as vigorously as he had before his strange illness. Memories of crawling under the stage floor, of being in the hospital, and of a little girl named Bonnie were pushed so far back in his mind that they would probably never be recalled again. At that moment, Denny only cared that he would be seeing his theater friends again.

TWENTY

Bobby, after waiting half an hour for his father, finally grew tired of studying the designs that circled the doors and racing up and down the grand staircase. Pouting, he walked over to a couch and bounced up and down on it, folding his arms. He wished his father would hurry and take them to the museum, like he promised.

"Don't know why he had to come to this dumb place, anyway," he griped.

Little Alec sat in the middle of the rich carpeting with the yellow stuffed dog in his hands, pretending it was walking around him. He banged it along the rug, laughing and making its ears flop up and down. From across the room, Bobby suddenly saw him stop and look up, his eyes wide.

"Watcha starin' at?" he asked, seeing nothing.

Alec did not answer, so Bobby lost interest in him. He did not know that his little brother was staring at a child hardly bigger than himself, standing before him in a white ruffled dress. She smiled at him, and he returned the smile, holding up the dog.

"What are you doing here?" she asked.

"Waiting for Daddy," Alec replied. "See my dog?"

The child nodded. Yes, she saw the dog. She had put it in that woman's locker. And the woman had died. Why were her children here now?

"Want to play?" Alec chirped.

Bonnie tilted her head. It had been a long, long time since anyone had asked her to play. There had been other children, but they had always been afraid. Then Denny—but he wasn't here anymore. And he had not helped her. He had been made to pay for that.

"Yes, I want to play," she said. She sat down. "I want someone to play with forever."

"I play with you," Alec said. "I be your friend."

Bonnie's head went back a little, and she studied him like some long-ago tyrant scrutinizing a subject.

"Come tomorrow night," she said. "Come tomorrow night and I'll make you my friend forever."

She disappeared. Too young to dissociate reality from fantasy, Alec simply waved bye-bye. Bobby saw the gesture and walked over to his brother with an exaggerated swagger.

"Who're you waving at?" he asked. "There's no one else in here."

"Little girl," Alec said. "She wants to play."

Bobby looked around the empty lobby. Then, with an exasperated sigh, he grabbed his brother's hand and pulled him to his feet.

"You've got a weird imagination," he said. "Come on and sit down."

Alec, poking a thumb into his mouth, followed his older brother obediently. He sat down, folding his two arms around the yellow dog, and began to rock back and forth on the couch, finally falling asleep. When Bobby suddenly decided he had to use the little boys' room he debated whether or not to leave his brother. But he finally decided it would be okay. Alec was asleep. He'd be right back. His father wouldn't mind.

As Bobby was climbing the stairs the little girl returned, taking a seat beside Alec. He intrigued her, this child who did not seem to fear her. Maybe, when she had her daddy, she could have a friend too. Then she wouldn't be lonely, and it would never be dark again.

Across the room one of the etched-glass doors swung open. Sander Bernaux saw Alec on the couch, curled around something small and yellow. At first it meant nothing to him, until the child stirred in his sleep and the dog dropped to the floor.

"No!" Sander cried. "No!"

His shouts woke up the little boy, and he sat upright with a gasp. Alec looked at Bonnie, seeing her, though Sander didn't, and then up at the actor.

"You can not have that yellow dog in this theater!" Sander cried. "It's bad luck—horrible luck! And the night before our debut! Get it out of here!"

He snatched it up and started to carry it towards the door. Alec, screaming, shot to his feet and raced after the man, tackling him head-on. The man was trying to steal his doggie!

Bonnie stood up and watched the scene in unemotional silence.

The doors to the vestibule swung open, and as a crowd of ticket-buyers watched in bewilderment, Sander pushed through the front doors and flung the dog into the street. A taxi, colored the same yellow, crushed the toy dog beneath its wheels. Sander gave his head a quick nod, then turned on his heels and walked back inside, as the ticket buyers whispered in shock.

Alec stood in the middle of the lobby, screaming.

This is how Joel found his two-year-old son. Tears were pouring down the boy's reddened cheeks, and he was waving his hands around him in a tantrum. But when he saw his father, he ran up to him to be taken into his arms.

"Took doggie!" Alec whined. "Man threw doggie in street!"

Joel looked at Sander, who was pacing the floor worrying about whatever bad luck had already befallen the production. When Nate and Adrian entered the lobby Sander stopped and announced, "Outsiders should not be allowed in here. That child had a yellow dog in his possession!"

"Big deal," Joel said. "It's a kid's toy!"

"An instrument of evil," Sander said.

Nate looked at both men, then held up a hand and said quietly, "Wait a minute. I think I know what Sander means."

"Then maybe you'd better tell me," Joel said, rocking his son as the boy began to calm down in his father's strong embrace. Joel looked around for Bobby. "Where's your brother?"

Alec shook his head in confusion. He had no idea what was going on.

"The yellow dog," Nate said, "is one of the theater's oldest superstitions. It brings bad luck to a production."

Joel frowned. "You took my son's toy because of some idiotic belief?"

"My beliefs aren't idiotic, sir," Sander said, straightening as if to ready for a fight. "And the dog means much more than my director is telling you."

Shut up, Bonnie called. *Don't say anything more! Don't ruin my plans!*

But Sander didn't hear.

"In medieval plays," Sander continued, "yellow was the color worn by the Devil. And to this day the presence of a yellow dog in the theater means someone in the company is going to die."

Adrian and Nate saw Joel blanch, and Adrian quickly added, "It's just a legend. Surely you don't believe in such things, Mr. Warner?"

Joel shook his head. He squeezed Alec closer to him and kissed the toddler's soft cheek. His son had been playing with that damned dog. He had·been playing with the symbol of Barbara's death...

He closed his eyes in disbelief.

"Judy Terrel found that thing in Barbara's locker," he said. "Are you going to tell me now that my wife wasn't murdered?"

The lobby was silent. Even Alec had calmed down, and now he watched the adults quietly, sucking his thumb. He noticed the little girl and waved to her. But she did not wave back. She was watching the mean man who'd thrown his little toy out to the street. And she looked angry.

"I don't know what to tell you," Nate said. "Except what you know already."

"Tell me you're going to close this place down," Joel said.

"No!" Nate snapped. "I won't close my theater! Opening night is tomorrow!"

Joel turned on him. "Is that all you care about?" he demanded. "Your frigging opening night? I don't give a damn about it! I only care about my Barbara—and seeing her killer punished!"

Bobby walked up to his father's side carefully, frightened by his yelling. It was bad timing.

"Where the hell did you go?"

"To—the boys' room," Bobby faltered.

"You couldn't wait a few minutes, at your age?" Joel demanded. "You left your baby brother alone?"

"Dad, I . . ."

But Joel was already delivering an angry whack to his backside. Nate cringed, picturing himself there, receiving punishment harsher than deserved from his own father. Bobby burst into tears, the first he had shed since the funeral. It was Nate who came to his rescue, grabbing Joel's arm before the second blow came down.

"You don't do that in my theater," he said plainly.

Joel stared at him for a moment, then relaxed.

"May I say something?" Adrian asked. "Mr. Warner, you really want to find your wife's—" She looked at the children and hesitated.

Joel nodded, understanding.

"Then let the show open," Adrian said. "The only way we'll succeed is if we let this person come here tomorrow night. And then we'll be able to catch him."

Joel looked down at his sobbing son. He knelt and took Bobby into his arms, closing his eyes and rocking him.

"God, I'm sorry," he whispered. "Daddy's so sorry."

He looked up at Nate.

"All right," he said. "Go ahead with opening night. I want the bastard caught, no matter what the cost!"

When Sander Bernaux entered his dressing room, he at first did not see the small child standing off in one corner, watching him. He sat at his vanity and checked his makeup kit. It was in a disarray, for Sander believed a tidy kit would make him look like an amateur. He had better things to do than worry about neatness.

He poked around the box, and mumbled "ahh," when he found a cellophane-wrapped crayon. He would use a brand-new set of makeup on opening night, as he always did. That again was an old theatrical superstition. Legend had it that once upon a time an actor became so angered at another actor's popularity that he stuck pins in the man's makeup stick. When the actor used it, he cut his handsome face to pieces. So, to this day, many performers insisted upon using unopened, untouched makeup.

The child suddenly reflected in the mirror. Sander swung around and demanded, "Who are you? What are you doing here?"

The little girl simply shook her head.

"Impudent brat," Sander said. "Why must it always be children who cause trouble? I've had enough with that little boy in the lobby!"

"He was nice," Bonnie said. "He wanted to be my friend. You scared him away."

"Nonsense," Sander said. "I merely averted disaster." He waved the back of his hand at her. "Now, get going! I won't have a child contaminating my dressing room!"

Bonnie threw back her head and began to scream.

"Stop that!" Sander ordered.

Bonnie lowered her head and looked into his eyes, her own dark and deep.

"You're a bad man," she said. "You gave them a warning!"

"Warning?" Sander sneered. "What are you talking about? . . . Never mind, I don't care! Get out of here! Go back to wherever you belong."

"You have to pay," Bonnie said. "You have to pay for what you did."

She picked up one of the new makeup crayons. Sander

smacked it away from her hand, then tossed his head and turned away from the sight of the hatred in her eyes.

It was the last mistake he'd ever make in his life.

She came around to the front of his chair, her small body wriggling easily between his knees and the vanity. Before Sander could pull away, she reached up and placed her hands on his cheeks. Sander froze, wanting to scream as horrible pain filled his head, horrible burning pain. But he couldn't move. Her eyes held him paralyzed, her eyes that looked up at him with a power such as he had never imagined existed. He began to tremble. And then everything grew dark and he was falling, falling . . .

"NNNNNOOOOO!!!!"

"You have to pay!" Bonnie screamed. "You must be punished!"

Sander found himself in his chair again, but he was not the same outraged, arrogant man as a moment earlier. Now he was meek, cringing as the child threatened to touch his flesh again. The thought of the pain terrified him. He would do anything to make it stop. He was completely in her power.

"You warned them!" Bonnie cried. "Now they know I'm coming—but they won't stop me! They won't!"

She picked up the new crayon Sander had been saving for opening night. The one he had not yet opened. She thrust it at him.

"Put on your makeup, darling," she said. "Put on your makeup for your first act."

Sander took the tube but did not turn his gaze from her. In the back of his mind, he knew this was not opening night. He knew there were no performances, and that rehearsals were over for the day. Yet still he unwrapped the plastic, obeying her, terrified of the pain and unable to fight.

"After you've done that," Bonnie said, her voice mimicking her mother's voice, "you'll go in the dark closet. You will go there because you were bad."

A memory came to her, and through glazed eyes Sander saw her cringe.

"Put it on," she said again, pointing to the crayon.

Sander raised it to his face and began rubbing it in. Habit made him turn from the child to the mirror, and he watched himself work. He wondered vaguely why there were red streaks on his face, why there were fine lines of stinging pain.

"Harder," Bonnie hissed. "You aren't putting in on dark enough!"

Without thought, Sander pressed harder and deeper. He did not seem to care that he was slashing his face to pieces with a nail that had somehow been embedded in a brand-new makeup crayon.

TWENTY-ONE
December 12, 1981

Opening night had come at last. In spite of all the trage-dies, in spite of the fears Nate had been unable to push away from himself, it was really here. People were already filing into the lobby, excited about being at a fashionable premiere. Reporters took notes on how the elite crowd dressed and the elegant Dysart Theater. They asked to come backstage, but Nate understood about first night jitters and wouldn't subject his cast to reporters before the performance.

While the crews took over the stage for a last double-check of their work, Nate made his way to each and every actor or actress, giving them a few words of encouragement. He was relieved to note that none of them seemed to detect the slight edge in his voice.

Let me get through this night, he prayed even as he patted one of the extras encouragingly on the shoulder.

He moved on to Sander Bernaux's dressing room. He smiled in spite of himself to see that the number on it was fourteen, although the room before it was numbered twelve. There was never a thirteen on anyone's dressing room door, let alone superstitious Sander's. Nate knocked, but there was no answer.

"He should be putting on his makeup," Nate thought. He knocked again, and when he was not acknowledged he tried the doorknob. It was locked.

A thought flashed through Nate's mind—he hadn't seen Sander since they were all in the lobby yesterday.

But he quickly shook his head to drive away any fears that

might surface. Sander just wasn't answering his door, that was all. Nate wouldn't put such eccentric behavior past him.

He walked on to Adrian's room, quickly forgetting Sander. He found her sitting before her vanity, dressed in a red and gold kimono, fussing with her red hair. He kissed her neck, which was free of makeup for the moment.

"How do you feel?" he asked.

"Nervous," she said. "And not just about my first Broadway play. The important thing is, how do *you* feel?"

Nate shrugged and pulled up a seat next to hers, speaking as she got ready for the first scene.

"I don't know," he said. "The way things are happening tonight, with everyone so excited and so much going on, I can almost believe none of the past weeks was real. None of the bad stuff, anyway."

"You know it was real, though," Adrian said gently.

"Yeah," Nate said, studying his hands.

Adrian unwrapped a makeup crayon.

"Have you seen any of the security guards yet?" she asked.

"They've been here for two hours," Nate said. "You wouldn't know it, though. They're dressed just like everyone else."

Adrian nodded. "That's good."

"I came up with a pretty logical reason for them being here," Nate said. "I told them that some of the women in the audience would be wearing expensive jewels, and that I was taking every precaution to make certain no one was robbed."

"Makes sense," Adrian said. She turned to him. "Kiss me before I'm not kissable any more," she said.

Nate put his arms around her and kissed her half-made-up face. For a moment, it seemed he would never let her go.

"Everything's going to be all right," she said. "With all those guards, our mysterious Bonnie won't be able to make a move. We'll catch her, and this nightmare will end."

Nate straightened up and backed away.

"Don't even think about that," he said, though he knew it would be heavy on her mind the entire night. "You're not Adrian St. John anymore. You're Daisy Bertrand. And Daisy doesn't have a care in the world."

We should all be so lucky, he thought.

"I'll knock 'em dead," Adrian said.

Nate kissed her again.

"Hey," Adrian said, pulling away, "you've got other actors to encourage. You'd better get going."

"I'll see you on stage at five-to-eight," Nate said. "I'm going to give everyone a pep talk."

"Shades of Knute Rockne," Adrian couldn't help teasing.

Nate finally left her, feeling just a little stronger. He was met in the hallway by Don, who held a clipboard and a pen in one hand. One of the stage manager's jobs was to be certain everyone was here, but he had been unable to locate Sander.

"His dressing room door was locked," Nate said. "He has to be in there."

"But he isn't answering," Don protested.

"You know Sander," Nate replied. "With all his superstitions, he's probably going through some preshow ritual."

"I still wish he'd just say he was in there," Don answered. "For a guy as respected in the theater as he is, Sander Bernaux is damned strange."

Nate patted his shoulder.

"Don't worry," he said. "He'll show up."

He *had* to show up!

But when Don had brought all the cast on stage for Nate's speech, he whispered in the director's ear that Sander still wasn't here. Nate felt something sour in his stomach. *Don't let it be starting,* he prayed. But for the sake of the actors around him, he bit his lip and steadied his expression.

"It seems Sander Bernaux has taken ill," he said.

A moan ran through the group, and Adrian raised her hand to her mouth. Nate looked at her only momentarily, as if to say she shouldn't indicate something more serious was wrong.

"Not to worry," he said. He pointed to Sander's understudy. "Think you can handle a first-night performance?"

"Of course I can," the understudy said.

"Good," Nate replied. "Don, do me a favor and announce that the part of Nigel Bertrand will be played by Patrick Smith."

Don walked over to the microphone, and in a moment the cast heard his clear voice. They also heard a rush of protests from the audience, but these lasted only a moment. Nate, satisfied no one was going to leave, began his speech.

"We've worked damned hard these past weeks," he said. "All of us. And what happens tonight is the proof of the pudding. I know you're all going to do your best. Remember to pause for effect after the jokes we discussed, but also remember some of them have to be shot out quickly. And another thing—those people out there will probably be talking about Sander's absence, so speak up during the first scene. You should feel your voices in your stomachs."

He gave everyone a final word of encouragement and wished them all luck, then walked off the stage. Actors and actresses hurried back to their dressing rooms to await their cues, and Adrian caught up to Nate in a hallway.

"What happened to Sander?" she whispered.

"I don't know," he said quietly. "Don Benson hasn't been able to find him. Don't worry. You'll get yourself too worked up to go on stage if you worry."

But she did worry, and to stop herself from bursting into tears Adrian threw her arms around Nate and kissed him warmly.

In the upstairs lobby of the theater Joel Warner bent to take a drink from a gilded water fountain. He moved through the crowd of people heading towards their seats and pulled his ticket out of the pocket of his best suit. From the corner of his eye he could see a man watching the crowd with a deadpan expression, and knew this was one of Nate's guards. Well, hell, he thought. I hope they do some good.

His throat was suddenly dry again. Joel was more nervous about this night than outward appearances revealed, and he had been unable to stop coughing. He walked back to the fountain for another drink. As he was bent over, a small child came up beside him. Joel straightened, fishing through his pockets at the same time for a mint. But his hand stopped moving when he saw the little girl.

She was clothed in a ruffled dress, and her black hair was pulled aside with a big white bow. Her feet were clad in white Mary Janes. She watched him with hateful eyes.

"Who are you?" Joel asked quietly, so that none of the others in the lobby could hear.

"You're going to die tonight," the child said. "You're going to pay with the rest of them when the dark comes again."

Suddenly, inexplicably, she vanished before his eyes. Joel took a step forward, his hands outstretched. He couldn't possibly have seen her, could he?

He didn't stop to think of an answer but broke into a run. Taking the curving staircase two steps at a time, he pushed by several latecomers and ran to the lobby. A door marked No Admittance indicated the hallway that led to Nate's office. He had found the child named Bonnie! He had to warn Nate that the show must not be started!

But a burly man grabbed him by the arm.

"No one is permitted backstage during the performance," he said.

"I have to see Nate Dysart," Joel answered. The man simply shook his head, so Joel pulled out one of his cards. "I'm a reporter. I have to see him."

"All you reporters want to see Mr. Dysart," he was told. "Sorry, but no can do."

Joel wrenched from the bigger man's grip.

"You're one of the guards he hired, aren't you?" he asked. "Look, I found the little girl. She's in the upstairs lobby. I have to tell Nate!"

"What little girl?" the guard asked. "What are you talking about?"

A few people looked their way, then decided they didn't want to be late for the curtain and walked through the etched-glass doors.

"Didn't Mr. Dysart tell you about the little girl?" Joel asked worriedly. The guard shook his head. "Look, she's the one who's going to cause the trouble tonight! You have to stop her!"

"Stop a little girl?" the guard asked incredulously. He took hold of Joel's arm again. "Come on upstairs with me, pal. We've got a nice little room where you can rest."

Joel struggled to get away, but the man's grip was too strong.

"You don't know what you're doing!" he protested. "You can't hold me like this!"

"Wanna see me try?"

The lobby was empty now except for the two men. No one saw Joel being pulled up the stairs. No one but a little girl who was waiting for the right moment to set her plans for revenge into motion.

Don Benson made a final check of the stage to make certain everyone was in their places. He whispered to Mike Woodson and was assured once again the lights were working just fine. Then, at Don's signal, Mike took down the house lights and brought up the footlights. As the audience clapped in anticipation, the curtain rolled up. Nate, standing just behind his stage manager, watched Adrian cross the stage. She was holding a newspaper, and in her Brooklynite, Daisy-Bertrand voice she said, "Will ya just looka what they got in the papers today?"

Nate watched in silence as the first act progressed, feeling a wave of satisfaction run over him as he heard the audience laughing at just the right moments. But after a few moments it was all lost to him. He closed his eyes and was brought back to a time when Meg was still alive, when he had that little off-Broadway production company.

He was with Jim Orland and Meg, standing on a bare stage.

"In just about two months," he was saying, "we're going to put on a show like New York's never seen."

"It's going to be wonderful," Meg said.

In the dark wings of the Dysart Theater, Nate's head went up and down.

Yes, Meg, he thought. *It's going to be wonderful.*

She should have been here today, to share this with him. And Jim Orland should have been here. And Denny and Barbara...

His father should have been here too, to see that his son was going to be a success after all.

In a small upstairs sitting room Joel Warner paced the floor and tried to reason with the guard.

"You don't understand," he said. "You were hired to make certain nothing happened tonight."

"That's right, pal," the guard said, lighting a cigarette. He offered one to Joel, but the reporter shook his head.

"And nothing's going to happen," he said. "So long as I've got my eye on you."

"But it isn't me you should be watching!"

"No kidding?"

"And nothing's going to happen," he said. "So long as I've got my eye on you."

"But it isn't me you should be watching!"

"No kidding?"

"There's a little girl," Joel said, for perhaps the hundredth time.

The guard sucked deeply on the cigarette and held in the smoke as he laughed.

"You want me to believe a kid is going to cause trouble here?"

"She's probably working with someone."

"Where is she now, then?"

Joel gestured towards the door.

"Out there somewhere," he said. "She..."

He noticed the amused look on the guard's face and shut his mouth. Damn it all, why did he have to run into a moron like this one? He sank down to a couch and folded his arms. For the time being there was no use in arguing. He would have to think of another plan of action.

Denny's hand squeezed the doorknob for nearly fifteen minutes before daring to turn it. Finally, convinced by her snoring that his mother was sleeping soundly, he left the apartment. He had momentary doubts about this, anticipating what might happen if he was caught. But then he remembered his friends at the Dysart Theater, that it was their big opening night, and hurried for the building's rickety old elevator. He knew that he'd miss the whole first act, but that was okay as long as he was there for most of the play. Nate would understand.

"Anyone see you?" Mikey asked when they met in front of Denny's building.

"Uh-uh," Denny said. "It's okay."

Paul rubbed his arms. "Let's get going. I'm freezing to death!"

The three boys walked in the direction of the nearest theater, where Mike and Paul had told their parents they would be for the next few hours. But just before they reached it, they descended a dark stairway into the subway station below. Except for a young couple heading into Manhattan on a date, they were alone.

To the sound of thundering applause, the curtain came down on the first act. Don called "Strike!" the signal for the stagehands to change the sets for act two. No one in the clapping audience heard him. Adrian rushed into Nate's arms and kissed him. The other actors hardly noticed her, each one too intent on the fifteen-minute intermission to care what another member of the company was doing. Adrian squeezed Nate tightly.

"We're halfway through," she said. "Halfway through, and nothing has happened. And they *loved* us!"

"You were wonderful," Nate said, rubbing her back. He could feel perspiration through her cotton dress, the result of working under hot stage lights. But he also knew she had been nervous on that stage, anticipating what could happen at any moment.

"Maybe we were wrong," she said. "Maybe there is no danger."

Nate kissed her again.

"Forget it," he said. "Just go back to your dressing room and relax."

As they were walking hand-in-hand, Don came up to them with Sander's agent, Tom Selton. Both men looked very worried.

"I tried to get backstage when I heard Sander wouldn't be performing," Tom said. "But some goon of a fellow wouldn't let me."

"I'm sorry," Nate said. "What can you tell me about Sander?"

"I haven't been able to reach him at his apartment since yesterday morning," Tom said, "when I called him to give him a word of encouragement. He told me then he was on his way to the theater."

"Yes, he was here yesterday," Nate said.

"Well, apparently," Tom said, "he never came home. We were supposed to go out for a few drinks last night, but Sander didn't show up."

Hearing this, Adrian took Nate's hand, a gesture not lost on Tom.

"Is something wrong here?"

"I don't know," Nate said. "What do you suppose happened to him?"

Let it be nothing, he thought. *Dear God, let it be nothing.*

"My client never missed a performance in all the years I've been working with him," Tom said. "This just isn't like him."

Don looked down the hallway.

"I say we check Sander's dressing room again," he suggested. "Maybe he's got a bad case of stage fright and couldn't answer us before."

"Not my client," Tom said. "Not Sander Bernaux. He's one of Broadway's greatest actors!"

"I saw him cringe at the sight of a cat once," Adrian said.

Nate, not wanting anyone to see the trembling that had begun to creep under his skin, hurried towards the actor's dressing room. They spent a few minutes knocking on his door and calling to him, until Adrian finally had to leave.

"Let's break the lock," Tom said. "If he's not in there, we'll know he may not be answering his phone at home. Then I'll go there and find out what's going on."

Don stopped an actress who was passing by and asked if she had a hairpin. She pulled one out and gave it to him, then headed towards the stage. Don bent the pin open and worked it into the hole beneath the glass doorknob.

"This old-fashioned lock should give way easily enough," he said.

In a moment, the door clicked open. Don switched on the light and led the other two men into Sander's dressing room. It was empty. The makeup on his dresser sat in its usual disarray, and there were papers thrown around the floor. Nate bent down and picked up a copy of *Variety*. Absentmindedly, he neatened the pages and put the paper down on top of a costume trunk.

"Well, he's obviously not here," Tom said. He looked at his watch. "I'll go over to his apartment."

"Call me if he's there," Nate said.

Tom left Don and Nate alone. Don looked around the room for a moment, wondering how any one individual could make such a mess, then said, "Do you think something's happened to Sander?"

Nate shook his head quickly. No. Nothing could have happened! Not on his opening night!

"Well, Tom will call us," Don said. "I've got to get back to the stage. Intermission'll be over in a minute."

In the lobby the lights flickered to signal curtain time.

Joel's own little prison went dark and brightened again. And he realized he had wasted over an hour.

"You have no right to hold me here," he said. "Do you know who I am?"

"I read your articles all the time, Mr. Warner," the guard said. "It doesn't give you the right to cause trouble."

"But I'm not..."

Suddenly, the lights went out again. And this time they did not turn right back on. Downstairs in the wings Don Benson looked out at the house and saw the audience was seated in darkness. He turned to Mike.

"Hey," he whispered. "Get the lights up!"

Mike punched buttons and flicked switches, but nothing happened. In a flash, the stage lights also went out. Confused and excited whispers ran through the groups of people on the stage and in the audience. Mike cursed under his breath.

"Damn! We've got another blackout!"

"Keep working on it," Don said. "I'll take care of the audience."

He hurried across the stage and through the curtains. Though he knew the audience couldn't see him, he called for attention and told them there was a power failure.

"But don't worry," he called out. "We'll be getting on with the play in just a few moments. Thank you for your cooperation."

In Sander's dressing room Nate had spent the last few minutes thinking about Meg and Jim. When the lights went out, he stood up from Sander's chair and moved towards the door to find out what was wrong. But as he approached it, he heard it slam shut. And then, a familiar childish voice said, "It's time. It's time, Daddy."

Nate backed up a pace.

"Who is that?" he demanded. "Who are you?"

His eyes adjusted to the dim light flickering into the room from the neon sign of the hotel next door, and Nate saw a little girl standing before him. She was smiling.

"Who are you?" he demanded again.

"I'm your little girl," Bonnie said. "Don't you know me?"

Nate shook his head.

"I have no little girl!" he cried. "What kind of sick joke is this?"

Bonnie took a step forward, her arms outstretched.

"I want us to be together again, Daddy," she said, taking both his hands.

But though Nate could see her hands in his, he could not feel them. With an angered cry he jerked away, stumbling backwards and falling against the closet door. It bounced open. Nate pulled himself away from it, grabbing the room's curtains, letting in more light from outside.

Light that revealed Sander Bernaux's hideously mutilated face.

"No," Nate whispered, too stunned to scream. He dropped to his knees. "My God, no . . ."

"He had to pay, Daddy," Bonnie said, her voice sweet. "He had to pay."

There was a noose around Sander's neck, and his body hung freely from a high bar in the closet. His face was a mass of blood and gore, a mixture of red and pale, pale green. His tongue protruded from his mouth, his eyes stared wildly; streaks of dried blood stained his face, blood that had dripped from deep cuts in his forehead.

"He was a bad man, Daddy," Bonnie said, taking Nate's hand as the director stared in wide-eyed silence at Sander's body. "He tried to interfere, but I wouldn't let him."

Nate didn't hear her. Somehow, all he could think of at the moment was his father. He could hear the laughter of the old man, high-pitched, hysterical laughter. And he could hear the words his father used so often when speaking to him.

"Failure! Failure!"

Maybe I am a failure, Daddy. Maybe I'm not supposed to be happy. Maybe things aren't supposed to go my way . . .

He felt two hands press on his shoulders. The little girl had come up behind him, and unlike the moments when she'd held his hands, he was aware of her palms touching him.

"Don't cry, Daddy," Bonnie said. "This is a happy time. We're going to be together again!"

Nate wanted to run away from her. He wanted to stand up and run out of here and get Adrian away from this place. He wanted to warn the others before it was too late.

But he could not move. Bonnie's small hands held him down like steel bolts. Slowly, he was falling into her power.

"The time has come, Daddy," she whispered.

*   *   *

Judy Terrel came running up to Mike Woodson as he worked on the control box, breathing heavily. Forcing herself to whisper, she hissed, "My God, we've got a fire backstage—and it's spreading!"

"Get the fire department here," Mike ordered.

"But the phones..."

"Run next door, Judy!" Mike yelled. He turned to the people standing near him. "Get fire extinguishers!"

He could smell smoke and, when he turned, saw the reflection of flames that poured over the sets and props behind the back curtain. It all happened in a matter of seconds when the flames suddenly shot out and overtook the wooden, painted sets on stage. Even as the actors ran to save themselves or to get fire extinguishers, the audience noticed the flames and smoke. Terrified screams filled the dark auditorium.

"Fire! Fire!"

Adrian hurried toward Nate's office, thinking that you were never supposed to yell "fire" in a crowded theater. Where was Nate? She hadn't seen him backstage. Was he hurt somewhere? Did he need her?

"NATE?"

Someone bumped into her in the darkness. She felt a sudden rush of cold when the back door was forced open as everyone made their way out of the theater. A shaft of moonlight barely illuminated the crowded hallway, and Adrian used it as a guide to find her way

"NATE, WHERE ARE YOU?"

Even as she ran along the hallways, crying out for Nate, the members of the audience were making their own mad dashes to safety. The walls and ceiling had come to a point of such intense heat that they burst into flame simultaneously. Pieces of the wooden ceiling dropped on the screaming, rushing throng of people. Black smoke curled up and caressed the gilded wainscotting and balcony trim

"Help me!" a man screamed.

"My children! My children!"

One young man knocked another aside to move ahead more quickly. The latter picked himself up off the floor just in time to miss being stepped on. But an elderly woman was not so lucky, and as the crowd pressed toward the doors she fell

forward. A thousand feet trampled her, a thousand ears
ignored her screams.

The mock columns to either side of the room ripped away
from the wall, no longer supported by wooden beams. A
series of loud crashes echoed throughout the building as they
fell to the floor. A man was knocked down and pinned under
it. He reached forward with a curling hand.

"Get it off of me!" he gasped. "Get it off!"

Then his gasp turned into a scream and his scream into a
sickly choking sound as the smoke made its way down his
throat.

Denny and his friends pounded up the stairs to the street,
glad the ride was over. In typical subway style the train had
stalled for twenty minutes, cutting short the time they could
spend in Manhattan. Eager to get to the theater, they ran
along the street, dodging crowds of people. They didn't pay
attention to the sirens of a passing fire truck until Denny
realized it had turned down the block where Nate's theater
was.

"C'mon!" he cried.

When they rounded the corner, it was to see the crews
from several other trucks already trying to put out the fire
that was claiming the Dysart Theater. The three watched the
scene in awe, too engrossed by the fire to think that the delay
on the subway might have saved their lives.

The fire department had worked quickly to get its hoses
into action and to save as many lives as possible. Some of the
cast and crew had come out to the street from the side alley.
Everyone was trying to comfort each other as they watched
the beautiful Dysart Theater's destruction.

In the crazed chaos, no one heard Joel's cries.

"What the hell is going on out there?" he demanded of the
guard. "Why do I smell smoke!"

"I don't know," the guard said. "But I'm going to get us out
of here."

He fumbled for his key and pressed his fingers on the door
to locate the keyhole in the blackness. The key slid in and
turned, but nothing happened.

The guard began to rattle the door.

"What's wrong?" Joel asked.

"It's jammed," was the panicked reply. "I can't get it open!"

Joel pulled him away and tried the door himself, to no avail. Then he started pounding on the wood, screaming.

"GET US OUT OF HERE! WE'RE TRAPPED! HELP! HELP!"

But no one heard him.

Not Adrian, who raced through the smoke-filled building in a desperate search for Nate.

Not Mike Woodson or Judy Terrel, who finally left the theater to the fire department and ran to safety.

Not the casting director, Virginia, who paused only a second in her flight to lift the theater's cat, the screeching Cartier, into her arms.

Not the fire fighters, nor the other actors and stagehands, nor the people still trying to get out of the theater.

Only Nate Dysart heard him, a voice faraway and faint. But he did not move to help him. He was frozen, staring at Sander Bernaux, holding the little girl named Bonnie.

"You have to remember me, Daddy," Bonnie said. "You have to remember the night I died."

She put her head on his shoulder.

"It was so, so long ago..."

TWENTY-TWO

Bonnie placed her hands gently on Nate's cheeks, hands that earlier had brought horrid pain to those who had angered the little girl. But Nate felt no pain—only the loving touch of a small child. Bonnie looked at him and saw not a Broadway producer, nor a man born some thirty years after her death. She knew him not as Nate dysart but as Philip Jackson, the daddy she had been taken from sixty years earlier on a fateful December night.

And now her daddy was back again, his reincarnated spirit locked within the mind of Nate Dysart, only now to be released on the anniversary of Bonnie's death. She kissed Nate's forehead and whispered, "Remember, Daddy. Remember what happened to me."

Nate felt himself being lifted up, and the room he was in

faded away. He was floating, floating through a long, dark tunnel. Faint voices reached his ears, sounding muffled and contorted like a tape recorder running backwards. There were screams and there was laughter. Flashes of light and pockets of deep blackness swirled around him, images wavered before his eyes like pictures in an old family album. There was the mansion, there his first car, there a toy boat...

For a long time he floated that way, experiencing again the phenomena of an entire lifetime, seeing images of his childhood, of Meg, of his father, of...

Suddenly, he was on his feet in a darkened room. He felt a small child's arms around his knees and said, "You just wait here. I'll be right back."

But the voice wasn't his. Nate moved to touch the tiny girl who hugged him...

...but it was Philip Jackson who stroked Bonnie's soft hair.

By way of a power only evil could conjure up, Nathaniel Philip Dysart became Philip Nathaniel Jackson. He had gone back sixty years in time to relive the night his daughter, Bonnie Jackson, had died. Nate watched the scenario like a person watching a play. And yet, strangely, he felt himself as part of the action, as if he were sharing Phil's body. It seemed as if his being had been split in two—one half as Nate Dysart, observer, the other as Phil Jackson, participant.

Phil Jackson stomped along the blackened hallway that led away from Bonnie's dressing room, waving the gun he held as his anger grew. In the deep darkness, his sense of hearing was sharpened, and he easily found his wife when he heard her whispering behind one of the doors. He put a hand on the glass knob, hesitated, then burst into the room.

Through the light of a hurricane lamp, Phil stared at Margaret. She was trying desperately to pull up the bodice of her silk dress. Her mouth gaped open when she saw the gun. Her beads (Phil had given them to her last Christmas) were tossed carelessly, almost contemptuously, on the floor. Nervously, Aaron followed Phil's gaze to the necklace, then he stopped fastening his suspenders and bent to pick it up.

"Phil!" Margaret cried, finding her voice at last. "What are you doing with that gun?"

Phil said nothing in response. With his lips set hard, he

walked across the room and delivered a hard backhand to his wife's jaw. Margaret screamed and fell back on the couch.

"How dare you?" Aaron demanded, stepping between them. He knocked the gun from Phil's hand, sending it flying across the room.

Without warning, Phil ran a blow to Aaron's stomach, sending him to the floor. Margaret's lover doubled up in pain, clutching his middle.

"You lousy little bitch," Phil hissed, enunciating each angered word. "What the hell do you mean, endangering Bonnie's life so you can have your fun with that bastard?"

"Phil, Aaron and I were only..."

Margaret had started to sit up, but Phil slapped her again. She brought a slender hand up to her reddened cheek.

"I found Bonnie locked in a closet," Phil said. "What did she do this time, Margaret? Did she scuff her shoes again? Did she spill her milk?"

"Phil..."

He couldn't resist another smack, hating her now more than he ever had. She had hurt his baby. She had thought screwing with Aaron was more important than Bonnie's welfare.

"Oh, wait," he drawled, his slicked-down hair glistening in the light of the hurricane lamp. "I know! Bonnie figured out you were up to no-good, huh? You locked her up so she wouldn't get in your way!"

Once again, he struck her. Aaron had got to his feet, and he tried to grab Phil's arm. With a gasp Margaret stood up and ran from the room.

Phil broke away from Aaron's grip, picked up both the gun and the hurricane lamp, and ran out into the hallway. He saw his wife turning a corner up ahead and hurried toward her.

"That child is more trouble than she's worth. You keep her! I hate her!"

"Margaret..."

But she began walking toward Bonnie's dressing room, shouting.

"BONNIE JACKSON, HOW DARE YOU BAD-MOUTH ME?"

"DON'T YOU HURT HER!"

Phil yelled at his wife even as she pushed open the door to

Bonnie's room. But it was empty! Phil followed her in and
moved the hurricane lamp around, seeing no sign of his little
girl. Across the room, the closet gaped like a demon's mouth—
waiting to devour a little girl.

"Son-of-a-bitch," Phil whispered, leaving the room. He
looked up and down the hallway. "BONNIE! BONNIE WHERE
ARE YOU?"

The theater was silent. So silent that the sound of footsteps
behind him made Phil turn with a gasp. Frustrated that it was
Aaron and not Bonnie, for a moment he lost control and fired
the gun. Aaron grabbed his arm where the bullet had grazed
him, barely making a burn on his shirt.

"You're insane!" he cried.

Phil moved quickly along the hallway, shouting, praying,
his heart pounding so hard it hurt his chest. What had
happened to Bonnie? Was she hurt? Was she even able to
answer him?

"BONNIE!"

He came to the stage and held up his lamp. Ropes and
sandbags cast weird shadows in the light, but it did not
find Bonnie for him. Phil looked up beyond the crystal
chandelier at the mezzanine, but no one was there. Unless
Bonnie was hiding, too frightened to let him know where
she was . . .

"Let's try upstairs," he suggested to Margaret.

Just at that moment, Aaron Milland walked on stage. He
took Margaret's arm and said, "I'm leaving."

"Aaron, no!"

"This isn't my problem," Aaron said. "I want no part of
you, or your daughter!"

Margaret, stunned by the changed attitude of the man
who'd said he loved her just a few minutes earlier, watched
Aaron storm from the theater. But she made no attempt to
follow him. Instead, she turned and ran after Phil.

She found him on stage. "You ruined everything!" she
shouted. "For once in my life I was happy, and you and that
kid ruined everything!"

"You really do hate Bonnie, don't you?" Phil asked,
incredulously.

"I never wanted a baby, and you know it," Margaret said.
"*I* was supposed to be the actress in this family. But what

happened? You got me pregnant at eighteen years old, and I was ruined!"

"That wasn't Bonnie's fault," Phil protested. "You could have . . ."

"God damn it, yes it *was* her fault!"

Suddenly, she grabbed the hurricane lamp, and in an effort to vent her anger threw it with all her might at the gold-and-white curtains that rose majestically to the striplights above.

"NNNNOOO!!!"

Phil's angry cry tore through the air even as the flames from the lamp devoured the curtains. He took a step forward, his hands outstretched, as if he could put the fire out. Then he caught hold of his senses and hurried off the stage.

Flames poured with lightning speed over the wood and curtains and ropes, destroying everything in sight, spreading wildly. Margaret ran toward a nearby office to phone the fire department, as Phil ran off in the opposite direction. He had to find Bonnie!

"BONNIE? BONNIE, FOR GOD'S SAKE, WHERE ARE YOU?!"

The hallway began to fill with black smoke. Tears stung Phil's eyes as he stumbled along the hallway, guided by the light of the rapidly spreading fire. He crashed into the lobby, already thick with smoke, coughing and yelling.

"BONNIE?"

The winding staircase beckoned him, and he raced up it, taking the steps two at a time. A quick, desperate search of the upstairs proved Bonnie wasn't hiding anywhere. Phil didn't even stop to catch his breath as he raced back down the stairs again, burning his hands on the metal railing, which had heated up in the last few moments. As he crashed to the bottom floor a line of flames raced along the ceiling above him, and one of the lobby's chandeliers collapsed. Axes began to pound on the stage door.

Moments later, a dozen firemen broke into the building. They helped Margaret to safety, trying to calm the hysterical woman.

"Margaret, I can't find Bonnie!"

But Margaret could only scream.

Phil hated her more at that moment than any other time in his life. With a loud cry that seemed to rip open his already pained throat, he pushed a fireman aside and ran to the hallway that led backstage. His daughter was hiding somewhere, of course. She was hiding because she was terrified of her mother.

"BONNIE?"

Just a few yards away, in the orchestra pit, five-year-old Bonnie Jackson coughed and regained consciousness. Weakly, with the last breath in her smoke-filled lungs, she cried out, *"Daddy?"*

Phil stopped in his tracks. The voice sounded so faraway that he didn't dare believe it wasn't a trick of the crackling flames.

"BONNIE?!"

He raced onto the stage. The ghost light had been knocked over, and unable to see in the darkness, Phil tripped over it and fell into the orchestra pit. His arms flung out and touched something small and warm.

"Bonnie!"

He gathered the little girl up into his arms, tears of joy racing down his flushed cheeks. But the joy was soon shattered.

Bonnie didn't respond to his hugs and kisses.

His little girl was dead.

"NNNNNOOOOO!!!!!"

Phil Jackson threw back his head and let out a scream of anger.

And at the same time, Nate Dysart also screamed, sitting once again in Sander's dressing room. Sixty years of time had flown by in a split second, and the present had taken over.

Nate screamed in terror, rocking the little girl in his lap. In that brief moment, he came to understand what he had been trying to know all these months. His theater was haunted by a little girl who should never have died, a little girl who was still looking for her daddy. And Nate was that daddy—Phil Jackson's reincarnated spirit. Bonnie had come back to the site of the theater to find him.

"Bonnie..." he whispered, somehow hearing Phil Jackson's voice.

"Daddy, don't cry," Bonnie said, her voice sweet. "We're together again. The dark isn't here anymore!"

Nate didn't hear her. As Phil Jackson he remembered. His

wife, Margaret, had died several months later in an asylum. By some freak of time and fate, Nate's wife Meg had also died in a mental institution, driven there by Nathaniel Sr. after the loss of her baby. Meg's maiden name had been Margaret Jackson . . . and Phil, the father who had so loved Bonnie that she looked for him even beyond mortal life, had shot himself in the head.

Nate brought his hands up to his own head and remembered the suicide attempt he'd made after losing Meg.

"Nate!"

The spell was broken when he heard someone shouting his name. He looked up to see Adrian in the doorway, staring wide-eyed at him as he held Bonnie on his lap.

"Nate, what are you doing?" she demanded. "That's her! That's the little girl!"

Suddenly, Adrian caught sight of Sander Bernaux's corpse, swinging from a rod in the dark closet, illuminated by the hotel lights outside. She covered her mouth with her hand and screamed in horror.

"Nate, what's happening here?"

Now Bonnie crawled from Nate's lap, a strange, bestial growl escaping from her small mouth. She lunged at Adrian, knocking her to the floor.

"DON'T!" Adrian cried in a panic.

"You won't take him away from me!" Bonnie cried. "You won't! You won't!"

She placed her hands on Adrian's face, sending intense burning pains over the woman's skin. Adrian screamed and struggled, unable to understand why Nate didn't help her.

"Nate, *please!*"

Nate sensed something was wrong as he watched the woman and child struggling, but under Bonnie's spell he could not move.

"*Nate!*"

The pain raced over Adrian's body, burning her and yet making her quake as if it were freezing in the room. Nate watched her struggle as if she were a figure on a movie screen, as if she were not a flesh-and-blood woman, a part of his life.

"NATE FOR GOD'S SAKE STOP HER!!!"

Abruptly, like the crash of thunder, the hypnotic vacuum

Nate had been in exploded. He saw Adrian writhing in pain. He saw the woman he loved being tormented.

"NO!"

He stood up and looked at Bonnie.

"STOP THAT RIGHT NOW!"

Shocked, Bonnie turned away from Adrian and looked innocently into Nate's eyes. Adrian, sickened, wrapped her arms around herself as the pain slowly subsided.

"Daddy?"

"What *are* you?" Adrian demanded.

Nate shook his head, locking eyes with the small child.

"Daddy, she was bad," Bonnie said. "She wants to take you away from me!"

"No . . ."

"Nate, what is she talking about? Who is she?"

Nate ignored her. He took a step toward Bonnie.

"What do you want from me?"

"You're my daddy," Bonnie said. "I want you to come with me."

"No," Nate said. "No, I'm not your daddy."

Bonnie threw back her head and screamed.

"You are! You are!"

"No!" Nate cried. "Your real daddy died a long, long time ago! I am *not* Phil Jackson!"

Adrian's eyes dripped huge tears as she watched this, unable to understand or believe what was going on.

"Please come with me, Daddy," Bonnie pleaded.

"I'm Nate Dysart," Nate said firmly. "I am not your daddy!"

"I want you to come with me!"

It wasn't right! The little girl couldn't believe his words. All these years in darkness, all the plans she had made. How could they fail now? How could he reject her so coldly?

"Daddy . . ."

Nate put his hands on her shoulders.

"Your daddy died a long time ago," he said again. "Maybe his spirit is in me—I don't know. But I do know I have a long life ahead of me. I'm not ready to give that up!"

"Nate, for God's sake," Adrian choked, rubbing her eyes.

Bonnie stared into his eyes.

"You're supposed to love me, Daddy," Bonnie said. "You're supposed to come with me now."

"No!" Nate snapped. "I don't want to come with you! I don't want to die! I am not your daddy—no matter what I was in 1921, I am *not* your daddy!"

Adrian moved inside the room and took his arm.

"Nate, I can see flames in the hallway!" she cried, pulling him.

"Bonnie," Nate said, his voice strangely calm, "you'll be with your daddy, one day. But the time isn't right now. And I'm not coming with you!"

"Then I'll wait, Daddy," Bonnie said. "I'll wait. Because I know you always come for me."

"I don't . . ."

She pulled him down a little and kissed his cheek.

"You always come, Daddy," she said. "I'll wait."

And then, suddenly, she was gone. Nate and Adrian stared at the spot where she'd just been, stunned. Then Adrian pulled Nate with all her might from the room. Flames were just reaching the doorway, flames that spread mercilessly in spite of the fire department's work. Nate and Adrian raced away from them, stumbling down the dimly lit hallway toward the back door.

A few seconds later they crashed into the backyard. The icy December wind struck Nate like a slap in the face, bringing him to his senses. He collapsed onto the frost-covered ground, his ears bombarded with the sounds of screams and sirens.

"Oh, Nate," Adrian said weakly. "What happened in there? Who was that child?"

Nate couldn't tell her right now. He began to cough, his lungs giving in to the smoke. Trembling, he turned away and buried his head in Adrian's chest. For a long time they sat in silence, protected from the smoke by a wind that blew in toward the front of the theater.

The theater . . .

Nate looked up at the building that had once been his pride and joy. But it had brought only pain to him, and in a strange sort of way he was relieved to see it haloed now in flame and smoke.

"She was looking for her father," he said softly. "She thought I was her father."

"Nate?"

Adrian kissed the top of his head, smelling smoke in his hair. She didn't understand what had just happened, but to her the most important thing was that they were safe.

"I looked everywhere for you, darling," she said. "Why didn't you answer me?"

Nate couldn't tell her he'd been in another dimension, unable to hear her.

"Just hold me, Adrian," he said. "Just tell me everything's going to be all right."

"I have to know what happened in there," Adrian said.

"She was a ghost," Nate said, as if that were the most natural statement in the world. "Bonnie was a ghost who walked the halls of my theater looking for her daddy."

"Nate . . ."

Adrian wanted to say that was impossible but stopped herself.

"Nate, let's not talk about her," she said. "No one would believe us. No one has to know what happened."

"But Joel Warner knows about her," Nate protested.

Adrian closed her eyes and gently told Nate the news.

"He's dead, Nate," she said. "He died from the smoke upstairs."

"Oh no . . ."

"Two other people died too," Adrian said. "And God only knows what happened to Sander in there! Let it be, Nate. If you start talking about ghosts, the police will think *you* set the fire! They'll put you away, Nate!"

Put you away . . .

The way Nathaniel Sr. had put Meg away . . .

"I don't want to die," Nate said weakly.

"You aren't going to die, Nate," Adrian said, crushing him to her. "You aren't ever, ever going to be hurt again!"

She rested her cheek on top of his head and stared at the shell of the Dysart Theater. As its life came to an end, she knew that the horror, too, was over.

EPILOGUE
Summer, 1986

So much had happened in the last five years. As if he had been reborn after the fire, everything had taken a turn for the better in Nate's life. He was married to Adrian now, the father of twin boys, and heading up a theater company he'd started in 1983. Much of the profits that he made went to compensate the families of those who had died in the fire. But money didn't really mean very much to Nate. He had everything he wanted in his little family.

Well, almost everything. It had seemed, after all the investigations were over and the fire declared accidental, that everything would be all right. No one even looked his way regarding Sander Bernaux's death. It was believed to have been a suicide, and the note lost in the badly burned dressing room. And so, with no worries, Nate should have been happy. But somehow, he knew something was missing from his life.

Though he loved his sons dearly, he couldn't stop thinking about the little girl named Bonnie. It amazed Nate, a man who had hated his father, that a child could so *love* her father that she'd haunt the earth for six decades in search of him. He often wondered, as he looked back on that December night, if he had done the right thing by rejecting her. And he always decided that he had. Life was too precious to him to be thrown away. His sons, Joey and Jimmy, were a constant source of joy to him. And they, he vowed, would never know the heartaches and cruelties he'd experienced in his own childhood.

Yet, still, the idea of having a little daughter became an obsession with him. But Adrian was at the height of her career and couldn't afford time off for another pregnancy. Still she understood Nate's feelings, and after many discussions and arguments, had finally consented to adopt. So today, on a warm July afternoon, they were heading toward the Goldmountain Foundling's Home for a prearranged meeting with its director.

"You don't know how excited I am," Nate said, squeezing Adrian's hand. "Just think—we might have a little girl soon!"

Adrian laughed. "It'll be a new experience for me, coming from a family with nine brothers!"

They arrived at the gate of the home, and George swung their Lincoln onto its gravel driveway. A few minutes later they were in an office, telling a stocky woman why they wanted to adopt another child when they had a pair of toddler boys at home.

At the end of the meeting, the woman smiled and said, "Well, there don't seem to be any problems, Mr. and Mrs. Dysart. We've looked thoroughly into your background. Now, would you like to look at some of our children?"

Nate grinned.

"Please," he said.

They were led out to a huge backyard, where several dozen youngsters played on swings and slides and chased each other through the garden. Nate put his arm around Adrian's shoulder and watched them in silence for a long time. They all seemed very happy.

But there was one little girl who sat apart from the group, swinging lazily in a tire that hung from an oak-tree branch. She was dressed in a red sunsuit, and her dark braids flicked over her slight shoulders. She turned, as if hearing a signal from Nate's mind, and stared into his eyes with big, black ones of her own. Nate smiled slightly at her.

"Who is that?" Adrian asked. "She's certainly a shy little thing."

"Strangest thing about that child," the woman replied. "She was left with us about five years ago, when she was a very tiny infant. No one ever came to claim her."

"But she's beautiful," Nate said, tilting his head to one side as he watched her play. "Why hasn't she been adopted yet?"

The woman signed. "The poor dear has problems. She's terribly shy, and she has a tremendous fear of the dark. Wakes up from nightmares almost every . . ."

But Nate wasn't listening. The word "dark" kept bouncing

back and forth in his mind. This little girl was afraid of the
dark. Just like Bonnie...

"Nate. It's a coincidence," Adrian whispered.

He turned to the woman.

"May I speak with her?"

"Why, of course!" the woman said. She hoped they would
like the child and would adopt her.

She walked across the yard and took the little girl by the
hand, leading her to Nate and Adrian. The child was hesitant,
staring down at her feet. Nate got on his knees and put his
hands on her shoulders. He said nothing but only smiled.
And in a moment the child returned the smile. She looked
into his eyes, her eyes filled with great innocence, and in a
sweet voice she said, "My name is Bonnie. Are you going to
be my new daddy?"

GHOST HOUSE
by Clare McNally

You won't be able to stop reading until the nightmare is over . . .

A dream house that traps a family in horror.

The beautiful old mansion on Long Island's South Shore seemed the perfect home for the Van Burens and their three young children. What happened to them inside that house is an experience you'll pray couldn't happen to you.

At first the Van Burens believed there had to be some natural explanation. Before it was over, they were fighting for their children's lives against an obscene manifestation of evil that engulfed them all in a desperate nightmare.

Not even *Flowers in the Attic* prepares you for

GHOST HOUSE

0 552 11652 1

GHOST HOUSE REVENGE
by Clare McNally

The Ghost House horror lives on . . . for revenge.

Only nightmares and broken limbs remained to remind the Van Burens and their three children of past terror. And when the physical therapist and his shy daughter arrived, the family dared hope for a return to normal life . . .

But somewhere within the ancient Long Island mansion, something was laughing, mocking, plotting . . .

They prayed it wasn't the same as before. It was not – it was much, much worse. Soon they were fighting for their lives against a shape-shifting horror of insatiable evil. A malevolence that lusted with hideous pleasure, and killed with raging delight . . .

0 552 11825 7

WHAT ABOUT THE BABY?
by Clare McNally

EVIL HAS COME FOR HER BABY

1824 A young mother returns home to find her infant son brutally murdered in his cradle. Her tortured grief led to a consuming desire for vengeance . . .

NOW For beautiful Gabrielle Hanson, 17, orphaned and pregnant, her lonely world becomes a place of unimagined terror. Bizarre chants invade her mind . . . Death plagues her dreams . . . Blood desecrates her room . . .

For she has been adopted by an undying evil from the past, an evil that has come for only one precious thing – her baby.

WHAT ABOUT THE BABY?

0 552 12691 8

SOMEBODY COME AND PLAY
by Clare McNally

For thirty years there had been peace beside the waters of Lake Solaria except in the rambling mansion where Myrtle Hollenbeck paced up and down like a mad woman, waiting for the return of her children.

But Myrtle's waiting is soon over: one night she is found hanging from her daughter's skipping rope. Everyone believes Myrtle's death to be a case of routine suicide; everyone, that is, apart from Cassie Larchmont, the ten-year-old child, who witnessed Myrtle's death, and Robert Landers, an investigating police officer who hears from Cassie how a dark shadow stood by Myrtle's side that fearful night.

At the same time, Nicole Morgan comes into Cassie's life. Dark-haired, malevolent, dressed in quaint old-fashioned clothes popular decades before, Nicole seems bent on luring the other children into Myrtle's haunted mansion. The fabulous playroom they discover conceals untold horrors, while outside the terror that has lain quietly on the lake bed for thirty years rises slowly towards them. Only Landers can save them before that evil kills them all . . .

0 552 13033 8

COME DOWN INTO DARKNESS
by Claire McNally

The house had been empty for twenty years. There was dark stories of murder and suicide told about it. But it was just what Doreen Addison was looking for – big, inexpensive and secluded. It was perfect for her child refuge.

At first it was just a crazy man in the woods and a dead cat on the back porch. But then the children started seeing and hearing a beautiful woman dressed in black and there was a terrible accident in the cellar. Something wasn't right about this house.

And then the nightmare really started as children disappeared and Doreen found herself confronting an evil power beyond her understanding. Only one thing could save her and the children from destruction: she must discover the secret of the woman in black who commands them all to: Come Down into Darkness.

0 552 13034 6

A SELECTED LIST OF HORROR TITLES
AVAILABLE FROM CORGI AND BANTAM BOOKS

THE PRICES SHOWN BELOW WERE CORRECT AT THE TIME OF GOING
TO PRESS HOWEVER TRANSWORLD PUBLISHERS RESERVE THE
RIGHT TO SHOW NEW RETAIL PRICES ON COVERS WHICH MAY
DIFFER FROM THOSE PREVIOUSLY ADVERTISED IN THE TEXT OR
ELSEWHERE.

All Corgi/Bantam Books are available at your bookshop or newsagent, or can be ordered from the following address:

Corgi/Bantam Books,
Cash Sales Department,
P.O. Box 11, Falmouth, Cornwall TR10 9EN

Please send a cheque or postal order (no currency) and allow 80p for postage and packing for the first book plus 20p for each additional book ordered up to a maximum charge of £2.00 in UK.

B.F.P.O. customers please allow 80p for the first book and 20p for each additional book.

Overseas customers, including Eire, please allow £1.50 for postage and packing for the first book, £1.00 for the second book, and 30p for each subsequent title ordered.